They stared at o

'Mrs Victoria Slade?
bow, and the bow wa

'I am. And you, sir?'

'I think you know very well who I am, Mrs Victoria Slade,' he said evenly.

Victoria Slade gave him a slight smile, and replied, 'Oh, indeed. You are Mr Gerard Schuyler, the Captain's grandson, are you not?'

'Oh, indeed.' And Gerard was smiling, too. A thin smile, the smile of a predator, the smile of a man who made no concessions to anyone, not even a woman as beautiful as Mrs Victoria Slade.

Dear Reader

We launch a Paula Marshall trilogy this month, following the Schuyler family, who are American, but base their lives in England. We begin with Gerard, a real buccaneer, and his efforts to discover the truth about Victoria. We have a wonderful romp from Elizabeth Bailey, and our two American authors are Donna Anders, with the first of her mother/daughter duo set on Hawaii, and Marjorie Burrows, with a story of Montana in 1876. A wonderful month's reading to welcome the Spring!

The Editor

Paula Marshall, married with three children, has had a varied life. She began her career in a large library and ended it as a senior academic in charge of history in a polytechnic. She has travelled widely, has been a swimming coach, and has appeared on *University Challenge* and *Mastermind*. She has always wanted to write, and likes her novels to be full of adventure and humour.

Recent titles by the same author:

THE CYPRIAN'S SISTER
MY LADY LOVE

THE CAPTAIN'S LADY

Paula Marshall

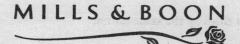

MILLS & BOON LIMITED
ETON HOUSE, 18–24 PARADISE ROAD
RICHMOND, SURREY, TW9 1SR

First published in Great Britain 1994
by Mills & Boon Limited

© Paula Marshall 1994

Australian copyright 1994
Philippine copyright 1994
This edition 1994

ISBN 0 263 78248 4

Set in 10½ on 12 pt Linotron Times
04-9403-78956

Typeset in Great Britain by Centracet, Cambridge
Made and printed in Great Britain

CHAPTER ONE

SHE was notorious. She only had to enter a room for every head to turn. A woman who owned and edited a feminist newspaper, who had been the mistress of the dead old man whose funeral was being held in the Collegiate Reformed Protestant Dutch Church of New York on this cold early March day in 1891.

But even without her notoriety, heads would still have turned, for she was, the watching man saw, beautiful.

He knew immediately who she must be. On his return to the United States after a long absence in England, she had recently been pointed out to him with a snigger and an obscene joke about the dead man, who had been his grandfather, by a man who had called himself a friend—but was a friend no longer. But today she was not walking down Fifth Avenue, but entering a church, and a church whose service she ought not to be attending.

A susurration of angry voices, a noise like a swarm of excited bees, hissed through the congregation, which was made up, as the newspapers said that night, of all that was swell in New York society. Old money, new money, members of the First Four Hundred, those who aspired to be members, politicians, and the parasites who always attended upon the wealthy and powerful, were all present to speed on his way to the grave Ghysbrecht Schuyler, always known as 'the Captain', who, living, had despised the lot of them, and had made himself the richest man on earth.

Rich enough to buy the beautiful woman on whom the hissing disapproval created by her presence had no effect. Nor did the words of the usher who had walked peremptorily towards her, and who was speaking to her — to no avail — for she appeared to be shrugging him off, so that suddenly he placed a hand on her arm.

The watching man, standing at the back by the font, who should, by rights, have been waiting with the family to process into the church behind the coffin, but had, instead, preferred to enter the church almost anonymously, to see that nothing went wrong, always a possibility when a man of such notoriety as the Captain was involved, sighed, and moved forward — heads now turning to watch him. In his own quite different way he was as notorious as the woman.

The last two heads which turned were those of the usher, his cousin, Perry Standish, and the woman with whom he was remonstrating. He had no eyes for Perry, only for the woman, and her eyes, great violet ones, were only for him. It was the first time that they had met.

They stared at one another. 'Mrs Victoria Slade?' he enquired, with a bow, the three words something between a statement and a question, and the bow was derisive.

'I am. And you, sir?' And her last sentence was a question, too.

For a moment it was as though they were alone together. On one side of an invisible divide stood a tall woman, dark hair piled high on her head, beneath a broad-brimmed black hat trimmed with violets, above an ivory face of a pure classic beauty. Her gown was black grosgrain beneath a broadcloth coat with a seal-skin collar, to which was pinned another bunch of violets, their clean scent filling the air.

On the other side was a tall man, who was so broad and powerful that his six feet and more of height was diminished by his width—but nothing could diminish his face. Improbably, although he was of Dutch extraction, he was very dark, with glossy black hair, a sallow complexion and a pair of eyes of a yellow-brown as feral as those of a tiger. There was nothing handsome about him, but he radiated an almost brutal power. Like the woman he was impeccably dressed, in a charcoal-grey morning suit made by an English tailor on Savile Row, and the collar of his perfect greatcoat was of sable, as black and velvety as his hair.

'I think you know very well who I am, Mrs Victoria Slade,' he said evenly.

Victoria Slade gave him a slight smile, and replied, 'Oh, indeed. You are Mr Gerard Schuyler, the Captain's grandson, are you not?'

'And I am wondering why you have chosen to come here. . .' was his only reply to that.

The usher, who stood in awe of Gerard Schuyler, spoke at last. 'And so I told her,' he said eagerly. 'Most improper, Gerard. There is no place for her at this sad ceremony.'

'Oh, indeed.' And Gerard was smiling, too. A thin smile, the smile of a predator, the smile of a man who made no concessions to anyone, not even a woman as beautiful as Mrs Victoria Slade.

'I would have thought that you would have had sufficient respect for my grandfather's family not to attend his funeral, even if the other proprieties had not restrained you. . .' Only for him to be interrupted by Mrs Slade, murmuring, her manner as cool as the air about them.

'I am present at the express wish of your grandfather, the late Captain Schuyler, who is being buried here today. I have his letter with me, and in any case I was not aware that one might be turned away from God's house. . .even if one were a sinner . . .particularly if one were a sinner. . . I had the belief that it was open to all.'

'But the family,' began the usher, 'will be disturbed by your presence. Good taste alone——'

'Now, now, Perry, I don't think that Mrs Slade is troubled by notions of good taste,' said Gerard, a derisive smile on his strong face. 'Is not that so, Mrs Slade? Otherwise she would have ignored my grandfather's wishes. He was never troubled by any notions about good taste, either.'

'Oh, as to that, it is a matter of opinion,' said Mrs Slade levelly. 'All I know is that the Captain wished me to attend, and so I am here.'

Gerard was suddenly tired of all this, of the prurient faces of the watching congregation as he argued with his late grandfather's whore. He leaned forward, murmured in a low voice, 'Well, that being so, madam, and since you *are* here, and appear determined to stay, allow me to seat you somewhere discreet. I trust you not to make a further scene, madam, no wailings, no hysterics.'

Victoria Slade had an answer ready for him. She seemed, Gerard thought, to have an answer for everything, which, considering her reputation, was not surprising. 'It was not I who made the scene, Mr Gerard Schuyler. I was prepared to sit quietly down. Your flunkey here caused the commotion.'

Gerard could not repress a grin as his cousin Perry, a self-important man, began to stutter, 'A flunkey. . . I am not a flunkey. . .'

'Don't be more of a fool than God made you, Perry,' Gerard said pleasantly. 'Go and do your duties. Leave Mrs Slade to me,' and he took her by the elbow, his strong fingers digging into the delicate flesh of her upper arm, gripping her so cruelly that even if she had wished to pull away she could not do so. They were now so close that he could smell not only the violets but a delicate aroma which was uniquely Victoria Slade's, and which had his senses reacting to it, as well as to the soft warmth of her body. He commanded himself to remember who, and what, this soiled dove was.

Quietly, the soiled dove said, through stiff lips, 'There is no need to manhandle me, sir. I must remind you again that any unpleasantness created on my arrival was due to the behaviour of a member of your family, not through any act of mine.'

Gerard almost laughed aloud. Only the knowledge of where he was prevented him from saying something unforgivable to this impertinent if

beautiful bitch who was flaunting her profession at
his grandfather's funeral.

Why, it might not be a bad idea to make an
assignation with her, on the spot, enjoy her as his
grandfather had done, except that that might cause
her to think that she had gained some advantage
over him, by persuading him to take advantage of
her all too physical charms.

'The unpleasantness is your presence, Mrs Slade.
To be quite plain, the family does not wish to be
reminded, today of all days, of the scheming dollymop my grandfather chose to entertain in his old
age.' And his voice was ice. The seat he had half-
dragged her to was at the side, well away from the
family, or from any other person of consequence
present. Victoria Slade could see very little, and no
one could see her.

As Gerard Schuyler pushed her into it, with an
almost insolent deference, using his strength to do
so, she looked up at him, prepared to remonstrate,
but Gerard was having none of her tricks.

By God, she was not going to use those amazing
eyes on him. He hissed through his teeth, 'Pray do
not attempt to exercise your lures on me, madam. I
am not an old fool in his dotage.'

'Nor was your grandfather,' she flung back at
him, also keeping her voice low, only to have him
reply,

'And pray leave quietly at the end, madam. That
should, I hope, conclude your unwanted association
with the Schuylers,' and he turned to walk away.

Gerard had barely gone two paces before her
voice drew him back. It was, he noticed, against his

will, as beautiful as the rest of her, low, perfectly modulated, not at all the voice one might have expected from the Captain's bit of fluff, who also happened to be a strident Woman's Righter.

'I think not, Mr Gerard Schuyler.' She seemed to be taking a perverse pleasure in throwing his full name at him. 'I am bidden to the will-reading this afternoon. And I have a letter from the Schuyler family's solicitor to prove that, too. I look forward to seeing you again. You may give me some further instruction in the proprieties, although it seems to me that you are the one in need of instruction, not myself.'

Gerard's stride faltered. He stopped. Enraged, he knew that she must have registered his shock, for he heard her low laugh.

He turned again: to stare at her, to give her the full force of his arrogance, for he was all Schuyler, the only one of the descendants of the dead old man who shared his ruthless and formidable will.

'You are sure of that, madam? Such is not my family's understanding.' He had a sudden delightful vision of his fat and pompous father's horror at the presence of the Captain's ladybird at the will-reading! Even in death the old devil was going to dominate affairs, his wicked and wanton voice coming from the grave. He wondered wryly what further shocks for them all might be in store.

'Quite sure,' returned Victoria Slade, and oh, what triumph there was in her violet eyes. 'It was your grandfather's express wish, and I respect him too much to defy him — even after death.'

Gerard could not restrain himself. Death or no

death, funeral or no funeral, church or no church, there was nothing for it, he threw his head back and laughed, a full-blooded laugh that had every head in the church turning in shock, handkerchiefs lifted from eyes, reproving 'Oh's and 'Hush'es coming from all directions.

'Respect, Mrs Torry Slade?' he queried, giving her, at last, the name by which she was most generally known. 'Respect! Is that the emotion you peddled when alone with my grandfather? I could give your cantrips a different name were we anywhere else but in the House of God. Remind me to do so later on, over the teacups and niceties of the will-reading. It will enliven a difficult and unpleasant day for me.'

His amusement was so heartfelt that it lit an answering spark in her, and Gerard could see at once what, beside her beauty, had drawn his grandfather to her. Oh, Mrs Torry Slade had spirit and humour, had she not? What was she thinking now, as he sobered himself again, pursed his mouth, became one of the respectable descendants of the distant Dutch peasant who had landed on a foreign shore, to pillage the inhabitants in creating a fortune beyond the dreams of Croesus, to become the wealthiest family in the world — as the Captain had been the wealthiest man?

Torry Slade, watching him walk away, his shoulders shaking, was remembering what the Captain had said to her once: 'The only one of the whole pack of them — ' meaning his family ' — worth knowing is young Gerard, and he doesn't want to know me.'

Now, why was that? she thought. For one thing

was plain to her. The late Captain Schuyler and his oldest grandchild had a great deal in common.

'Here? She is coming here? How dare she come here? Have you done nothing to stop this. . . Gerard? Are you listening to me, Gerard?'

Typically, Mrs Joris Schuyler, wife of the Captain's eldest son, was appealing not to her husband but to her son. She knew only too well that an appeal for action to Joris Schuyler was useless. Browbeaten by his stern father in youth, he had retreated into inaction and gormandising as he grew older, and, incapable of making money himself, preferred to live on the fortune which his wife had inherited. He sat on various of the Captain's boards, but had never been known to open his mouth.

Gerard, who carried on the family tradition by being the exact opposite of his father, raised his heavy eyebrows, said, 'No, Mother, let us keep matters in perspective. I have no authority to send her away. Van Rensselaer tells me that the Captain laid it down that she must attend the will-reading. What I have done is order Marchant to show her to the small drawing-room with orders to serve her tea and to keep her there until the lawyers are here to read it. The library has been prepared for the ceremony.'

He sighed again. Today, had he remained in England, he had been due to go to Tatton Park to be a member of a house-party graced by Edward, Prince of Wales, where Gerard's latest mistress, Lady Daisy Gascoyne, was also to be present, her husband having been sent by a considerate Prince to do some diplomatic finagling in Portugal, leaving the coast clear for the guilty pair.

Instead, here he was, called back to dismal New York surrounded by large numbers of people for most of whom he did not care a jot. Now that the funeral service had been held he had had time to appreciate the nonsense of it all — and the hypocrisy.

The Captain had been laid to rest beneath a highly inappropriate and simpering marble angel, holding out a wreath, presumably to be carried by him on his journey to whatever Valhalla his God might choose to send him.

Not, thought Gerard, who could hardly restrain his irreverent laughter, not only at the sight of the monument, but at all the grieving mourners, most of whom had hated the dead man's guts, as he had hated theirs, that Ghysbrecht Schuyler had ever believed in anything but himself.

Afterwards, the family, and all those who might have an interest in the dead man's will, had adjourned to his mansion at the corner of Fifth Avenue and Sixth Street. It was a copy of the Château de Chambord, built in the Loire Valley during the French Renaissance, and was filled with treasure looted from every great house in Europe whose owners needed money to support their life-style, diminished by their loss of income after two decades of agricultural depression in Europe.

The drawing-room in which the mourning party was gathered was two storeys high, and the painted ceiling, shipped over from Italy, showed Zeus in glory, surrounded by the gods, being handed wreaths of flowers and fruits by Aphrodite, Pallas

Athene and Hera. Whatever, thought Gerard, looking around him, had his grandfather made of the palace his architects had built for him?

However beautiful the furniture and the works of art with which it was filled, none of it was designed to be comfortable, but to display the wealth and power of the man who had caused it to be built.

Gerard's mother, formerly Miss Mamie Dodds of Pike's Place, Nevada, where the silver lode which had made her miner father a multi-millionaire had been discovered, still reproaching her husband and son alternately, sank down on to a Louis XV bergère. She patted its ornately carved arms gently, ready to assume its ownership, and the ownership of everything which surrounded her. No one had the slightest notion of what the Captain's will contained, and until it was read, in an hour's time, speculation as to whom all this would pass was general and rife.

The universal consensus was that the Captain would hardly leave his fortune, estimated to be over two hundred and fifty million dollars and the largest in the world, away from his eldest son, even though he had never seen eye to eye with him, and had no respect for his judgement, either personal or financial.

Deeming her smile of pleasure at the thought of sitting here and entertaining assorted Vanderbilts, Astors, Whitneys and Goulds to be inappropriate to the occasion, Mrs Joris thought it polite to place her handkerchief to her eyes again to display a more suitable grief, giving a loud sob as she did so. Irreverent Gerard laughed. He knew only too well that his poor mother had both disliked and feared her father-in-law, the Captain, and wondered where all this grief was coming from.

Unexpectedly, he had found himself regretting that he had never been on terms with his grandfather. His decision to live in England, after making a fortune for himself in dealings on Wall Street, had been based on a desire to be free of the Captain, the Schuyler family, and the family's influence.

Well, that was the past, and only a fool harked back to the past, when the present was there to be lived, and the future lay before him to be planned and anticipated. He had no hopes from the will himself, and was sufficiently wealthy not to regret the fact. His own fortune would have seemed remarkable to most men, and only the magnitude of the Captain's wealth was able to diminish it. His cousin, Brandt Schuyler, a man of his own age, came up to him. Brandt was what Gerard thought of as a flunkey, someone who could not make money for himself but was used by other men to help them to do so. 'Is it true?' he asked, 'that that woman will be here for the will-reading?'

'So van Rensselaer says,' replied Gerard a little sharply; he was growing tired of constantly explaining about Mrs Slade, but his unsatisfactory father had, as usual, abdicated all responsibility for everything to do with the Captain's death as soon as Gerard had set foot in New York. 'And before you go on, there is nothing anyone can do about it.'

'Not good enough,' growled Brandt. 'It was a damnable business that an old man of eighty, who ought to have been thinking of the life to come, was running a creature like Torry Slade at all. A Woman's Righter, of all things, encouraging all women to immorality. Irreligious——' Brandt was by way of being pious '—and the old man putting up the money for her paper, and helping her to gamble on the Stock Exchange. A woman stockbroker—whoever heard of such a thing?'

'I didn't know that,' said Gerard, struck. 'Gambles on the Stock Exchange, does she? Makes much money?'

'Oh, with the old man running her, a fortune, they say.'

'They say, they say,' said Gerard impatiently. 'They say a lot. How much of what they say is true is another matter.'

Brandt shrugged his well-tailored shoulders: all the Schuylers, even fat Joris, were well turned out, dressed perfectly for every occasion. 'Well, it's true that she was the old man's mistress. They went everywhere together. She even lived at Seahorses with him last summer.'

This did surprise Gerard. His heavy brows rose yet again. Seahorses was the Captain's seaside home at Newport, Long Island, a palace built for him by the same architect who had designed his Fifth Avenue mansion. He had never before taken his women there, not even after his wife had died, ten years before his own death.

'He *was* smitten, then.'

'Of course he was. Did you think that the family was making a fuss about nothing? All that money going begging when he died, and that woman virtually his wife. . .'

'The family's been worried about women before, and it always came to nothing.'

'Not this time.' Brandt was brief. 'This one's. . . different.'

'Different! How different? Dollymops—they're all the same.'

'Well, the way he went on with Torry Slade was different. You never saw them together, did you? Too busy enjoying yourself in London.'

Gerard was suddenly impatient. Whores who were different! What next? 'All this is hot air, Brandt. Wait for the will to be read *then* have hysterics about it—if necessary.'

'Oh, it'll be necessary, you'll see. She'll have inherited something, you may be sure. Point is, how much? You know, the old man cut us all off these last few years—but, of course, you don't know. Cut yourself off too.'

'Well, I'm back now,' offered Gerard. But he had no intention of staying. The worship of the family, as though they were descended from European grand dukes at the very least, which everyone but himself went in for, he found tiresome. Like this conversation. He was reasonably sure that Brandt's gloom was unwarranted. The old man had not been in his dotage. A week before he died he had brought off a coup involving his interests in copper mining which had netted him a small fortune.

Gerard's father had spoken to the Captain's doctors immediately after his death. They had told him that until the very moment when the massive heart attack had struck him down, dying, appropriately, while he was standing at his desk in his Wall Street office, he had been in a remarkable state of health and sanity for a man in his early eighties.

He told Brandt so. His cousin's reply was a grunted, 'Well, if even your father was worried about what the Captain might have done with his money, you may be sure that there *is* something to worry about!'

Gerard smiled wryly. His father's sluggish idleness and lack of mental acuity was so markedly in contrast with the Captain's furious energy which he had retained into old age, to say nothing of his almost Machiavellian cunning, that he could not take offence at Brandt's acid comment — but he did not like him the more for it.

He was saved from any comment himself, and from further dooming by the worried Brandt, by a gentle tap on his arm. It was his seventeen-year-old sister Kate. The thirteen-year gap between the two of them occasionally had him suspecting that his dilatory father had only favoured his wife with his presence in her bed on the two occasions on which he and his sister had been conceived.

'Gerard!' she exclaimed — lively Kate always exclaimed. 'I've hardly spoken to you since you landed! What with Pa worrying you about Grandpa and you having to arrange the funeral and all, and Ma saying that young ladies should not be seen at all in times of family grief, and confining me to quarters, I haven't had a chance to talk to anyone. I'm surprised that I'm even allowed to be here. Oh dear, and now I'm smiling! Ma *will* be annoyed! Tears only allowed today! How the Captain would have laughed!'

In looks, Kate was very like Gerard, very dark in the face and athletic in the body — only pretty, their mother had once said. They both took after the Captain, bearing no resemblance to their mother, or to their obese father, who stood mournfully plucking his lower lip, a habit of his which had infuriated the Captain.

'Well, the Captain directed that you should be here, and since we *are* talking, Kate, how is life treating you?'

'Abominably. Everything a dead bore,' said Kate frankly. 'I hate being groomed by Ma to be a young lady. Especially since I'm sure that Ma is picking out a poverty-stricken English earl for me to marry, and will want you to take me back with you to London in order to hook him! Although today is different. Tell me, Gerard — ' and she waved her hand around the ornate room and the people who filled it ' — is it really true that that woman will be here for the will-reading?'

Her brother gave his tenth sigh of the day and put out a hand to tuck a straying black curl into Kate's neatly bound coiffure, thinking that to try to turn her into a sedate and characterless young lady was a hopeless task.

'First of all, you shouldn't know, or should pretend not to know, that Torry Slade so much as exists. Secondly, I'm tired of being asked if it is true that she is here. Yes, she is. I've had her put in the small drawing-room and she'll only appear when the will is read, and will be politely escorted out of the house the moment that it is.'

'Oh, bully, I'm dying to see her close up,' cried

Kate eagerly. 'And oh, it is good to have you back, Gerard. No shilly-shally about you. Such a relief after Pa's inability to make up his mind about anything. What would have happened if you hadn't come home to sort things out I can't imagine!'

'Oh, Brandt and the rest would have seen to it all quite competently.'

'Not like you,' said Kate. She put her head on one side. 'You know what, you're just like the Captain must have been when he was your age? Like the picture over there.' And she pointed to the giant oil over the hearth showing Ghysbrecht Schuyler in the pride of his youth.

'God forbid,' he said instinctively. The thought had haunted him for as long as he could remember. Everything about the hard old man frightened him, because he could discover the same traits in himself. The furious energy he had brought to life. The driving ambition, the brute power of him as he crushed everything which stood in his way, and the procession of women who had passed through his life, satisfying that appetite for living, too.

Was it true? Was he like that? Had he not gone to England to live a different life, to try to deny it?

Oh, yes, he shared so many things with the Captain, including the women—especially the women. And, thinking this, he had a sudden vision of Torry Slade, elegant and proud, mocking him in the church, and felt a spasm of desire, so shocking in its intensity that it provoked his instant arousal. Could he really be missing Daisy Gascoyne so much? Kate was speaking again. He must listen to her, since no one else did. She was only a Schuyler woman being groomed for a dynastic marriage.

'All I can say,' and her voice was earnest, 'is that everyone thinks so. And you've made your own fortune, independent of him. Not like Pa living on what the Captain gave him and what Ma inherited from Grandpa Dodds. Oh, I wish I were a man to do what you and the Captain did, and not be handed over like a parcel to some Haw-haw of a Limey!'

Reproving heads turned again as Gerard laughed out loud. 'I promise you, Kate, they'll not sell you to some aristocratic wastrel in order to have a title in the family. And you're the spit image of the Captain, too. Next thing you'll want to be a female stockbroker on Wall Street.'

'Just like Torry Slade—and I could run a newspaper the way she does. I just know I could, Gerard.' Kate's vivid face was alight. 'Say you'll help me, Gerard; go on, do! Oh, wouldn't that be bully?'

'Not now, Kate, later.' Gerard was dismissive. Marchant, the butler, was coming towards him with the news that the lawyers and the library were ready for them. The will-reading was about to begin.

CHAPTER TWO

MRS TORRY SLADE put down the china teacup from which she had been drinking, rose to her feet and surveyed the elegant room to which she had been brought by the Schuylers' butler — as a form of banishment, presumably.

The thought made her shapely mouth curl. There was an elegant Renaissance mirror over a Chinese lacquer cabinet and she carefully checked her appearance in it. It would not do to arrive at the will-reading looking less than perfectly turned out. Nothing, but nothing, must suggest the dishevelled courtesan or the shrieking sister demanding the Rights of Women.

Nothing did. The woman she saw there was as splendidly turned out as any of the women in the library where she would shortly sit and who belonged to the society on whose edge she had lived with the Captain.

The memory of the formidable old man who had been her protector softened her face, increased her smile. She could imagine what he might say to her if she felt like faltering before the massed ranks of respectability. 'Now, girl. No need to feel yourself inferior. All women sell themselves for money. They have to: it's the way society is run. What they do for it and the reasons for doing it are different —

23

everything else remains the same. No need for execuses — head high, and damn their eyes.'

She knew what he would say because he had occasionally said it, and if she ever faltered she reminded herself of him and his pithy and sometimes barbed comments on the world he had exploited so successfully.

Securing her broad-brimmed hat more firmly on her high-piled hair, tucking in the odd black tendril — her own hair was nearly as black and glossy as Gerard Schuyler's, she had noticed, but nothing like as springing and coarse; the Captain's must have been very similar before it grew white with age — she heard the butler enter, coughing respectfully. Whatever he thought of her, and he knew her from the many occasions on which she had been here with the Captain, nothing moved on his shrewd old face.

'I am to take you to the library, madam.' And he inclined his head and indicated the door, face still impassive. Only, as she walked by him, her violet scent drifting on the air, he said quietly, so quietly that she thought she might have imagined it, but knew that she hadn't, 'Good luck, Mrs Slade,' and then processed her, as though she had been a visiting princess, to the library, where she and the Captain had frequently played crib for bonbons from one of New York's finest shops, except that if he won he always commuted his for whiskey. The Captain had been a light drinker, only indulging himself at night when business was over, never in the day. 'Only a fool pours stuff down his throat to addle his brains,' he had once commented trenchantly.

Marchant opened the door and she walked into the library, aware that everyone in the room — she was the last to enter — was watching her. Gerard Schuyler, his face now impassive, although Torry thought that she detected a twitch on his mouth, came forward to meet and to seat her, nearer to the centre of things this time.

But he placed her firmly on her own, the seats on each side of her empty — so that she should not pollute anyone by her presence, she supposed. The thought, and what the Captain would have said, were he, or his ghost, present at his own will-reading, amused her so much that she smiled again, involuntarily, lighting up her face so that the watching Gerard drew in his breath, understanding a little why this particular woman had had her hooks in his grandfather for so long, when most of his other women had shared his busy life only briefly.

Oh, a proper jewel of a whore was Mrs Torry Slade, and any red-blooded US male would be proud to have her in his bed, walk out with her on his arm!

He made his way to his own seat at the front. The Family — he always thought of it with the formal capital letter, so solemnly did they regard them-selves — were assembled behind him. It was as though the few years since the Captain had acquired his money and power had been sufficient to turn them into a dynasty at one with the Hapsburgs and Romanovs of Europe.

Van Rensselaer, a minor member of a family

whose own name did go deep into the roots of New York and American history, rose from his seat behind a desk which had come from an Austrian palace — at least the Schuyler possessions could claim an imperial or aristocratic origin — and surveyed the assembled men and women before him.

If he thought, as he undoubtedly did, that they were a collection of parvenus, Johnny-come-latelies, whose immediate ancestors, including the dead man, had recently been mere toiling clods unworthy of a genuine Yankee aristocrat's attention, he gave no sign of it.

'You all,' he said, in his precise old voice — he spoke like the English ruling class whom his ancestors had driven from the land now owned by such as the Schuylers, 'know that you are gathered together to hear the last will and testament of the late Gysbrecht Gerhardt Schuyler, and you are all here at his expressed invitation. I must stress that in his own hand he listed all those whom he wished to be present. I say this to clear up any small misunderstandings.'

He coughed, paused and stared stonily at them. Or rather, Gerard thought, he stared stonily at Torry Slade. He could almost feel her presence, although she was seated several rows behind him. Why had the old fool stopped? Did he expect anyone to challenge him? No, he was probably enjoying his one brief moment of power after years of being bullied and dominated by the Captain.

Everyone in the room either coughed, echoing van Rensselaer, or moved uneasily, thinking with Gerard, Why don't he get on with it? Don't he know that we all want to find out where we stand, what the old man might have left us? But the new manners which the senior members of the family had painfully acquired and the junior ones had imbibed with their mother's milk kept them polite and attentive.

Van Rensselaer coughed again, began to read, occasionally pausing to enlarge on or to explain something which might appear opaque. The beginning of the will was unexceptional, listed small monies left to old retainers, friends, still living, from the Captain's own youth.

The lawyer reached the end of the second page, looked up, and said, almost sardonically, 'That concludes the minor portion of the disposal of the Captain's fortune. May I remind you all that what I am now about to read was written by Mr Ghysbrecht Schuyler himself, and has nothing to do with my law office, other than that we advised him to set down his wishes in such a way that it was legally sound? Ahem! I recommence, "In disposing of my fortune, I bore in mind that my greatest wish was for it to remain intact, and that it was not to be frittered away among those who had shown by their conduct of affairs that they had no idea of how to keep it, or to increase it. I have therefore passed over all members of my immediate family, including my son, Joris Schuyler, when disposing of it. I have already bestowed large sums of money on him, and he is a virtual multi-millionaire by reason of his marriage to old Dodds's daughter. The same goes for my other sons and my daughter, Theodora.

'"Instead, I propose to reward those of my family

and friends who have shown gumption and spirit and who will not frivol away what I choose to bequeath them, but will increase it."'

By now the noise in the library was beyond the original nervous coughing and feet-shuffling of the beginning. Joris Schuyler had jumped to his feet and had begun to protest. His two brothers, Hans and Franklin, rich men by virtue of their employment in various Schuyler enterprises, but who had hoped to be richer, were also protesting.

'I shall have the will broken,' Joris shouted. 'The old man was in his dotage—he must have been to inflict his whore on us.' Joris was beyond considering that there were ladies present and that he must suit his speech to them. His perceived wrongs were too great for that.

Gerard, who had been grinning, for he, if no one else, had anticipated this, although not the exact terms in which his dead grandfather might choose to insult his unsatisfactory descendants, rose.

'Let us,' he said, and he raised his voice, which was, Torry noted, both powerful and beautiful, quite unlike the dead Captain's harsh tones—but then, Gerard had been educated at Harvard, the Captain by life, 'allow Mr van Rensselaer to finish the reading. Courtesy alone. . .yes, Father, courtesy alone must prevent us from saying what we think until he has concluded. Nothing will be served by turning this into a brawl—other than to convince New York that the Schuylers are still unmannerly peasants.'

Silence fell. Most of Gerard's contemporaries liked to think of themselves as the flower of society, and were deeply conscious that if news of this. . . unseemly shindig got out New York would both laugh and sneer at them.

'Thank you, Mr Gerard Schuyler,' said the lawyer repressively, 'and I must remind you all that before this will was made, anticipating such trouble, the late Mr Ghysbrecht Schuyler had himself inspected by a panel of doctors — you will allow. . .' And he began again.

'"First of all, I leave to my good friend and the companion of my old age, who has lightened my life for me, Mrs Victoria Alexandra Slade, the sum of two million dollars and my villa, Seahorses, at Newport, Long Island, in the hope that she will think of me a little when she is there.'

That did it! That really did it! One of Mrs Joris Schuyler's dearest dreams had been to preside at Seahorses, entertaining various members of New York's swell set, the First Four Hundred. She let out a shrill scream, cried, 'Oh, no-o-o. . .' half rose and then fell back into her chair. 'Oh, how wicked! How could he. . .?' And her emotions were echoed around the library as she subsided into hysterics.

Torry sat, immobile, shocked in her seat. She had thought, given that she had been invited to the will-reading, that he might leave her *something*, but not, after leaving his sons and daughter nothing, that he would make her such a princely present.

No, she did not want it, not at all. Except. . . except that hearing the raised voices, feeling the anger of the jilted family, she thought with a burst of rebellious pride, Well, I made Gis happy, and it's quite apparent that none of *them* did. They had never considered him at all, except as a money mine, so why should he consider them?

'Flesh and blood cannot stand this,' declaimed Joris loudly. 'To be passed over, while he rewards his whore. Let her leave at once. Her interest in this is over. I demand it.'

It seemed that the company agreed with him. Gerard, who had expected nothing, even if in his secret heart he had often wondered what he would do in the unlikely event of him inheriting a mere fraction of the Captain's wealth, was wryly entertained by the brouhaha, and turned to inspect Mrs Slade's reactions.

She was, he was amused to see, quite composed, if very pale, and was looking coolly at van Rensselaer, until, suddenly aware of his gaze on her, she stared straight at him, quite unrepentant, he was happy to notice. Serve all his mealy-mouthed family right, was his swift and irreverent thought!

'I cannot,' announced van Rensselaer, who had begun to enjoy himsef, 'ask Mrs Slade to leave, since a further and major portion of the will concerns her, too.'

'What?' shrieked Joris, who, having been pulled down by brother Hans, now rose again. 'You mean that there's more of this. . .wickedness to come?'

'If you will allow.' Van Rensselaer bent his head and began to read rapidly. '"Bearing in mind that I wish my estate and all my possessions to remain as one, and not to be squandered, I direct that my grandson, Mr Gerhardt Ghysbrecht Schuyler, the eldest son of my son Joris, shall inherit the entire remainder of all of which I stand and die possessed, and which is listed as an annexe to this will, on condition that within three months from the date of my death he takes in marriage the said Mrs Victoria Alexandra Slade, since I have frequently deplored his unmarried state, and, wishing the Schuyler line to continue through its most able living member, I can think of no better way to ensure it.

'"Failing this marriage, he shall inherit nothing, and the estate will pass into a trust fund, the details of which are listed below, whose headquarters shall be my home in Fifth Avenue where this will is being read.

'"I trust in God that Mr Gerhardt Ghysbrecht Schuyler will continue to demonstrate the common sense and gumption, which no one else in the family appears to have inherited, will carry out my wishes, and that Mrs Victoria Slade will also heed them. Her future needs to be secured beyond the trifle I have left her."'

Silence, as van Rensselaer finished, then, 'Trifle!' wailed Mrs Joris, echoed by thirty other voices. 'He dares to call Seahorses and two million dollars a trifle, when he has left us nothing. Oh, Mr Schuyler, I am about to faint; help me.'

'Stow that,' said Joris Schuyler, reverting to the coarse speech of his ancestors, sounding for once like the dead Captain. 'Can't you see who has influenced him? The conniving bitch! She worked on the old fool to gain a fortune and a husband. Well, I'll make sure that she'll gain nothing.'

The only silent person in the room was Gerard, surveying his unwanted prize. The old devil, he said to himself. He left his dollymop two million and

Seahorses, and then tried to make sure that even *that* stayed with the rest, by, in effect, bequeathing her to me. Well, be damned to that! Even to gain two hundred and fifty million dollars, I'm not marrying the old man's leavings, and that's flat.

CHAPTER THREE

'So, Mrs Torry Slade. A fine plot for you and the old man to hatch between you. Did you conceive it between the sheets instead of children? I can imagine that it must have enlivened the night hours between you, given the inevitably flagging energies of an eighty-year-old.'

Gerard could not help himself. At first, his grandfather's last black joke, his last trick practised on his wretched family, to leave no one but himself anything, and that conditional on his marrying his own grandfather's mistress, had half amused him.

The worst of it was that he had expected nothing, would have been satisfied with nothing. Only to have the whole lot dangled before him — and then snatched away by a condition that no self-respecting man could fulfil. . . *That* had him boiling.

From the moment when the reading concluded shortly afterwards, and van Rensselaer had said, 'I must ask Mrs Slade and Mr Gerhardt Ghysbrecht Schuyler to meet me in the late Mr Schuyler's study,' he had been overcome by a rage which turned the world red about him.

Stiff-legged, a pulse beating in his temple, murder in his heart, he had defied all canons of politeness, had walked from the room to leave *her* to walk behind him, unattended, to run the gauntlet of stares, sneers and vengeful looks from his betrayed family. The famed coolness which Gerard brought to all aspects of living had disappeared.

He had even snarled at van Rensselaer as he rose, 'My name is Gerard,' giving it the soft G in preference to the hard one which van Rensselaer had adopted, whether to emphasise his difference from a man who clung to his European origins, or to remove any resemblance to his dead grandfather, he did not know.

Hatefully, his rage was almost sexual in nature, anger and sex being closely intertwined, or so his Harvard studies had taught him. For as, perforce, he was compelled to let her walk into the study before him, or be branded by van Rensselaer as the peasant scum he was, the scent and nearness of her brought on a spasm of desire so powerful that it actually caused arousal.

God, that he should be lusting after the whore his grandfather was seeking to force on him in marriage! If he could merely have bought her, enjoyed her, and then, as one did with such creatures, passed on, the whole thing might have been endurable.

But no. The Captain, may he rot in hell, had decided, nay ordered, that if the Schuyler fortune were to remain with the Schuylers she was to be the mother of his children. What bee had buzzed in his bonnet—or, more accurately in his night-cap, or in his. . .?

His thoughts were growing so disgusting that he suppressed them, since the cause of all this was standing quite steadily before van Rensselaer, then was sinking into the chair he held out for her, her face as grave, serene and lovely as though she were a nun fresh from the convent instead of. . .no, in the inelegant language of your silly father, Stow that, no point. The point is. . .what is the point?

Gerard gave up, refused the chair van Rensselaer was offering to him as though *he* owned the Schuyler mansion—which come to think of it he probably would do, to all intents and purposes, if the Captain's hateful plan failed, since he would certainly be the lawyer who would organise the trust which would supplant them all.

'No,' he ground out, trying to control himself. 'I prefer to stand. What is it now? Is there more to come? Can there be more? Hasn't the old fool done enough?'

Van Rensselaer allowed his shock to show. 'I thought better of you, Gerard,' he said stiffly, 'than to refer to your dead grandfather in such a manner on the day that he has been laid to rest.'

'Well, I haven't been laid to rest,' he said, vigorously, and was that a smile he detected on the bitch's face? 'And I am not likely to be at rest, seeing what he has seen fit to do to me. Couldn't you have stopped him?'

'As well stop an avalanche, as you of all people surely know. Come, this is useless and you are forgetting Mrs Slade. . .'

'Forgetting Mrs Slade! I am not likely to do that.' He swung on the woman, the faint smile still on her face—a very Mona Lisa, damn her, but she had enough to smile about, did she not? 'I could not forget you, madam, could I? Even without what the Captain has done your many attractions are so manifold that ——'

'Gerard, Gerard,' van Rensselaer wailed behind him. 'Enough. I am bidden to read the Captain's letter to you both, and you must both sign various documents which will allow his many enterprises to continue until the three months is up, and you have either married—or not.'

Mastering his anger—and why should he be so consumed by such rage that he had forgotten himself to the degree that the woman's steady eyes on him were a reproach?—Gerard said, 'Very well, then, read the letter, produce the documents.'

'The documents first, the letter second.' Van Rensselaer was determined to demonstrate his authority and Gerard restrained himself from taking the man by the throat. After all, it was not his fault, for who could ever have stopped the Captain in full flight—any more, added a small voice at the back of his mind, than anyone can stop you?

So, later, the documents were signed, the letter read, which directed that the proposed happy pair— God save the mark—should meet after the will-reading to introduce themselves and to discuss— rationally, the writer had hoped—the condition laid out in the will.

'And if I leave you alone——' van Rensselaer was officious '—I trust, Mr Gerard, that you will remember that Mrs Slade is as surprised as you are by all this,' for Torry had not uttered a word while Gerard had fumed at him, but had sat there, quiet, turning her lustrous violet eyes from one to the other as van Rensselaer had read and Gerard had commented.

'That,' said Gerard, swinging on her again, 'I beg leave to doubt.' He paused, then said, ungraciously,

'Oh, very well. We must, I see, be civilised. I shall pretend that Mrs Slade is both innocent and virtuous — will that do?'

The insult was quite intended on his part, for Gerard had developed a passionate wish to break the unnatural calm the woman before him was displaying. Damn her, she had no right to be cooler than he was — but, of course, if she had known what the old man intended, as he suspected she had, then she had had plenty of time to prepare herself to be cool.

It was this which drove him to be quite so scabrous towards her as he was when van Rensselaer had left them, so that he had twitted her, joking tastelessly about her being in bed with the Captain, laughing with him about the mayhem they intended to inflict on the Schuyler family.

His tone was so savage that Torry Slade rose to her feet, walked towards him, held him with her eyes, and said, still cool, but the felt passion in her whole posture carrying its meaning for him, 'I had nothing at all to do with the way in which Gis drew up his will. This afternoon came as much as a surprise to me as it did to you. More, I suspect.'

Gerard was beginning to recover himself a little; nothing would be gained by blackguarding this. . . this. . . Words failed him again, but he was pleased to notice that his speech had returned to its normal sardonic indifference when he replied, 'So you say, madam, so you say. Forgive me if I don't believe you.'

'Believe what you please. I know what the truth is. Had I known what Gis, the Captain, intended, I would have tried to talk him out of it. Which is presumably why he did not inform me.'

Gis! Gis! How dared she inflict on him the nick-name which she had used to the Captain in his erotic bouts with her? No one in the family, nor any of his previous lights-of-love, had ever dared to speak to or of him so familiarly in public. And how dared she lie to him, and do it with such a lovely face on her? She made Daisy Gascoyne seem commonplace.

'But, in any case,' she continued, 'more to the point, what are we to do about the situation in which the Captain has placed us?'

'Do, madam, do?' And he bit the words savagely at her. 'What do you expect *me* to do? Accept my grandfather's leavings? Never. No, let me rephrase that — I would not marry you for you to be the mother of my children. In other circumstances I would have taken you for an evening's pleasure — you seem eminently beddable to me — but for any-thing more. . .'

Torry Slade could not help herself. She shook before the force of Gerard's thick-voiced contempt.

'No,' she said, her voice still low, but trembling now. 'I do not deserve this. And the Captain was wrong about you. He said. . .he said. . .' and despite herself she could not prevent herself from expressing her sorrow for the dead old man by at last allowing the tears to fall '. . .he said that you were a new kind of Schuyler, a peasant turned gentleman, but with the peasant's shrewdness and determination. But there is nothing of the gentle-man about you, to speak to a helpless woman so. . . so. . .' And her voice faltered into silence, and she turned away from him so that he should not see the fast-falling tears which she could no longer contain. And then, suddenly, all pride, she faced him again. 'I wonder, thinking of me as you do, you can bear to think of touching me, even in lust.'

By heaven, she should be on the stage — she was Sarah Bernhardt's best! The sight of her, head thrown back, proud body taut, the lovely length of her legs, the pride of her bosom plainly visible to the connoisseur in womanhood which he was, was too much for him.

The desire which was so inconveniently attacking him at the sight of her, as though he were a boy of sixteen again, aroused by every female form he saw, discovering the joys of sex and his own mastery of it, impelled him to sudden and unwise action.

'Lust, madam! Lust! I'm sure you know all about *that*, and yes, I should have no difficulty with *that*. Love is the problem, lust is simple.' And he was on her, his hands gripping her shoulders, his mouth coming down on hers, the sight of the shock and fear suddenly in her eyes adding to his fever, so that the kiss he gave her was as fierce as he could make it, and the stunned woman in his arms could feel not only his hard body against her, but the erect and rigid strength of his arousal.

The thought of her dallying with the Captain, the temptation which she represented, the anger and rage he felt at the trick which the pair of them had played on him and his family had driven all notion of common decency out of his head.

Worse, as the kiss went on, he knew that it would not be enough for either of them, and he felt her hands, which had begun by pushing him off, slacken, felt the closed mouth begin to open beneath his, proof that she too was sharing in his suddenly aroused and inconvenient passion.

Why, if this went on, they would progress at one bound from being hard at odds with one another to consummation on the floor of the very room where she had doubtlessly dallied with the old man.

Common sense, mixed with disgust, moved in him. What was he doing? By such actions he was giving the bitch a chance to work her wiles on him. The sweetness of her, the delicate scent, the soft mouth, the shapely body beneath him could only help her to trick him out of what little dignity the Captain had left him. For the whole thing was an affront to his dignity, was it not?

But before he could withdraw she was moving, began beating her gloved hands on his chest, trying to twist her mouth away from his, and only the knowledge that were he to continue he would be well on his way to something akin to rape stopped him for very shame.

He stood back, breathing hard, his face flushed, as was hers, her mouth bruised and swollen by the force of his passion, and yes, of hers, for between the first refusal and the last she had been his most willing partner, and, by God, he could see why the old man had favoured her. He had always liked them wild, and he had no doubt that this one would be wild, once she had removed her decorous mask.

'Beast,' she said, all her composure gone. 'A beast. Is that what living among the aristocracy of Europe has done for you? If so, I cannot say I care for it or you, and as for marrying you, why, you may all live in poverty for me; the Captain knew what he was doing when he disinherited the lot of you.'

Gerard had the grace to feel a little ashamed. But, damn her, she had provoked him to it, and he returned her contempt with interest. 'Content yourself, madam. I am not like to starve. My fortune may not be as large as the one the Captain left, but it is bigger than most, and I intend to increase it — aye, and marry the woman of my choice ——'

'Oh, spare me,' she interrupted, scrubbing her lips with her hand from which she had removed her glove. 'I had intended to refuse the house and the money he left me, but you have quite changed my mind for me. I have to hope that Gis thought he knew that what he was doing was for the best, but for once in his life he was mistaken. And you may tell your cousin Brandt that I shall have no hesitation in publishing to the world the hypocrisy of your other cousin, the Reverend Homer Blackwood. It is time that the general public knew how such creatures as you and he are treat women.'

She turned away from him for the last time, to leave the room not by the door, but by a secret exit in the panelling which the old man had once shown her, and which he had often used to fox people who thought that he was safely in his study when he was engaged in some of his more devious business.

Gerard watched her go. Now what was all that about? What was Homer up to *now*? What new scandal, what fresh piece of folly had he committed, and did the damnable woman intend to publish it in her rag of a paper? And how did she know of Homer's delinquencies? But no need to ask that question. The Captain had told her, of course.

'And what new folly,' said Gerard to Brandt, who had come fussing up to him when he had left the study, and had tried to start a conversation with him on the iniquities of the will, 'has Cousin Homer being committing such that the Slade woman is about to pillory him in her newspaper?'

He had no intention of discussing the will with Brandt or anyone else. He knew that he would have to bear his father's and mother's wailings on the subject, but he would be damned if he would endure anyone else's wittering about it.

Diverted from his original desire to ask Gerard what he proposed to do to save the old man's fortune for the Schuylers, since he assumed that if, somehow, Gerard did inherit, he would ensure that the family received its share of the loot, Brandt said, in disgust, 'Oh, that! I've been trying to put a stop to it, on the family's behalf, of course. You'd not credit it, but the Captain gave him away to her, told her of his latest affair, said, in front of witnesses after listening to one of Homer's sermons denouncing sin and immorality, that he didn't mind a saint rebuking sinners but he was damned if he was going to be battered about the ears by an unrepentant old lecher like Cousin Homer — he knew too much about him. Virtue was one thing, hypocrisy another.

'He put her up to exposing the old fraud in her damned paper. Only the old man dying so suddenly has delayed its appearance. Apparently she's been collecting chapter and verse about Homer's goings-on over the last twenty years, particularly his affair with his secretary Merton Spencer's wife, and the secretary conniving at it. . .'

Brandt finally ran out of breath; he had become so enraged that foam and spittle ran from the corner of his mouth.

'Oh, he's been going the pace for years.' Gerard was his usual sardonic self again, recovered from his recent bout with the lady editress, as he inwardly dubbed her, to exorcise a little the powerful sexual attraction which she had for him. 'You're saying that she has some real hard evidence, she's not relying on gossip?'

'So I understand. Incriminating letters — God knows where she got them from — or so she claimed when I spoke to her on Homer's behalf. I asked her to think of his family, and of ours, before she destroyed his reputation, and all she could say was that the whole world ought to know what a hypocrite he was. Denouncing immorality for the public, she said, while practising it himself in secret. Had the gall to say that she was doing it on behalf of all women exploited by men, and it was time that the double standard was hauled down, and men like Homer were exposed for the sham that they were.'

'A crusader,' said Gerard, 'but I wonder how she justifies her own position as the Captain's mistress, while denouncing Homer for doing what she and the Captain did?'

'Oh,' ground out Brandt, 'she had an answer for that when I twitted her about it — the damned woman has an answer for everything! Said that she and the Captain didn't hide their relationship behind a mask of virtue, as Homer did, and, whatever else he was, the Captain wasn't a hypocrite.'

Well, that was true enough, thought Gerard, and, come to that, neither was she. He thought of the woman's unmovable calm, broken only once in his conversation with her, and for a moment he felt nothing but admiration for someone who had the courage to put her principles into practice, however dubious those same principles were.

Aloud, he queried Brandt, 'You say that she has hard evidence, and I assume that she's speaking the truth, or she wouldn't dare print these accusations for fear of legal reprisals.'

'Exactly,' said Brandt wearily. 'And the old devil we buried today was undoubtedly helping her and advising her; he hated Homer and he didn't mind what trouble he caused.'

'Hmm.' Gerard was thoughtful. Desperate situations called for desperate remedies, and the last thing that the Schuyler family needed, after the scandal of the old man's will, was another scandal involving a member of the family, even a distant one. 'I'll try to think of a way to spike her guns. We could put it to her that now that the Captain's will has almost made her a member of the family, so to speak, she ought to give up the idea.'

'No chance——' Brandt was shaking his head '——unless you marry her, of course. You'd keep the fortune in the family and shut her mouth at the same time. She could hardly carry on with it if she were a genuine member of the family.' The look he gave Gerard was hopeful.

'Oh, I wasn't thinking of anything as drastic as marrying her,' murmured Gerard, whose devious mind, so similar to that of the dead Captain, had already shuttled through a whole series of possibilities relating to silencing the scheming Mrs Slade, while at the same time he continued to refuse to discuss the Captain's will any further, merely saying as he parted from Brandt, 'Trust me, I have a notion of how to go about things. Leave it to me.'

As he had expected, once he had returned with his parents to Joris Schuyler's home lower down Fifth Avenue — a mansion which was so similar to the one built for the Captain, though much smaller in scale, that Gerard had once thought that it looked as though the Captain's had pupped, and set the unwanted offspring down for his equally unwanted son to live in — his father and mother began immediately to press him about it.

'No, Mother,' he said resolutely to her, 'I absolutely refuse to discuss the Captain, the will, my possible marriage, or anything to do with the Schuyler fortune,' and when his father had snarled at him,

'At least, when I begin a legal action to break the old dotard's will, I hope you'll give me your full support,' he had replied wearily, in much the same tone that the Captain had always used to him,

'You may throw good money after bad, Father, but I have not the slightest intention of helping the Schuyler family to become a circus turn, either in the law courts or in the Press. We have absolutely no hope of winning such an action, no hope of proving that the Captain was mentally incapacitated when he made the will — he took good care of that — and, as for providing that any woman could have unduly influenced him, no judge or jury would ever believe any such thing of him.'

His mother gave another series of loud sobs, and sank on to a *chaise-longue*. 'Oh, Gerard, I never thought that you, of all people, would be compelled by the old man to hand yourself over like a Christmas present to his. . .fancy piece, or that we should all be doomed to watch his fortune go out of the family.'

His father, goaded at last into activity by the contempt which the Captain had openly expressed for him in his will, said, harshly for him, 'All I can say is that if you won't back me in a legal action to break the will then you'd damn well better marry her and have done with it. Surely two hundred and fifty million dollars is worth *some* sacrifice? And if she's not to your taste, being married never stopped any sensible man from enjoying himself outside of it.'

His wife's wails redoubled. 'Oh, what next, Mr Schuyler,' she sobbed, to have him roar at her,

'Damn you, woman, I'm sick of your nagging. Come to that, I'm sick of the lot of you. What with my father despising me and my son looking at me down his nose, I've had enough. I'm off to Kate Fielding's for the night. At least I shall find some enjoyment there!'

'Oh, you can't mean it,' wailed Mrs Joris, seeing the worm turn at last. 'To go to a bad house, and to tell me of it. . .'

'Well, I've been there often enough for a little

comfort,' said her husband coarsely, 'and it's about time you knew. A good evening to both of you. I'll see you at breakfast.

He was gone, leaving Gerard to comfort his mother, and to face his own lonely destiny. Not for the first time he realised that great wealth seemed to bring little happiness with it—but he certainly didn't wish to be poor, for that didn't answer, either. Meantime, he had to pick up the pieces of the life which his grandfather had shattered when he wrote his monstrous will.

Torry Slade was also thinking hard about the Captain's will. She had known nothing of what was in it, despite what the Schuyler family thought, and had no particular wish to be handed over to that high-nosed monster Gerard Schuyler, who, although he physically resembled his dead grandfather, seemed to bear little other likeness to him. On the other hand, she hated the thought that she, by her mere existence, was cheating the whole family out of the Captain's millions.

She spent the two days after the will-reading preparing her paper, the *Woman's Banner*, for its next edition; it came out once a week. She had already decided that her exposé of Homer Blackwood's lechery would have to wait until the excitement generated by the Captain's death and its consequences had died down. She had no wish to be accused of being a vulture, preying on the family. It could wait.

She had seen her second-in-command, Judith Reis, who had been in a mad state of excitement, for the news of what the old man had done could not be hidden, and had flown round New York in a flash, reaching the daily papers, and Torry had barricaded herself in her office on Fourth Street, refusing to give interviews or to offer any opinion as to whether or not she would marry Gerard Schuyler.

'No comment,' she had said, and Judith too.

In private Judith had said eagerly, 'I hear he's quite a masher, friend of the Prince of Wales, one of the swell set. Does he look like the Captain?'

'A little,' she had answered coldly. Gerard's assault on her had shaken her badly. She had thought herself immune to men, but her own response, initially cold, had suddenly begun to change, so that her cheeks flamed at the very thought.

'We shall be putting back the Homer Blackwood story,' she said at last, more to silence Judith than to offer information. 'Now is not the time, but later, yes.'

'And marrying him, so you both get the fortune,' Judith went on, not to be silenced. 'What a temptation.'

Torry refused to make any answer. Usually she was on the best of terms with Judith, laughed and joked with her, but she, like Gerard, had no wish to discuss the predicament in which the wilful old man had landed them.

She remembered now that he had once hinted to her something of what he had proposed to do. She had been playing the piano for him one evening, the songs of his lost youth, and he had said at the end, reminiscently, 'That was good, Victoria. Reminds me of how old I am, and that I ought to bring my will up to date. . .' And then, after a pause, 'I think it's going to interest you.'

'No, Gis,' she had said, rising from the piano, shutting the song-book, and turning towards him. 'You are not to leave me anything. I won't have it.'

'My money to do as I please with, girl,' he had said with the infuriating grin which he used against friend and enemy alike, to tease and to taunt, something else which she now realised he shared with Gerard. 'I shall do what I want with my own, and damn the lot of you.'

She had known that it was always useless arguing with him when he was in that mood, so she had said nothing, and since he had never raised the matter again she had thought he had forgotten about it, or might heed her wishes, but, of course, he hadn't, and she should have known that he was immovable once his mind had been made up.

How like him was Gerard? She asked herself the question while she and Judith worked, and then, later, in the apartment which the Captain had insisted on buying for her, and which her legacy would allow her to keep, she asked herself the question again.

She remembered that Gerard had spoken to her about Homer and what she proposed to do. He had not threatened her, but she had felt his anger, and she wondered what the Captain would have done in a similar situation, if he had wanted to stop her from exposing his relative instead of encouraging her to do so.

Her knowledge of Gis, and of his unscrupulousness, of his rumoured daring, particularly when he had been Gerard's age, provided her with an answer which she did not like, and quite coldly and suddenly, as though a hand had touched her, or a cloud had passed over her brain, she knew that Gerard was capable of doing such a thing as she had imagined, and if so then she must act, for she had possibly left herself vulnerable.

She looked at her watch, rang for her maid to call her a cab, and, putting on a light coat, for the evening was warm, picked up her bag, and after seeing that she was properly equipped for any emergency she ran downstairs and told the cabbie to drive her to her office as fast as he could.

Gerard had already decided on action. He had spent his two days examining the books relating to the Captain's fortune, and talking to van Rensselaer and the old man's financial number one, a shrewd operator by the name of Jevons Shreve.

'The old man still had all his faculties,' Gerard observed at the end of a tiring afternoon, 'but. . .' And he frowned thoughtfully.

When he did not continue, Shreve said, a trifle bluntly, 'But what? Or would you rather not say?'

'He was a man of his time,' returned Gerard, 'and I see that he has made no plans to invest in Public Utilities; probably didn't appreciate that they were the coming thing if money-making in the Nineties is your game.'

'Not for the want of telling,' replied Shreve, blunt again. 'But you're right, he was slowly beginning to be a dinosaur; he had stopped seeing new possibilities. Do you want in?'

'Yes,' said Gerard briefly. 'What's good enough for Harriman and Whitney is good enough for me. Buy — but discreetly. I don't want the price forced up. I want to improve on what the Captain left, not just hold on to it and pray.'

Shreve was bold. 'So, you do intend to get it by marrying the. . .lady.'

'Haven't made my mind up yet,' said Gerard truthfully, turning his strong face towards Shreve, who thought, Well, as long as Gerard Schuyler lives, old Gis ain't dead. 'I've one or two other things to settle first.'

One of them, he thought, taking a cab back to his parents' home, is how long I stay here. Is it worth while acquiring my own apartment now that the will-reading is over? God-dammit, before all this I had intended to return to England on the next boat, but now. . .

First things first, though. There was Cousin Homer's business to settle. As soon as he had left Torry Slade after the will-reading, he had tracked down a private detective whom he had employed when he had last been in the States, and had given him several missions. One of them was to discover the address of Torry Slade's newspaper office, and then, within twenty-four hours, to make a plan of the building it was in, and the rooms she occupied, and let him have it.

Once back in his own room, he fetched it out, stared at it, made up his mind. He walked downstairs to find his mother, whose eyes were still puffy from two days of almost constant weeping, and told her as kindly as he could that he proposed to skip dinner and the visit to the opera to which he had half committed himself, because, 'I have business to conduct.'

'At night?' said the daughter of one of America's leading robber barons acidly.

'Now, Ma,' he said, kissing her. 'You know as well as I do that the best business is often done at night.'

'Depends on the business,' she had sniffed at him, but Gerard could always get round her, and she loved him dearly, was always lamenting his absence in England, and had hopes that now he was back he would settle in New York for good.

'It can't wait?' she queried.

'No,' and he was as curt and definite as the Captain had been when he was on some dubious venture, so she sighed and sped him on his way.

She might have been a little surprised, if she had followed him to his bedroom, to see him strip off his fine clothing, go to a bag at the back of his wardrobe and begin to pull from it the clothes of a hoodlum from the Bowery, down to the heavy boots and a battered brown Derby hat, its ribbon greasy from long use. He hid it and his thug's clothing under his greatcoat, which he then threw on the chest in the hall — there being no one about to see him — before he went into the night, to be lost and anonymous in the busy streets full of people bent on pleasure.

New York, by virtue of the settlement there of the newly rich capitalists who had made their pile from America's mineral wealth, its systems of transportation, and the money broking that centred in the city, had become America's capital in actuality, if not in fact. Once the new dynasties had settled there, Washington, always something of a provincial town, had become even more so.

Worse, the real power in the country now lay with the Captain and his kind, and it was the politicians who did their bidding, not the other way round. He, and the rest, bought and sold senators and presidents, and Gerard had spent the afternoon discovering whom exactly the Captain owned, and how he, if he married Torry Slade and succeeded him, might use them.

Walking briskly towards Torry Slade's offices in his disgraceful clothes, having stopped to black his face merely by running his hands along one of the ledges of the shop fronts he was passing, and then smearing them across his cheeks, he pondered sardonically on the difference between his thoughts and his appearance. He carried a pistol stuck in his waistband and in the capacious inner pockets of his ill-fitting coat instruments designed for house and safe-breaking quite different from anything which the young man-about-town he had been in the daylight hours might be expected to know of.

Once in Fourth Street he slipped down one of the side-alleys which led to the back of the tall buildings which fronted the street. As usual, the contrast between the Imperial façades which the ordinary passer-by saw and the slum-like conditions at the back of the buildings impressed him all over again. Symbolic, he thought, of the Captain's façade which he showed the world and the harsh reality which had lain behind it.

He supposed himself to be similar, given what he was about to do. He made for the rickety fire-escape at the back of the *Banner*'s offices, mounted it lightly, stopped on the landing to put a filthy bandanna across his face, and then forced an entry through one of the back windows, but not before consulting the map in his head which he had put there after reading his detective's report.

The room he sought, Torry Slade's personal office, was at the front of the building, and contained, he already knew, a safe, which he intended to crack. The moon was high and powerful, filling the room with light, a bonus for him.

There was just a chance, if the safe were one he could open, that the papers relating to Homer Blackwood were there, waiting for him to steal them—and perhaps others which might interest a man who wanted to gain hold over the woman his dead grandfather had tried to force on him.

He went on his knees, inspected the lock, discovered to his pleasure that it was one which he could easily manipulate, and began his nefarious work. Long ago, when a very young man, he had paid a cracksman to show him how to open locked doors, break into safes and strong-rooms, prise open strong-boxes, even to the extent that he had learned how to use explosives to smash open anything particularly stubborn.

'Why, young feller?' the man had asked. 'You're rich enough not to need to do this. It's poor devils like me that have to learn such skills.'

'Knowledge is power,' he had said, and the man had had to be content with that.

The lock proved stubborn, and he swore a little as he worked at it, until, suddenly, a strong twist of the wrist, and the door swung open under his hands. The safe proved to be only half full, but the documents he wanted were there, as well as others which looked interesting, and, stuffing them together, he decided to take the lot. Yes, knowledge was power, he told himself contentedly, and prepared to go. Mrs Torry Slade's guns were well and truly spiked. She could hardly expose silly Homer to the world if all her evidence had disappeared.

But there was another saying which Gerard Schuyler might have more usefully quoted to himself, and it went, Pride goeth before a fall, for even as he rose, prepared to lock the safe door again, so that discovery of what he had done might be delayed, there was a movement behind him, the office was flooded with light, and a woman's voice said coldly, 'Stand up, whoever you are, put your hands above your head, and turn around. I have a gun trained on you, and I'll blow your middle away if you as much as make a wrong move!'

CHAPTER FOUR

IT WAS Torry Slade. Slowly, the papers still firmly clutched in the right hand which he raised above his head, Gerard turned to face her. He saw her face change, and triumph and shock pass over it at the sight of him. She recognised him immediately despite the bandanna, his dirty face beneath it, and his disreputable clothes.

'I knew it,' she breathed, 'I knew it. It was exactly what Gis would have done when he was your age. You came here to steal the evidence, didn't you? As I came here to take it to a safer place.'

Then as he began, astonishingly, to grin at her, she said sharply, 'Drop the papers on the desk, and then put your hands above your head again, Mr Gerard Schuyler, you dirty thief in the night.'

Gerard's grin grew broader. She was standing there, erect, both arms stiffly held in front of her, both hands holding the Colt which was trained steadily on him.

'Oh, come,' he drawled, for he had no intention of allowing the fact that she had so neatly trapped him to affect either his speech or his demeanour, 'this is no Bowery melodrama. We are not on the stage, and you have no intention of firing that thing, I am sure,' and he dropped his hands and began to move confidently towards her.

Torry Slade swivelled a little as he started his

detour around her desk, tightened her finger on the trigger, and, at the last moment, fired away from him, a little to her right, so that he felt the passage of the bullet as it buried itself into the wall just above and a little to the left of his head.

He raised his hands again, said coolly, 'So, I was wrong. I apologise. Was that another trick the old man taught you, in the intervals of teaching you quite different ones?'

'Yes,' she answered, as cool as he, he was fascinated to note, 'Gis taught me. He said I might need to use a pistol against villains, and so I do, for have I not caught you, Mr Gerard Schuyler? Shall I shoot you dead, the evidence of your theft about you, and say that I surprised you, and shot you before I knew who you were?'

'A little drastic, don't you think?' said Gerard, but he was careful to do nothing which might provoke her into firing at him again, and this time winging him or worse, such pistols being notoriously inaccurate, even at short range. 'You really don't have to shoot me in order to turn me down. Even the Captain might have thought that a bit too Draconian.'

If he was admiring her coolness, there was suddenly no doubt that she was admiring his. A little of the tension went out of her, and he decided to take advantage of it.

'What the well-dressed woman is wearing to repel intruders,' he said mockingly, parodying one of Macy's advertising slogans, and his eyes ravished her as he took in the elegant gown of deep violet which she was wearing, and the matching coat above it, open just enough to display her *décolletage*. 'May I say how much that colour you are wearing suits your eyes?'

'Oh, don't try to talk me round,' she said, suddenly showing emotion. 'You did come here to dispose of the evidence, did you not?'

'Useless to deny it,' sighed Gerard, 'seeing that I'm caught here with the damned stuff in my hands and the safe open. Tell me, now that you have caught me, what do you intend to do about it?'

'You can hand over the papers at once, and properly this time,' she replied smartly, waving the pistol at him, so that he capered about in mock-alarm, but still hung on to them.

'Do you want another demonstration of my willingness to shoot? And while you're about it you may as well put the weapon which you're surely carrying on the desk,' she said, and at this Gerard, realising that he was the bone in the dog's mouth, the king on the chessboard, neatly mated by the queen, placed the papers and his own Colt on the desk for her to pick up, she still holding the gun in her right hand tightly trained on him. 'May I put my hands down now?' he pleaded. 'I'm growing tired.'

The woman opposite him considered him gravely. 'You're not about to apologise,' she said crisply, 'for having tried to rob me? Suppose I called the police?'

'Well, you could,' admitted Gerard, 'but think of the scandal. Gis's mistress shooting and turning in Gis's grandson. Do you really want that sort of field day in the Press?'

'Not really,' she said, 'and nor, I think, do you.

You may sit down, Mr Gerard Schuyler, provided you put your hands on the desk before you, and make no attempt to jump me.'

'I would never jump a woman holding a pistol,' said Gerard fervently, sitting down. 'Too risky. Kindly point it away from me. You're making me nervous.' But he showed no signs of being so, and he continued to ravish her with his eyes, so that she said sharply,

'You may stop that; it won't get you anywhere.'

'Stop what?' he said innocently, although he knew exactly what she meant and was being quite deliberate in his attempt to disconcert her.

'Raping me with your eyes.' She was deadly cold, he saw, and was in no mood to allow him to try tricks of any kind on her.

Surprsingly, she now sat down, opposite him, a little way from the desk, the Colt in her lap, but she was, he knew, quite ready to train it on him again.

Silence followed. Neither of them seemed to wish to talk, and Gerard wondered why she did not simply order him to leave, probably through the window and back down the fire-escape, which she must have guessed he had entered by.

'I have been thinking,' she said at last.

'Congratulations, madam,' was his answer to that. 'Too few women make the attempt.'

Torry's magnificent eyes glinted and she murmured dangerously, 'Does everything have to be a joke with you, Mr Gerard Schuyler? Are you never serious?'

'Oh, I'm deadly serious,' he riposted, 'as who

wouldn't be in my position? But as the poet said, "And if I laugh. . .'tis that I may not weep."'

'Gis with education, I see,' she said, almost beneath her breath. 'Yes, ever since I heard what he had done to us, I have been thinking, and I have come to some conclusions. Would you care to hear them, Mr Gerard Schuyler, or would you prefer to crack jokes?'

'Hear them,' he said promptly. God, what a magnificent specimen she was; no wonder the old man had run her, his last, best bit of not-so-dry goods!

Something of what was passing through his mind reached her. 'And none of that, either,' she ordered sternly. 'I can tell what you're thinking. Pay attention to what I am about to say. Contrary to anything you might believe, I had no desire to inherit any of Gis's wealth, and, while I might have swallowed Seahorses and the two million dollars, since I obviously made his last days happy, I am loath to be in a position where my acts might rob the Schuyler family of his wealth.' She paused, then added, 'Never mind that few of you seem to deserve to inherit it, from what I heard of the family while I lived with him. So, I would make you a proposition, which you may accept or not, as you please——'

'Oh, very good of you, I'm sure, madam. You don't intend to force it on me at pistol-point, then?'

'Not at all,' said Torry magnanimously. 'And if you could pause a moment from this insistent merry-making, which is most inappropriate to the occasion, I may add, I will tell you what I have decided.'

Gerard decided to behave himself. He had discovered that whenever he was with her he had only one idea in his head, and that was to break her perfect calm. It was for that reason, as much as any other, that he had jumped on her in his grandfather's study. And now the same desire was growing, parallel with the unwanted sexual urgings which the mere sight of her seemed to provoke.

He leaned back in his chair and drawled, 'I am agog, madam, positively agog. Pray proceed.'

'There is one way out,' she said, face stern, picking up her gun as she spoke and training it on him, on his chest this time. Good God! Did she really intend to dispose of him? Apparently not, for she was continuing.

'We could, you see, appear to fulfil his wishes by marrying, except that it would be simply a marriage of convenience, never consummated, and at some date in the future we could divorce. We should be cheating Gis — but then, he should never have put us in this position, should he? And *he* wouldn't have hesitated to cheat, if it suited him. I should expect you to sign an agreement of non-consummation with me, for I am sure, after all you said three days ago, you have no desire to marry me at all.'

'True,' said Gerard gravely. 'Bedding you now, yes, but marriage, no. Which would make a white marriage difficult, you think?' And his eyes on her were watchful.

'Oh, no,' she replied decisively. 'I should leave you with perfect freedom of action with other women, of course. I would not be a dog in the manger.'

'Bitch,' corrected Gerard sweetly. 'Bitch is the correct term for you to use there, I think.' But all the time his busy brain was working. For here was a way out of the impasse — and he supposed that she supposed the agreement as to the non-consummated marriage would remain their secret.

As if she was reading his thoughts exactly, she assured him that that was what she intended.

Well, if she wanted to be a sacrificial goat to save the Schuyler millions for the family, who was he to stop her? He knew that all the family expected him to marry her, whether she had been the Captain's mistress or not. And if he did then somehow, before he got rid of her, he would make sure that he did bed her — but it would avail her nothing, for he was certain that he was the prize she was after, and that the Captain had intended all of this. . .might even have written the book, as though he were composing for an improbable Italian operetta!

No, he had no intention of making her Mrs Gerard Schuyler in the real sense of the title. When he finally married for good, to provide himself with an heir, he would choose someone whom he could trust, as well as love.

Something again of what he was thinking must have reached her. She said, and her expression was wry, 'Oh, I can see that you're a hard man too. Just like Gis. He said that you were, but I couldn't quite believe him — all the other Schuylers are such soft creatures.'

Gerard smiled. 'Flattery,' he said, and his voice was jeering. 'Did he teach you that in the long night watches?'

But he saw immediately that he could not dent her composure by such comments. She shook her head. 'You have not yet given me your answer, Mr Gerard Schuyler. I want one now. I do not propose to spend days waiting for you to make up your mind. The decision is a simple one, after all. Such a small sacrifice to gain the Captain's millions. Save them from a bloodless trust.'

'Would you believe me,' he replied, his voice almost idle, 'if I told you that I had not looked to inherit anything and even now I am not even sure that I want the Captain's fortune if the price I must pay for it is too high?'

'Oh, I believe both halves of that statement. Or, at least, I believe that you have persuaded yourself that that is what you do believe. I am not sure, however, that, offered the Schuyler millions, you have any doubts at all. No, I am sure that you would be prepared to pay almost any price to get them.'

Gerard threw his head back and laughed again as he had done in church, the noise echoing around the small room.

'Now, what cat-house were you bred in, Mrs Victoria Slade, to be so cynical? I should dearly like to know.'

'Oh, I'm certain that one way or another you will make it your business to find out. But you are still dancing me around. If you don't make up your mind soon, I shall take it that the answer is no.'

'Then you take it wrong,' retorted Gerard, rising to his feet. 'I am prepared to meet your terms, contract and all, but we shall need to draw it up ourselves if secrecy is to be maintained. I want no further handles for gossip about the Schuylers to entertain New York, and nor, I am sure, do you. I will meet you in my office in Wall Street tomorrow.'

'Certainly not.' Torry had risen to face him, the pistol still in her hand. 'The proposition was mine. You will meet me here to agree on the details of our settlement. There are a number of points which we shall need to decide. Then, and only then, can we announce our decision to the world.'

'To provide another gala day for the Press,' he smiled. 'No matter, we cannot escape one, I fear; the Captain saw to that when he bequeathed you to me.'

'If you like to think of it that way. . .' she began.

'Now, what other way is there to think of it?' wondered Gerard. 'But I do have one condition, which I must make plain straight away, since it is not negotiable, and that is that you do not publish anything that is in there.' And he pointed to the papers which branded the Reverend Homer Blackwood liar, lecher and hypocrite.

He was fascinated by the sudden play of emotion on her face, the struggle with herself which was obviously taking place.

'You are asking me to surrender a principle,' she said in a low voice.

'Oh, come.' Gerard was impatient. 'Like it or not, you will be one of the family if you marry me. You cannot throw Homer to the wolves; it would be neither decent nor proper.'

'Since he is neither,' she flashed back, 'it makes no odds. Take care, Mr Gerard Schuyler, lest you push me too far.'

Gerard was growing bold; he leaned forward as if to touch her, saying, 'If we are going to pretend to be man and wife, you might at least call me Gerard; such formality as you are employing will raise suspicions.'

In a flash, as he made to touch her arm, the pistol came up again, rock-steady. 'Oh, no. Keep away. I don't trust you an inch—no, not a centimetre. I wouldn't put it past you to pretend to agree to my proposition, if only to get the Blackwood papers back, and then laugh in my face. . .'

'If I did, the laugh would be on me,' said Gerard gently, 'to the tune of two hundred and fifty million dollars—while you, madam, still gain two millions and Seahorses.'

'Fleabites,' said Victoria stonily, 'to what I shall expect from you when we divorce! Oh, yes, there is a price to pay for my offer, Mr Gerard Schuyler, and you will pay it. You did not think that I came free, did you?'

'No,' smiled Gerard, 'but then, whores never do, do they?'

The pistol shot up as he finished speaking, and for one heart-stopping moment he thought that she was going to shoot him where he stood, in return for the insult. It was a risk he had taken when he insulted her so grossly, but he was a risk-taker *par excellence*, and if one day the dice fell wrongly, or he miscalculated the odds, then he would have lived his life on his feet before he died, not crawled through it on his knees as his father did.

'Be thankful,' she said, 'that I didn't shoot you on the spot, and don't intend to withdraw my offer. If

I am a whore, sir, then you are a thief and a cheat, a night-hawk caught in the act, your loot about you, and from what I have heard this is not the first time that you have engaged in some felonies. Beware: one day the pitcher will go too often to the well.'

'Ah, yes, but before it does think of all the lovely water it will have drawn,' drawled Gerard. 'You will allow me to leave by the front door, I hope. I have no mind to negotiate the fire-escape a second time.' He was as cool as she, and as determined not to be faced down.

For the first time it occurred to him that he and she were two of a kind, little to choose between them, and for some strange reason the thought was erotic. So far, the sexual chemistry which had been generated between them on their first encounter had been missing, replaced by the cut and thrust of an argument about the solution to their mutual predicament.

But, now that that was over, it was slowly being replaced by something else. Danger ended, for Gerard was sure that it was, even though she still held the pistol loosely trained in his direction, there was now time for them to look on one another as man and woman, and not as two adversaries, sexless inside the logic they were both practising.

He had time at last to register the perfection not only of her face and body but of her clothes, for all that she must have sped across town to catch him in her office — and what caused her to guess that *that* was his intention? No matter; what mattered was the trim ankle he could see below her skirts, the shadow of the cleft between her breasts revealed by her low-cut dress — she must have been preparing to dine when the fit had taken her to check the security of her office — and the beauty of her high-piled hair under her broad-brimmed hat, a model from Paris, France, he was sure.

He wanted to pull down her dress, to reveal the beautiful breasts completely, unpin the lustrous black cloud of her hair, let it down to make a semi-transparent cloak through which the perfection of her bosom would shimmer. If, flaunting her beauty before him, she thought that he would keep to any agreement relating to a celibate marriage, she must be mad.

He did not think that she was mad; he thought, rather, that Mrs Victoria Slade was eminently sane. Too sane, perhaps. Despite her denials, he was sure that she had put the Captain up to binding him over to be her husband so that she could gain either her share of the millions or a rich and powerful husband, to give her at last the respectability so long denied her.

He walked towards her, ignoring her pistol, and his, which still lay on the desk in front of her, until they were almost breast to breast. For a moment she half raised her own weapon, to train it on him again, and then laid it on the desk beside his.

'You are wrong to trust me,' he said huskily. 'For I could use my superior strength, now you are unarmed, to take the papers and go, leaving you nothing.'

'But yourself with less,' she said. 'No Schuyler millions then.' Her voice was faint, so faint that, near to her as he was, he could barely make out what she was saying.

'Something to seal our bond,' he said, 'before we part—to become mere business partners,' and, taking her gently by the shoulders, he bent his head to kiss her, only, exercising all his will, he avoided the perfect mouth, to kiss instead the flawless forehead, making the embrace as passionless as he could, to deny the powerful pull of her, so that she could not think she lured or tempted him in any way.

Vain hope. The spark in her eyes, the dilated pupils, told him how aware she was of him, and of herself in relation to him, and that just as he was controlling himself so was she, so that, although he heard her shuddering breath, by no movement of face or body did she betray that she might be nearly as aroused as he was becoming.

Danger past—a danger shared by men and women, either on the same side, or another— carried a different danger—that of an erotic response, as the life force demanded fulfilment and payment for what it had endured.

And, knowing that, he would do nothing more.

'Until tomorrow,' he said, releasing her at last. 'I will be here by ten-thirty and you will be alone. Send everyone away. Neither of us wants any witness to what we are about to do.'

She nodded, stepped back, and they stared at one another, like two knights before single combat, each testing the other's will and resolution.

The conceit pleased him. He laughed a little, saw

her face soften and an answering smile dawn there
as he bowed and turned away, to hear her call after
him, '*Arrivederci*, Mr Gerard Schuyler; tomorrow is
another day.'

CHAPTER FIVE

PREDICTABLY, perhaps, only one person was shocked by Gerard's sudden capitulation to the Captain's wishes. As soon as he announced that he and Mrs Slade had agreed to marry, he was deluged with congratulations, most of them cynical. He thought that he had never endured so many winks, ironic back-slappings and 'Attaboy, Gerard's in his entire life.

His mother alternated wailings and moanings with rather tearful good wishes; his father said tersely, 'Seen sense, have you? I thought you would.' When he went to the lawyer's office to begin the legal arrangements which would accompany the wedding, van Rensselaer became the only person to offer him congratulations with a straight face.

Shreve, presenting him with details of his buyings in Public Utilities, was also commendably brief, merely grunting at him, 'Common sense, Gerard, common sense; the Captain would have been proud of you.'

No one suspected the truth; everyone took the marriage for granted, assumed that once he and the Slade were finally hitched they would settle down to begin producing the heir of which the Captain had dreamed, and for which he had planned.

No one except his sister Kate. He was dressing for dinner two days after the news had been announced, probably his last formal engagement as a single man, when there was a tap on the door.

'Come,' he shouted, imitating the English aristocrats among whom he had been living, to see Kate put her head round the door.

'Could I speak to you, Gerard?' she asked timidly. 'Privately.' And her eyes slid over Timson, his English valet.

Timson needed no instructions. A nod of Gerard's head was enough. He vanished into the dressing-room — which was as large as most people's ground floors.

'What is it, Kate?' he asked. 'More trouble about arranged marriages?'

'In a way,' she offered. Head bent, she was running the toe of her black pumps along the intricate pattern of the beautiful carpet. 'Only it's not mine, it's yours.'

'Mine?' Gerard did not betray his surprise. 'How mine?' and continued fastening his black bow-tie.

'Why are you doing it, Gerard?' she cried, suddenly and passionately. 'I know you, if no one else does. You can't really want to marry Grandpa's. . . bit of stuff.'

'Oh, but think what comes with her,' he said carelessly, avoiding her eyes.

'No need to talk to me like that, Gerard,' she said sorrowfully. 'You're doing it to keep the money in the family, aren't you? Does she know? Is it. . .is it. . .? Yes, I'm sure it is. . .it's a trick, isn't it?'

Startled, Gerard swung round. 'No, Kate,' he denied, for he must not let her become aware of how shrewd her guess had been. 'Of course not. She's very attractive, you know.'

Kate stared at him, and he thought suddenly that when she had said that she wished she had been a boy she had been doing no more than express her knowledge that intellectually she was as bright as he was, and that there were few among the male Schuylers to match her. What freak of inheritance had passed the Captain's intellectual legacy to himself and his sister, and to no other descendants? he wondered, not for the first time.

'Don't marry her if you don't want to,' continued his sister earnestly. 'Oh, I know she's clever, and I think that the family is wrong to see her as a schemer who ran Grandpa, but all the same don't sacrifice yourself to keep the money in the family. They'll never thank you.'

'Come now, Kate,' he said, grinning. 'You flatter me. I'm no altruist. I'm doing it to get the money for myself.'

'That, too,' agreed Kate. 'But all the same I'm sure that's not the whole story.'

Gerard turned away. 'I can't help what you're thinking,' he said, 'but don't say it to anyone else, OK? Not advisable.' He hesitated. 'Never give away what you know if you think no one else knows it.'

'Oh, I won't.' Kate was fervent. 'And Gerard, I was right about Ma wanting me to marry an aristocrat. I think there's one coming over soon to have a look at me — or rather at how much money Pa is prepared to settle on me as my dowry.'

'Any idea who it is?' asked Gerard, satisfied at last that his appearance was all that it should be.

'After all, I know most of your possible would-be suitors. I can't say that I think much of any of them.'

Kate hung her pretty head, contemplated the carpet as though some vital message for her were written on it. 'Someone called Otmoor. Justin, Earl of, or so Mama has said.'

'Otmoor!' Gerard was struck by the name. He was Daisy Gascoyne's penniless brother, who owned a big barracks of a country house falling into ruin and a whole raft of barren acres somewhere north of London, and little else. No better and no worse than most young peers strapped for money who were prepared to marry the daughters and granddaughters of men whom they would not have condescended to know if they had not possessed millions to their name.

'You know him?' said Kate, who read him aright.

'Yes,' said Gerard briefly. 'You may even like him. Wait and see.'

'And that's all?' said his sister bitterly. 'Wait and see?'

'You must marry someone, Kate; no life for you as a spinster, and marriage is a lottery, even if you think that you love your future partner madly.'

The dinner bell rang then, cutting off further discussion leaving Gerard to shoo Kate out and summon Timson to approve of his appearance, for to do otherwise would offend the man, however satisfied Gerard was with what he had done for himself.

Walking down the vast staircase, brought over from Italy in two pieces and reassembled here in New York, Gerard had time to reflect on all that had happened between himself and Torry Slade since she had presented him with her remarkable proposition.

Beautifully turned out, quite unlike the grubby man who had sat in her office and bantered with her, he had gone to see her the following morning.

He was glad that he had taken some care with his appearance for she had dressed so elegantly that he could see, all over again, what had drawn the Captain to her.

She had been coolly ladylike, her clothes absolutely suited to the occasion. She had been neither under nor overdressed. She had not worn anything which smacked of mourning, but for that matter neither had he. Her gown was a simple one of shot-silk moire in grey and rose, trimmed with black velvet bands—her sole concession to the Captain's death, he supposed. Her hat was of cream straw decorated with pink silk tea-roses, and the coat which she had discarded over a neighbouring chair was of grey wool, also trimmed with bands of black velvet.

Pinned to one lapel was a brooch in the shape of a bunch of roses, and if the jewels in it were, as he supposed, real emeralds, rubies and pearls he was sure that the thing was worth a king's ransom. Another of the Captain's presents, he presumed.

Beside her, at her desk, had been a young girl, neatly dressed in the regulation office uniform for young women of black dress and white collar, her hair simply knotted at the back of her head. She had given him a cold stare, made even colder when Torry Slade had said to her, 'This is Mr Gerard

Schuyler, Judith; I have some private business with him, nothing to do with the paper. Perhaps you could go over to Queens for me and check that story about sweated female labour in the clothing industry there. We can run it this week instead of the Blackwood exposé.'

The look Judith Reis turned on Gerard on hearing this was one of hate. 'I suppose that you're thinking of dropping it altogether now,' she muttered. 'Is that what he's here for?'

Torry Slade's response was as cool and measured as everything about her. 'It may be,' she said, 'that circumstances may compel me to drop that story altogether. We can't always do exactly what we wish, Judith, even in the newspaper world. There will be other stories.'

'I could sell it elsewhere,' returned the girl, only for Torry to say, still cool,

'You wouldn't get very far without any supporting evidence, Judith, and I've no intention of passing that on to you.'

'Well, I don't like seeing you give way to pressure from such as him,' Judith retorted, indicating Gerard with a jerk of her head, but failing to provoke any reaction from him, if that had been her intention. Piqued at his lack of response, she shrugged her shoulders and flounced out.

Gerard watched her go, thinking that she was much more like the stereotype of the advanced feminist woman than Torry Slade was—except that he suddenly wondered whether, for all her brave words, she would have held him at pistol-point as the fashionably dressed beauty sitting opposite him had done.

'I have been thinking,' he said, and his parody of the words Torry had used to him the night before was intended.

Torry did not take him up, even though he had deliberately and mockingly paused to give her the opportunity to do so; as a target for her scorn it was perhaps too obvious a ploy.

He continued, 'There are a number of points on which our understanding must be clear.' And he paused again, for her to say, this time,.

'Do go on, for I, too, have thought of several which ought to be debated.'

'Mainly,' said Gerard, and as she moved to stand again, to lift some papers from a shelf, he caught a whiff of her perfume, wild rose today, he noticed, 'to do with the relationship which we must establish both before and after marriage. We must,' and his voice had become more sardonic than ever, 'seek to convince others, if not ourselves, not only that we have come to some *modus vivendi*, but, unlikely though it might seem, we have also come to some kind of. . .amorous understanding; that the marriage, while mainly one of convenience, is not wholly so. It would not do for anyone to assume that once married we are immediately seeking to undo it, even if that is our ultimate aim. There could be complications. Van Rensselaer, who stands to gain by becoming the guardian of the trust if we do not marry, might challenge a marriage which was too obviously contrived to defeat him.'

'So?' said Torry Slade, and said no more. She was

determined to give him nothing, he saw, and his admiration for her grew. Either she had always possessed this extreme self-sufficiency, or she had learned it from the Captain, whose hallmark it had also been. Yes, she was a whore of choice, was Mrs Torry Slade. Living with her was going to be an adventure. Getting her into his bed was going to be another one to which he looked forward with pleasure.

'So,' he continued, trying to ignore the strong effect which, as usual, she was having on him. 'So, we must behave, I think, as though, having conquered the Captain by your charms, you have now conquered me, and I must appear only too happy to be conquered. In private, of course, it will be a very different matter.'

'Oh, of course.' Torry Slade's sardonic smile matched his own. 'And shall you have much difficulty, Mr Gerard Schuyler, in assuming such a role?'

'No more than you will, I dare swear,' was his answer to that, his own smile broadening, 'seeing that you have kept up such a farce in pretending to care for the Captain. I imagine that we shall both gain a kind of mutual pleasure from such a double act, rather like trapeze artists passing in mid-air while performing double somersaults thirty feet above the ground!'

'Or a lion tamer entering the cage with only a chair for a weapon,' she agreed, obviously determined not to be bested in any battle of wits, and beginning to shuffle through the papers before her.

'I have set out a form of agreement here,' she continued, 'by which we undertake to enter into this marriage binding ourselves not to consummate it in any form recognised by any church, religion or custom of society, now or in the past. Furthermore, I have laid down that at the end of any such marriage the only reimbursement for my loss is sharing the custody of the Schuyler fortune of two hundred and fifty millions, which I confidently expect that we shall increase by our joint efforts, will be the sum of ten million dollars paid into my bank account on the day the dissolution of the marriage becomes absolute.'

Gerard whistled as he picked up the document which she passed over. Perfectly typed, neatly set out, he realised as he read it that, whatever else, Mrs Torry Slade had the mind of a high-powered lawyer and a will as resolute as his own.

'Bravely and fairly stated,' he said courteously when he had finished reading, the violet eyes hard on him the whole time. 'Did you prepare this yourself? Oh, of course you did.' He smiled to forestall an indignant rebuttal. Not that one was forthcoming—she was as cool in the face of insults as he supposed that she might be when graced with compliments. 'You have had legal training?'

Torry Slade smiled—oh, the woman was a very Sphinx, her smile was so subtle, gave so little away. And then she gave something away—or did she? 'My late husband was a lawyer; I occasionally acted as his clerk.'

'Yes?' said Gerard quickly and encouragingly; he had frequently discovered that such a ploy often drew an answer unintended by the speaker, but Mrs

Torry Slade was not going to be trapped by such easy birdlime.

She said sweetly, 'So, you see, I had some little experience in drawing up documents, and I think you will find that this one is watertight.'

'Ah, yes,' he said gravely, 'but suppose that I did not want it so, wanted loopholes? Would you be able to find them if I tucked them in, I wonder?'

The eyes which met his when he finished speaking were so level that he felt suddenly ashamed of every half-taunting word which he had thrown at her since he had entered her office. 'I think so,' she answered gravely, 'but I had supposed that, like myself, you would wish this agreement to have no holes in it, either loops, or any other kind — that we might part in mutual amity, having achieved our intention of tricking the trickster. Do you think that the Captain is looking down from Olympus, laughing at us — has he any other tricks up his sleeve, do you think?'

'Up from hell, rather.' Gerard was suddenly savage. 'By God, how did you stand him? I suppose the money and the power made up for everything?'

'Would you believe me,' she answered him steadily, 'if I told you that I cared for him? No, I can see that you wouldn't. We waste breath, Mr Gerard Schuyler. We burn daylight. Sign the document or go without signing and kiss your millions goodbye. Up to you; always up to you.'

She was the first woman he had ever met who bargained like a man. Direct, unemotional, uncompromising. Take it or bloody leave it, as the Brits said, appeared to be her motto. What on earth would his London friends make of her? he wondered.

Well, there was one who would undoubtedly appreciate her, if only for her beauty, mixed with novelty, and that was HRH the Prince of Wales himself, old Tumtum. He had a sudden irrepressible wish to take her with him, launch her on London society, see what execution she would do there.

By God, he thought he would; it would pass the time until they were ready to part, and alone, in a foreign country, she might be disorientated, give way. . . He burst out laughing, aware of the look of surprise on her face.

'Something amusing you?'

'This, everything,' he choked. 'I might have guessed that the old devil would not have left me an easy life — until we part, that is. We shall do him out of his grandchildren, but that is all. I can imagine him anticipating this, Mother's tears, Father's impotent anger, Brandt and the rest fulminating and roaring, wondering if I marry you and inherit whether I shall be an easier mark than he was.'

'The same,' she said, direct still. 'He knew you, I am sure, as. . .'

She had checked herself sharply, and Gerard knew why. 'As you are beginning to know me,' he said softly. 'I see that I must have been indiscreet. I must remedy that. Or else you read all men easily. Oh, Mrs Torry Slade, read this, I beg you, and tell me what it means.' And with one stride he rose, crossed the space which she had put between them, lifted her from her seat and began to kiss her with a passion which at first was savage and then softened.

His hands were in her hair, his mouth on hers, his eyes closed involuntarily, and as his hands dropped to hold her by the shoulders, as before, he felt her beginning to melt, before she pulled away, breathless, to stare at him, eyes wild. 'That was not in our agreement and you know it, sir. It is expressly forbidden. Do you wish to withdraw from the bargain?'

Desire ran through him, unwanted, for he was in its grip, could not control it, or himself, as he wished, and he was a man to whom all control was precious.

'I have not signed yet,' he said hoarsely, 'and I wanted to sample, if only briefly, the goods I shall not be allowed to touch. Once I have signed, I shall behave myself, you may be sure of that. I have no wish to throw away what I hope to gain. That was . . .inoculation.'

His impudence, she thought, was unparalleled, his lack of scruple so patent that she knew, beyond a peradventure, that if he could gain what he wanted by breaking every clause in their agreement, or in any agreement he might make with anyone, he would do so. That being so, she must never trust him, never. He was like a cat physically, and the resemblance held good mentally. Throw him up, toss him away, and he would come down on his feet, teeth showing, claws out, armed and ready for the fight.

Gerard saw, once again, that she knew him. He picked up the pen from its stand on the desk, signed the document and its exact copy with a flourish, and handed the papers to her.

'Signed, sealed and delivered,' he laughed. 'We have a bargain, madam, and now you must sign, too,' and as she did so, handing him his copy silent, wordless, he gave another crack of laughter.

'Why, madam, I know of no document so water-tight that a rogue may not breach it. All's fair in love and war, Mrs Torry Slade, and since we are not engaged in the first then let us have at each other in the second. You are the worthiest adversary I have ever had, and, by God, one way or another I shall have you before our bargain ends, be sure of that.'

Well, that had been a piece of bravado that in retrospect he could not approve of. For she had recovered herself completely from the shock of his unexpected kiss, and had said, composed again, her manner as tranquil as though she had been at a garden party, 'It's a pleasure to me, Mr Gerard Schuyler, sir, to see you live up to all the worst expectations I have of you and your kind——' and, still intoxicated by he knew not what, he had rudely broken in, to take her hand and kiss it in farewell, uttering as did so his valediction,

'My kind? I have no kind, Mrs Torry Slade, I am custom built. Remember that, and let us deal as equals—since that is what you wish. Tomorrow afternoon at two of the clock be at the Captain's ugly palace to meet van Rensselaer and the lawyers so that they may begin the long finaglings they will feel it necessary to concoct before we tie our own knot. I am sure that you wish our marriage to be as speedy as possible.'

'Of course, and I shall be there.'

'And loving, Mrs Torry Slade—be as loving as you can compel yourself to be. We have been struck by a *coup de foudre*, lightning flashes all about us, the Captain has created our romance for us, and we may have the laugh on them all. I bid you good-day.'

Loving! The pair of them had fooled everybody. Van Rennselaer, jaw a little dropped, had watched them do their stately minuet of mutual adoration around the Captain's study the next afternoon.

'You see,' drawled Gerald, slipping an arm around Torry's waist, and feeling her stiffen, aware that she could not move away, if the farce were to be kept up, 'once Mrs Slade—no, I mean my dear Torry and I—had the chance to meet this week, we discovered we had so much in common that we knew at once that the old man, far from putting us in a predicament, had, in fact, been prescient. He must have known that what would please him would please me.'

He smiled soulfully into Torry's enraged violet eyes, tightening his grip and dropping a chaste kiss on the end of her nose. 'Oh, I forget myself, my dear; pray forgive me for being so demonstrative,' he said remorsefully, 'but, as I am sure you will understand, the wedding cannot come too soon for me. To think that I have delayed marrying all these years, unable to make up my mind, only to have my dear grandfather make it up for me so successfully.'

He did wonder whether he was not doing it a little

too brown, but his expression of besotted male, suddenly presented with a trophy which he had not expected to win, seemed to be fooling van Rensselaer; but all the same he reminded himself not to overdo things. Others might not be so easily deceived.

To his secret delight, Torry decided to take a hand in the game, too. 'Oh,' she said tenderly, 'my sentiments entirely. I feel exactly the same about dear Gerard as he does about me. I had never thought to meet anyone so like the Captain in everything.' This two-edged compliment had Gerard grinning to himself, and her next words nearly had him engaging in Rabelaisian mirth quite unseemly for a man preparing himself for a society wedding.

'And yes,' she went on, 'I cannot bear the notion of the wedding being delayed for very long, either,' and she gave the great sigh of someone who could hardly wait to get legitimately into bed with her betrothed. 'I do hope all the legal business will not be too lengthy. Oh, and the wedding will be a private one, I trust. It is so soon after his death, but I know that the Captain would want us to fulfil his wishes as soon as possible.' And she fluttered her eyelashes at Gerard and then at van Rensselaer, who was beginning to understand how she had managed to hook first the Captain and now his grandson, for after she had finished speaking Gerard had assumed an expression so sillily loving that it would have fooled anyone.

Anyone but Torry Slade, who had, dreadfully, begun to enjoy herself, and on looking at his ridiculous face she had the gravest difficulty in preventing herself from bursting out laughing on the spot.

To hide her own amusement, she leaned forward and gave him a light kiss on the cheek, being then rewarded by Gerard taking her hand and kissing her gloved palm, saying the while, in a voice choked either by emotion — or laughter — she could not be sure which it was, 'Oh, darling. . .darling.'

'Darling?' she murmured back at him, only for him to respond like one of the all-absorbed lovers in a *Punch* cartoon she had once seen.

'Nothing, darling, just darling, darling!' Risking the chance that the bedazzled van Rensselaer had not also seen it, and would recognise the parody.

Fortunately for both tricksters, united for once in cheating others and not each other, van Rensselaer's reading was confined to higher things, but, not for the first or last time, Gerard and Torry were compelled to understand that, while many things might divide them, one thing which united them was a common sardonic humour which manifested itself mainly in a desire to deceive those about them.

For a brief moment something moved in Gerard, if that were so, then after what fashion was Torry Slade privately amusing herself by deceiving *him*? The moment disappeared, and he contented himself by giving her a discreet if gentlemanlike embrace which had her pulling away from him. This, she thought, was going too far for her, and perhaps for the watchers, too.

She placed a reproving finger on his lips. 'Patience,' she murmured sweetly. 'After all, it will not be very long now before we are man and wife,' and when they had finally walked out of van Rensselaer's office, most of the legal formalities having been concluded, Gerard holding her arm so tenderly that even this light touch conveyed to the watching lawyers his impatience to get his beautiful prize, she muttered savagely in his ear, 'No need to overdo it, Gerard,' only for him to answer, 'Every need, my dear. Van Rensselaer and his minions are, after all, the ones whom we are most required to deceive.'

Nevertheless, Gerard felt Torry detach herself from him as quickly as she could, and before they parted she said in a voice so cold that it would have had icicles forming in the Sahara, 'You will, I trust, remember the document which you signed, Mr Gerard Schuyler? I thought this afternoon that you were in danger of forgetting it; that you might be substituting the truth for the falsehood.'

'Good,' he replied. 'I was seeking to give the impression of barely contained passion. So glad that I was so successful that I deceived you as well as van Rensselaer!' Which Gerard knew was a thundering lie, seeing that to be in her company, let alone lay so much as a finger on her, was enough to send him up in flames!

And that statement, he immediately saw, did not for some reason please Mrs Victoria Slade at all. He could have sworn that her lip momentarily trembled, and whether in anger, frustrated passion or regret he could not be sure.

He was sure of only one thing in their relationship, and that was his own desire for her; all else was problematical. And she? What, he wondered, did she feel for him? That was a thing he could not be certain of. A little of what she had felt for the Captain? Oh, come Gerard, do not be a ninny noddy! For sure, she had felt nothing for the Captain, but for his wealth, now, that was quite another matter!

Because he was a man who must know things, knowledge being power, Gerard was determined to know the truth of her past, if nothing else. As soon as he had signed his bargain with her he had employed a man, a Pinkerton's detective, to sniff out her history for him. Mrs Victoria Slade knew all about him, of what he had done, whom he had squired around, of his life in London, mingling with the great of Europe, as everyone in the States did, but he knew nothing of her — until his man reported back to him — and how soon would that be? He had told him that speed was desirable, since before he married her and began his campaign to bed her he must know every last disreputable fact about Mrs Victoria Slade.

Torry Slade, walking up to her apartment — she had refused Gerard's offer to see her up the stairs to her door — was beginning to regret the strange bargain which she had made. Considering it beforehand, she had thought herself capable of controlling the Captain's grandson. After all, she had coped with the Captain, and God knew that he had been as artful as a wagon load of monkeys. But Gerard possessed two things, one of which the Captain had long lost, and that was his youth, and the other was something which the Captain had never stirred in her.

The second was the worse of the two, for Gerard had begun to disturb her in the oddest manner, a manner in which no man had ever disturbed her before, and, what was the worst of all, she had begun to experience sensations which she thought the experiences of her youth had made it impossible for her to feel. She found herself looking forward to meeting him, to seeing the slight twist of his lip which signalled that he was about to say something outrageous.

Oh, but it was more than that, more than a mere quirk of appearance; it was something deeper in him which called to her, and was nothing less than her power to recognise in him violence contained and controlled, a violence which should have frightened her, as it must frighten others who saw it, but which, dreadfully, attracted her instead.

If Gerard, unknown to her, wanted to breach her apparently unbreakable calm, then she wanted to provoke him, to see if she could smash his perfect control of himself, to see what would happen if his contained violence spilled over into action. Once or twice in their passage of arms when he had broken into her office, she had thought that she had unleashed the tiger in him, only for him to exercise his will and control to prevent it from running free.

Now, why should she want to do such a dangerous thing? For would not the unleashed tiger eat her, as the Captain would have eaten her had she met him when he was Gerard's age? Why did the thought of Gerard, reaching for her, out of control, excite her so that merely thinking of it, as she gained her door, she gave a long shudder and leaned against it for succour and support?

What perverse impulse was making her legs, her bowels even, turn to water at the very thought? Was it fear? No, not that; she would not put a name to it, for passion was something which she had long ago determined that she would never feel for any man, least of all a cold-hearted, self-serving brute like Gerard Schuyler.

And here she was placing herself in the tiger's power, in easy reach of his powerful paws, and, even if she thought that she had muzzled him by making him sign the document which bound them both to a white marriage, she knew that documents, oaths and promises were nothing to the wild man who lived behind Gerard Schuyler's civilised façade.

But then, he did not know what lay behind hers!

Gerard, squiring Torry about New York, being seen with her in his carriage in Central Park, seated beside her in the Schuylers' box at the Metropolitan Opera House, walking with her in the famous and beautiful colonnade at Madison Square Gardens, knew that he was no nearer to solving the enigma of Mrs Victoria Slade than he had been that first time when he had seen her in church.

She was always perfectly turned out, completely appropriate for every occasion, and he imagined that the Captain, that connoisseur of female beauty, had felt as proud as he did to have such a perfect specimen of it by his side. She knew how and when to talk, what to say, and was as gracious and charming as the aristocratic Englishwomen whom he had taken as his mistresses during his long stay in England, and her sense of what was fit for public usage was as great as theirs.

Now, had she been chaste. . . For like all men Gerard knew that when he came to marry in earnest he would demand of his bride that however he had behaved she would be stainless when she came to him, a virgin to give him sons, and if, later, she would demand that like him she might go her own way, providing only that she did so discreetly, he would allow her then, and only then, the same sexual rights as himself.

Oh, some men, once married, became the faithful lovers of their wives, never looking again at another woman, but Gerard could not imagine that he would ever be one of them—and certainly no such soiled dove as Torry Slade, or whatever her name was, would, or could, ever gain such love and allegiance from him.

For Gerard's detective had brought him his first report on her mere hours before the wedding-day, which was to be celebrated not in church but privately in the late Captain's palace which would be his, once the ceremony was over, and from that report he had learned—precisely nothing!

Mrs Victoria Slade had no past. Like the goddess Pallas Athene springing into life, fully grown, armed at all points, from the head of the god Jupiter, her father, she had arrived in New York similarly accoutred, in her early twenties, four years ago.

Shortly afterwards, the Captain had made her his last, most beautiful and most notorious mistress. 'Nothing more than this?' said Gerard to the man, flinging down the papers he had given to him. 'I can't waste my time reading this stuff. Tell me, in your own words, and make it brief.' He was rude in his anger and disappointment from not discovering at what cat-house Mrs Torry Slade had learned her trade.

The Pinkerton's man, who was used to Gerard and his little ways, was not at all put out, Gerard was amused to note, and said slowly and mildly, 'In a nutshell, I can find nothing at all about her before she surfaced in New York nearly five years ago, calling herself Mrs Victoria Slade, a widow, although I have no information as to whether that is her true name or not. She possessed enough capital to hire a small apartment in an unfashionable district and live without other visible means of support before she found work. There is no record of any man in her life until she met your grandfather——'

Gerard interrupted him irritably—this was not at all what he wished to hear. 'Enough money to start the *Woman's Banner*?' he enquired, his voice so sardonic that it could have served as a model for the word.

'No,' said the detective. 'She got that first from the Captain; the banks would not lend her anything until he sponsored her—and then they fell over their feet. . .'

'Of course,' said Gerard, who felt for some reason an overpowering urge to act as an unpleasant Greek chorus to this remarkable story.

'And after that,' went on his man, 'she didn't need his direct help; she financed the early days of the paper with what she gained from her own successes on Wall Street. . .'

'Helped again, one supposes, by the Captain,' interjected Gerard; this saga, far from relieving him of anxiety, was, on the contrary, in some strange, slow way, enraging him. 'And before that,' he added, caustically, 'nothing? Nothing at all? She must have come from *somewhere*.'

The detective kept his good humour — one of the reasons why Gerard always employed him. Nothing Gerard said or did fazed the man before him, and no mission Gerard gave him was too *outré* for him to perform. 'As you, know, Mr Schuyler, thousands arrive each year in New York with no history, and Mrs Slade is one of them.'

Gerard rose to his feet, walked to the window, looked out at the busy scene below — Wall Street was at its most populous in the early afternoon. 'No home in the sticks? No husband? Nothing to tell us whether he is alive or dead? No parents, loving or otherwise?' He paused, remembering their conversation in the *Banner*'s office. 'She spoke once of her late husband, said that he was a lawyer — that might help you to discover where she came from, you think?'

The detective nodded. 'Might do,' he said. 'I've certainly traced the whole of her life here before she met the Captain. She just appeared, stayed for a few days in a rooming house before buying her apartment — the landlady remembered that she was very silent about her origins, wasn't short of ready money, and was employed as a reporter on the

Daily News before leaving that when she set up the *Banner*.'

'To have got a job on the *News*,' Gerard commented, 'must have required that she give some sort of background. Could you find nothing there?'

'No.' The detective shook his head. 'She started there as a freelance, a stringer, turning in little stories, until she gave them a brilliant eye-witness account of that robbery and killing on Fifth Avenue, some five years ago—you were out of the country at the time, I believe. The *News* scooped everybody with it, and her descriptions helped the police to find the perpetrators. The owner, old Cyrus Mackeson, gave her a contract and after that she worked for them full-time until she left. My information is that old Cyrus introduced her to the Captain, but there was no gossip about the pair of them, and believe me, if there had been, I would have learned of it. Oh, a discreet lady is Mrs Victoria Slade; even her life with the Captain is a blank, except for their public appearances. I couldn't find an old Schuyler servant to say a word against her, or about her goings-on with the old man—begging your pardon, Mr Schuyler.'

'No need for that, man.' Gerard was direct. This beat everything! He threw the papers he was holding on to his desk. 'Good God, did the woman never say anything to anyone about where she came from?'

'Close-mouthed, Mrs Slade. Not like most women in any way. Probably why the Captain valued her so much.' He looked sideways at the man who employed him, who was about to marry, wonder of wonders, his grandfather's sphinx-like mistress, knowing nothing of her but that one fact: that she had been his mistress.

'Do you want me to go on trying to investigate her? I warn you, I think it is probably hopeless; I keep running up against dead ends.'

Gerard aware that he was feeling unwontedly out of control of his life, and suddenly conscious that he was giving that away to the detective, straightened himself, squared his shoulders. He would not be beaten by the bitch, he would not; if it cost him the rest of his days he would discover who she was, and why she was what she was, and discover into the bargain why she was the one woman whom the Captain had invited completely into his life, making her his constant companion and confidante, as well as his mistress, when always before his women had lived on the periphery of his life.

And he was to marry her tomorrow in total ignorance of her and her past, while she knew everything of him, so that they were embarking on their life together on unequal terms, a condition which he had never before been in with anyone, male or female — especially female, for the phrase 'if you give men little, you give women nothing' had always been his motto.

No matter, for, in the end, it would come down to bed, and bed alone, between them, and there he knew that he would conquer, as he had always conquered. With him, between the sheets, she would learn to forget the Captain, be his, Gerard's, and only his. What matter if he knew nothing of her past if it was to be he who determined her future?

CHAPTER SIX

THE New York daily papers shrieked out their
headlines across the city, the newsboys howled on
every corner. Deplore it though they might, the
Four Hundred, New York's finest, were compelled
to recognise the powers of the newly voracious
Press, the first of its kind in the world's history,
whose methods were soon to be copied by every
other advanced industrial nation.

SCHUYLER HEIR MAKES TWO KILLINGS IN ONE
DAY! roared the banner headlines. For this was
Gerard's wedding-day, and not only was he inheriting his grandfather's fortune by marrying his mistress, but he had cornered the major share of the
new market in Public Utilities and his succession as
the true heir of the Captain was assured. He had
done, in one short fortnight, as much, and more, as
the old man had ever done and was now an enor-
mously rich man in his own right.

His competitors raved and grumbled. It was a
trick, a scam which Gerard had committed, on a par
with the behaviour of a barker at a fairground; all
this and more in the way of insult was thrown at
him, but Gerard cared not a jot; as a result of
working in tandem with Jevons Shreve he was going
to be able to walk to the altar on his wedding-day as
a man with a potential far beyond the millions of
dollars which marrying Torry Slade had brought

him — and that was a source of such satisfaction to him that even as Timson settled his morning coat on his broad shoulders, privately thinking that Mr Gerard Schuyler looked more like a prize-fighter in mufti than a man of what could only be called a sedentary occupation, the grin on his face seemed pasted there.

'A little solemnity would be expected of you, sir,' said Timson, who knew how far he could go with his master, and that far was a very long way indeed. 'It is customary, sir, for the groom — the Benedict, I believe they call it here — to be perhaps a trifle grave — although with a certain gleam in his eye.'

'At the prospect of delights to come,' remarked Gerard naughtily.

'Exactly so, sir. As usual, you have gauged the matter correctly, and permit me to say, sir, the lady is very lovely.'

'Exactly so,' said Gerard, mimicking his man's tone so accurately that Timson's own grin grew broader, matched his master's.

'And further permit me to say, sir, that it is the opinion of all your staff that the lady will do very well.' He paused as he saw Gerard stiffen — for Gerard was always unpredictable, and for a moment he wondered if he had gone too far.

But apparently not. 'So glad,' drawled Gerard, in his English mode of speech, 'to learn that my servants approve of my doings. The icing on the cake, is it? I should be devastated, positively devastated to learn that you were all secretly disapproving of my choice, which, damn your eyes, is, as you know, no choice at all.'

So, he had got away with it, thought Timson, who knew a delicious truth — or thought that he did — about Mrs Torry Slade which he was pretty sure that his master did not know, not being one of the servants, and therefore only being privy to a certain amount of knowledge and not to all.

There were times when he had thought of telling his master what he had discovered, but always, in their mutual doings, Gerard had had the better of him, being as artful as the devil and ruthless with it, so that it was a pleasure for Timson to know something which his master did not, but was sure to find out sooner or later. In the meantime, Timson could permit himself a small secret smile.

Gerard caught the smile, and, like lightning, seized Timson by the collar. 'Now what,' he almost roared, 'is *that* for? You sly devil, Timson, I know that expression. Explain, or I'll have your guts for garters.'

Timson cursed his tell-tale face and merely remarked as coolly as he could, to give the smiling devil before him no inkling of the real truth, 'Why, Mr Gerard, I was inwardly enjoying the stories of your latest exploits which the public prints here have blazoned across the city. We are not so frank about our doings in London, more's the pity.'

'Now why,' demanded Gerard, releasing Timson's collar, 'do I not believe a word of all that? No matter; I'll sort out what about my wedding-day gives you such an accursed fit of the sniggers later on. Or is it just the fact that I'm hooked at last — and by a hooker — which is causing you such satisfaction? No, do not answer me, I shall be late for the minister and the ceremony, and that would never do.'

'No, indeed,' agreed Timson suavely, thinking he had got off lightly. 'No call to create gossip, sir. And now you are ready, and have seldom looked more, more. . .gentlemanly, if I may be so bold.'

'What a liar you are,' said Gerard pleasantly, good humour restored. 'I never look like a gentleman and never will. I leave that to Cousin Brandt and the rest. Now had you said bruiser, I might have agreed with you, but you are too devilish sly to speak the truth and my wedding-day is not the day to start. Now, lead me out to where Cousin Brandt is waiting to be my best man; I have a desperate desire to discover what my bride has seen fit to wear!'

What Torry had seen fit to wear, he discovered when he entered to the strains of Wagner's Bridal March, was a deep cream silk, so deep that it was almost a lemon shaded with the palest ochre, which, although eminently suitable as an attire for a widow remarrying, bore no resemblance to that worn by a virgin bride. Pearl buttons ran from below her waist high, high up to the tiny band from which rose the perfect column of her neck. The skirt was discreet too, no elaborate padding being allowed to mar the lovely lines of her body. He had a savage bet with himself that every man in the room was mentally stripping her and every woman was hating her with a hate reserved for any woman who dared to look as she did, denying everything which she was.

A wreath of pale lemon carnations on her glorious

hair held down a small veil which did not cover her face but cascaded to her shoulders, and the tiny bouquet which she carried was also of lemon carnations, pure in their simplicity. Her taste, as usual, was perfect. There was nothing garish or overblown about her; one might have thought that she had just emerged from a nunnery to be offered up, a virgin sacrifice to the lusts of men.

That she had chosen to dress and behave so was, he knew, done to impress not only him but the world; to show that Mrs Victoria Slade, *grande horizontale* that she was, was serious in this marriage, and would say and do nothing to offend the manners of the world to which she would belong once the ceremony was over. What she might choose to do so far as the morals of that world were concerned, thought Gerard, still savage, was quite another thing. Thus the display of perfection in taste which she was offering to the world.

Which was more, he thought, than could be said for the taste of the artist who had designed the ballroom in which the ceremony was taking place, with its ornate white and gold columns and its painted ceiling where obese goddesses and over-muscled gods disported on rather weighty clouds, giving the impression, he naughtily thought, of mixed bathing in a Turkish bath in a cat-house — which, guessing at the bride's origins, however pure she seemed on the outside, was not, perhaps, inappropriate.

Her one bridesmaid was Kate, wearing a simple Kate-Greenaway-style dress in pale green, to complement Torry's deep cream, for Torry had insisted that the wedding ceremony be as simple as possible, and she had successfully fought off Mrs Joris's plaintively expressed wish for half a dozen bridal attendants and some six flower girls, whose sole duty would have been to strew rose petals before a bride who would rather have been married in a small office in her ordinary clothes than take part in the mummery which always accompanied a Schuyler wedding.

But at least, she thought gratefully, unaware how much she had pleased the groom by doing so, she had succeeded in making the ceremony as simple as she could, and in return had gone some way towards acceding to Mrs Joris's desire for her to look 'like a proper bride, my dear'.

And, of course, all the Schuylers were desperate to make the wedding look as little as possible like the thing it was — a legal arrangement by which the groom might get his hands on the Schuyler millions, so that they should not be lost to the family.

The minister's beam on them both as the ceremony began betrayed no sense of cynicism, of the reality of the situation — quite the contrary, he might have been Father Christmas, about to bestow presents on deserving children, and if the bride had to suppress a tremendous tendency to giggle the groom, for his part, had to suppress an equal tendency to burst into laughter at the most inappropriate places.

Except that, to his horror, Gerard found that the ceremony was beginning to affect him strangely, and that something inside him was rebelling at the difference between the words he was uttering and the unpleasant truths which lay behind them.

Reaching the lovely phrase, 'With my body I thee worship,' he had a sudden desperate wish that he was meaning what he said, and that the woman beside him was not someone foisted on him but someone for him truly to love and cherish. Such sentimentality was so unlike his usual self, was so unwanted, that he blinked, lost the meaning of what the preacher was saying, and had to be prompted fiercely by Brandt, who was astounded to see Cousin Gerard wool-gathering.

I shall get drunk tonight, thought Gerard, who had refused a traditional stag night with Brandt and the rest because he had been unsure of what he might say or do if he had consented; had been fearful of what he might have said if he in any way lost control of himself. If I get drunk tonight, on the other hand, no one will know, not even the bride, he told himself now.

'Are you quite well, Gerard?' Torry was whispering in his ear, and then, mockingly, 'It is usually the bride who is overset, most rare for the groom to have the megrims—but then you are a rare sort of groom.'

Black rage seized Gerard by the throat. 'Enough of that,' he muttered beneath his breath. 'We are not all as brass-faced as you are, madam.'

How dared she mock at him? Was he not mock enough for being compelled to swallow his unruly grandpa's leavings? He had a mind to forget all documents, all agreements and take the dollymop by force once they were alone. Dammit, the minis-

ter had maundered over them to some effect, and
why should he not take his pleasure with her? He
would show her what worshipping a woman with
one's body meant, and no mistake. But his worship
would be in the form of a Black Mass, meant to
violate, not to honour. . .

Sanity took over, mainly because he could hear
Cousin Brandt agitating over him at his back; he
was pushing the ring into his hand, and then was
watching him while he slipped it on the bride's
finger, as though he was fearful that something
might yet happen to prevent him from getting his
share of the commission for dealing with the
Schuyler fortune on Gerard's behalf, once the knot
was well and truly tied, and Gerard had inherited.

And then it was all over, the small string band
was playing some treacly sentimental tune, and they
were processing side by side down the aisle, through
the massed ranks of Schuylers, Whitneys,
Rockefellers, Astors, Goulds and the rest, the same
new and old money which had supported the
Captain's obsequies so recently.

Only the wedding breakfast to get through now,
and the speeches, and the mocking congratulations
of all who were there. At least they had been spared
processing through the streets to make a disgraceful
show of themselves for the mob, as had happened
at a recent Vanderbilt wedding, where the bride,
groom and family had had to push through milling
crowds outside the Episcopal Church.

Neither would there be any kind of similar pan-
tomime after the wedding breakfast was over, for
they had, sensibly, decided that the honeymoon

would be spent here at the Captain's home, or rather Gerard's home, for that was now what it was, the wedding which brought it to him accomplished.

As he sat eating food which he could not taste, drinking fine wine which might as well have been vinegar, smiling, always smiling, giving off an impression of supreme happiness, the deviousness which he had inherited from the old villain who had landed him in this pickle had never, Gerard thought, been so welcome or so well exercised.

His loving bride looked gloriously happy, too. She occasionally turned towards him and gave him an expression which could only be described as soulfully hopeful! The third time that she did it, just as they were about to cut the monstrous five-tiered bridal cake which his mother had insisted on, he swapped her grin for grin, saying, beneath his breath, 'One more look like that, Mrs Gerhardt Ghysbrecht Schuyler, and I shall consider that you wish our bargain to be broken tonight.'

'Oh, come now.' And Torry's answering whisper was sweet poison. 'Nothing to that, Gerard. We agreed, did we not, that we are to appear five fathoms deep in love? I consider that so far I have been somewhat restrained.'

'Restrained!' he hissed back, giving a smile at the end of his speech to deceive the eager watchers. 'If what you have been favouring me with is restrained, then God help me if you had decided to be a little . . .undone. The guests would have left screaming at the show, Kate Fielding's cat-house translated to Fifth Avenue, and in public, too.'

Torry rode even that. She put a soft hand on his

mouth as he finished, and murmured teasingly, but loud enough so that those around could hear her, 'I know how you feel, Gerard, but consider—it will not be long now before we are alone,' and her wicked eyes defied him to say or do anything in reply which would give away the game that they were playing.

Well, if she was able to play out this disgraceful charade with such finesse, then the least he could do was match her, or better her. Let her begin to dodge his arrows rather than that he should be compelled to try to avoid hers!

Obedient to Brandt's instructions, he placed his hand over Torry's in their joint cutting of the cake, for as usual at Schuyler celebrations Brandt was the Master of Ceremonies. He ought to hire himself out, was Gerard's sour and inward comment; he was better at it than playing financial games, and was fluttering around the bride and groom as though he had made the marriage as well as having organised the ceremony.

True to his inward determination to master her, as well as himself, when he finally released the hand of the blushing bride, he raised her blushes to an even higher level by seizing her round the waist and giving her a long and passionate kiss on that delectable mouth.

Protocol thus breached, which was not wholly unexpected—all the Schuylers knew that Gerard was a law unto himself—he stood back and announced cheerfully, 'Sorry, everyone, and you too, my dear,' turning to Torry, 'but I couldn't wait any longer to pay my best respects to such a lovely vision of delight as the new Mrs Gerard Schuyler.'

This brought clapping and cheers from everyone. 'Good old Gerard, saved the money for the family, hasn't he? Deserves his fun tonight as well, doesn't he?' being the general sentiment, since everyone assumed that any woman whom the Captain had favoured for so long must be a performer of some magnitude, and every man in the room was jealous of him.

Knowing this, told of it publicly by the uproar which followed his action, and the expression on the faces of the assembled men, Gerard's smile at the enraged Torry, whose wreath had been knocked sideways by the force of his apparently ill-suppressed lust, was almost a jeering one, defying her this time to say or do anything which would reveal the truth.

Torry, whose physical reaction to his sudden embrace had suprised and shocked her even more than usual, for she had had no time to prepare herself to resist the attraction he unwantedly posed for her, clutched at her bouquet, raising it slightly, as though she was about to strike him across the face with it.

Her husband, smiling still, saw the small movement of her hand, and, as he later realised, strangely and unwontedly sensitive to everything she said, did, or which might be passing through her mind, took the bouquet gently from her, murmuring, 'Allow me to relieve you of your burden for a moment, Mrs Schuyler; we do not want it to be crushed. After all, it has yet to be gifted to your bridesmaid as a token that her happy day will not be long in coming.'

He saw Kate's face change as she heard what he said, a look of horror pass briefly over it, and he knew that whoever else they deceived they were not deceiving Kate. He closed his eyes. The last thing he had intended to do was to distress his innocent young sister. Kate deserved better of him than that. He determined to have a word with her after the reception was over, and further that he would stop taunting Torry, and discourage her from taunting him — if he could.

Kate came up to him later. He had left Torry to circulate separately before they came together again to shake hands in a goodbye salutation to all their guests, and he had been slapped on the back and congratulated by every rogue who had made money on Wall Street out of America's expanding industrial growth. He wondered wryly how many congratulations he would have received had he refused his grandfather's last present to him.

In the middle of these dark thoughts, not helped by the knowledge that tiredness and the strain of the day were beginning to leave their marks on his face since even the arch-dissembler that he knew himself to be could not be on guard every moment of such a long day, he saw Kate bearing down on him.

'Gerard.' Her light voice was purposeful, her face also bore, he saw, the marks of a sleepless night and of sorrow. For him? Her first words told him that she knew what he was doing, had done.

'Oh, Gerard, how could you? To sell yourself for

Grandpa's money. You have, haven't you? You don't care for her at all, do you? It's all a pretence. . .'

'Now, Kate,' he began, 'you heard what I said——' for her to interrupt him.

'Oh, yes. I heard what you *said*, but I can also hear what you really mean. Every word you say, and she is as bad, can be read quite differently. I sometimes think that the whole world is deaf! No, Gerard, you may deceive others but you can never deceive me. I hope you think that your bargain is worth it.'

Gerard suddenly knew something which cut him to the quick by its unwanted nature. He had always shared a strange rapport with his little sister, ever since he had first picked her up and held her as a baby. And, piercingly, it came to him that the rapport he undoubtedly shared with the wife he did not want was exactly the same. And why was that?

Bargain! Kate had said bargain, but she could not know, she could not! And speaking to her again, listening to her passionate repudiation of what he had done, he knew that although Kate had no true understanding of the bargain which Torry Slade and he had struck she intuitively understood that *something* of that nature existed between them, only the detail was unknown to her.

For the first time in a career of almost contemptuous buccaneering and disregard for the feelings of others, Gerard felt a strange sense of shame, of guilt, something which he had never experienced before. The knowledge that others might be hurt by his actions, and that their hurt was as real as his own, was harshly forced upon him.

He would have given anything, anything, to assure Kate that she was mistaken, that he was not practising a monstrous deceit on the world, that what he felt for Torry Slade, and she for him, was true love, forced into flower by the Captain's action. Equally, he knew that he could no longer lie to her, however much he might be able to lie to others — including himself.

'Yes, Kate,' he said at last, the weariness on his face now in his voice. 'Yes, but for God's sake pretend as I do. The deed is done, we are man and wife; I have made my bed, and I must lie on it.'

Even as he spoke the double — and lying — meaning of his words struck him hard, hard. He saw Kate's face change, oddly, not to sorrow, but to something almost approaching happiness. She stood on tiptoe, and so tall was he that he had to bend a little so that she might fulfil her intention, which was to kiss him on the cheek.

'Oh, thank God, Gerard, that you have stopped lying to me. I could not bear it; bad enough that you should deceive others, but I am your sister, Gerard, and I know you as no one else does. You must not destroy yourself — as the Captain did. You are worth more than that.'

He did not want to ask her what she meant; he doubted whether, in her inexperience of the cruel world, she even knew, but it was as though he had been offered balm after poison, an antidote to the self-disgust which he had been feeling ever since he had woken up that morning.

'And Gerard, you will be kind to her, won't you? I know she's not what you would have chosen for a wife, but she was kind to the Captain, she made him very happy. Let her make you happy, Gerard.'

She had lost him, but he would not let her know that. Her own understanding of the world was so naïve that she could not be aware of what being compelled to marry such a woman as Torry Slade meant to him.

It was his turn to kiss her, which he did, just as Mrs Gerard Schuyler, for so he must learn to think of her, came up to him, saying in her cool way, 'Brandt is beginning to grumble, Gerard. He says it is high time that we stopped socialising among our guests and prepared to bid them adieu.'

Her look took in Kate, who said fervently, 'Oh, I am so glad that you chose a simple bouquet, Victoria, for, knowing that you will throw it to me before the first guest to leave shakes your hand, I would have hated one of those large vulgar ones. It is. . .' And she hesitated, and then said — and why not, for was it not the truth? 'It is as calmly beautiful as you are.'

To Gerard's surprise, Torry's eyes filled with tears. She looked at her husband over Kate's head, said simply and humbly, 'Why, Kate, that is the nicest compliment anyone has paid me today, and alas, as a poor return, I must rob you of your brother.' And she held out her arm to Gerard, who took it, and walked her silently back to the small dais where they were to stand, forbearing to twit or taunt her, content to be by her side, thinking of Kate and of her lost illusions.

Was what he felt for Kate pure, unerotic love?

Was that why he was so protective of her, so regretful that it was he who had robbed her of innocence? Would he ever feel for any woman an erotic love as selfless and as pure? Was he even capable of doing so?

In the hurly-burly of their necessary and protracted farewells such strange and new emotions were forgotten — to return later, when he was alone, to reproach him and to disturb him. He, who was never introspective, lived only for sensation and action, was compelled at last to recognise that there was another side to life — and he disliked the knowledge fiercely.

Mr and Mrs Gerard Schuyler's first meal together was long-drawn-out and neither party had much appetite for the splendid food placed before them. Both, considerate of those who served them, made an effort to eat at least a little, to show enthusiasm and thanks for it, even though the chef and his helpers stared at the half-full plates, shrugged their shoulders and said, in apology for their betters, 'Ah, well. They have other things on their mind.'

Which of course they had, if not exactly what their staff imagined. Gerard toyed with a fancy that he would have, for once, preferred life to be like a play: that the curtain would have fallen at the end of the act when the last wedding guest had left, only to rise again on the next act, taking place, as the programme said, two weeks later, the intervening action having occurred in limbo, to be remembered, not experienced.

No such luck! Every last moment had to be

endured. . .and the ones which followed. After the meal they retired to the vast drawing-room, the pair of them lost in it.

Gerard had changed into a velvet smoking-jacket and charcoal-grey trousers; whatever happened in life, bad or good, one had to assume the correct uniform in which to endure it. Torry was wearing what was always described as a tea-gown, a loose flowing thing in rose *peau de soie* with a wrap-over neck, lightly draped over her bosom, which made a woman look uncorseted, and consequently, to Gerard, sexually desirable.

He was not a great reader, but one of his English mistresses had had pretensions to literature, and when, once, undressing her, he had told her he preferred her in flowing robes of soft silk, not in the architectural and stiffly fashionable fabrics which made a woman look like a marble monument come to half-life, she had repeated to him the words of a long-dead poet: '"A sweet disorder in the dress Kindles in clothes a wantonness. . ."'

She had quoted something else in the throes of passion, and walking over to his wife, who sat opposite to him, a book in her hand, as composed as though she had sat with him these thirty years, he bent down, took the book from her hands, and when she lifted her head, startled, eyes glittering, he kissed her on the lips but not before murmuring, to her further surprise,

'"Whenas in silks my Julia goes,
Then, then (methinks) how sweetly flows,
That liquefaction of her clothes."'

Gerard laughed soundlessly at the look she gave
him, for she was not sure which shocked her the
most, his unexpected knowledge of the poem, or
that he should quote it to her. 'Oh, I am not a
totally unlettered savage, Mrs Gerard Schuyler, fit
only for the money markets of the world, but do not
ask me where I gained my knowledge of *that*.'

'No, indeed,' agreed his bride. 'Most unwise to
be curious, I have no doubt.' She picked up her
book, opened it again, dismissing him from her
consideration. Enraged, Gerard bent down and
took it from her.

'Not now,' he said, his voice thick. 'It is, after all,
our wedding-night, and dressed like that you look
ready for liquefaction yourself. . .'

Torry's eyes were watchful. She could not take
the book back because he had tossed it on to the
sofa opposite them. 'In name only, we agreed,' she
replied, and oh, by God, the bitch was as cool as
ever—did nothing move her? Did she, could she,
know how she was moving him?

She was still speaking. 'You will not forget that
we had a bargain.' And she rose and made for the
door.

Gerard caught her up. He took her by the
shoulders and swung her round to face him.

'Look at me, Mrs Schuyler. That old fool well
and truly tied the knot for us this afternoon. Are
you really telling me that you wish to continue with
the ridiculous farce agreed between us in your office
and later? We are a grown man and woman, I want
you, and you, I am sure, want me. Let us tear up

the agreement in bed together where we ought to be, man and wife.'

He had not meant to plead, but something in him, some last residue of the innocent boy he had once been, suddenly wanted this to be a real wedding-night, maudlin fool that he was. And if she refused him, then it would be war, straight war, a war he intended to win, and willy nilly, agreement or no agreement, he would have her in the fullest sense — but this way might be better.

The eyes on him were shuttered. He could have sworn that for a moment there had been an answering gleam in them, but the spark had died.

'No,' she said, rock-steady. 'I meant what I said and signed if you didn't. I will not be your partner in lust.'

'For God's sake, woman, we are married.' The words were forced from him. 'I could take you, here and now. No one would deny my right.'

'Rape?' she queried, eyebrows lifted — would nothing shake that marmoreal calm? Had she no feelings? Did *grandes horizontales* who existed only to please men have any feelings of their own? He must never forget what she was.

'You could give me what you gave the Captain,' burst from him.

The expression on her face was so strange, almost he could have sworn she was about to laugh. To laugh? What was there to laugh at? Gerard Schuyler, for being an importunate fool, when he had decided to be quite otherwise.

The faint smile disappeared. 'There is always that, of course,' she said. 'I thought, I thought. . .'

She paused, and Gerard's treacherous body was now so roused that he could hardly control himself. The folds of the tea-gown had fallen apart and he could see the cleft in her bosom quite plainly; were it to part a little more. . .he might. . . He blinked, shook his head. 'Yes, madam, what did you think? You do too much thinking for a woman.'

'Oh, the Captain liked me to do that,' she offered carelessly. 'Perhaps you do not resemble him so much, after all.'

'Come to bed with me, Mrs Schuyler, and let us find out!'

'I thought. . .that for me to give you what. . . I gave the Captain. . .was not what you wanted. You made that very plain.'

'I have changed my mind,' he ground out.

'It is the wedding,' she said regretfully, 'and being here alone with me. . .that has. . .excited. . .you.'

'Yes, all that.' Gerard was fierce. 'And by God, Mrs Schuyler, were it not my wedding-night, and we supposed to be — what was it you said? Five fathoms deep in love — I would be off to Kate Fielding's on the instant, but since that is denied me. . .'

'Then I will do?' she finished for him, oh, so smoothly.

'Yes — no. I did not mean that at all.' By now, Gerard hardly knew what he did mean.

He had not expected this, that he would behave before her as though, as though. . .he were a child deprived of a lollipop. And what a luscious lollipop!

'There is one thing,' she said gravely, cool eyes never leaving him, but had he seen her hands they would have told him a different story, for, however outwardly calm Torry Schuyler might appear to be, her clenched fists would have betrayed her, shown him that she was exercising her own will to stand him off, not to melt and swoon towards him.

Liquefaction! What a word. And it was plain that both of them were heading for that state at the rate of knots, like a liner on an Atlantic crossing sailing into a predicted storm.

Not even to be offered what she had offered the Captain! But then, he had foolishly told her, many times, had he not, that he despised that and her? What in the world had happened to clever, predatory Gerard Schuyler, the sexsmith who had taken them, used them, and left them, that he should so foolishly lust after this one woman, who, face it, Gerard, was really no different from any other? he asked himself.

'There is nothing either good or bad, but thinking makes it so', that Englishwoman had told him once. Then think, Gerard; you surely don't want this particular woman so badly that you cannot stop putting yourself at a disadvantage with her, when there are so many others who would fall into bed with you, without argument, on the instant. He had seen the half-invitation to dalliance on the face of more than one woman since he had returned to New York—and Daisy Gascoyne was still waiting for him, back in England. He must have gone mad.

'I think, Gerard, it would be simpler,' said his wife gently, 'if I went to bed.'

'Simpler!' Gerard almost roared. 'How simpler?

And it's only nine-thirty. We have to sort out how we are to deceive Timson and the rest, you know.'

'True,' returned Torry gravely. 'Let us go and do so, and, having done so, I can retire with a book, and you can cool down.'

With a bottle, doubtless, thought Gerard furiously, as they mounted the stairs together to the suite which the Captain had shared with his wife, and later, presumably, with Mrs Torry Slade.

Which made it all the more strange that she stared about her with such interest, inspecting the dim paintings on the wall, brought from some Italian palace, admiring the hangings on the great bed which had also been transported from Europe, but exactly where no one knew.

There was another room opening off what Gerard irreverently thought of as the State Bedroom, which also had a double bed in it, ready prepared, and two dressing-rooms opening off them where Timson and a lady's maid, hired for Torry, somewhat against her will—'But you are a Schuyler now,' Gerard had said doggedly, 'and cannot be expected to dress yourself'—were waiting for them.

Torry allowed Miss Clarke to undress her—and then dress her again, in a splendid nightgown covered in lace and pink ribbons, which concealed more of her than a balldress usually did, and even then there was a négligé-cum-dressing-gown to slip over that, so that Torry thought she was nearly as well prepared to go for a stroll down Fifth Avenue as to bed, where doubtless her husband was expected to remove it all.

Gerard declined to allow Timson to undress him.

'I'm not ready yet, dammit,' he said irritably, 'and when I am I'll undress myself. Good God, I suppose we've got to decide which room we're sleeping in. Go to bed yourself, Timson. You've had a long day.'

Timson bowed acquiescence and retired without speaking. He was the perfect valet, always discreet, knew when to hold his tongue and when to speak. There were times when his perfection annoyed Gerard, and he could have done with a little less tact tonight. . .or. . .or. . .what the devil was he doing, drivelling to himself about his *valet*? That showed what arranged and convenient marriage did to you. Softening of the brain, no less.

Walking, still fully dressed, into the main bedroom, he found Torry already in bed, reclining against the pillows, the splendid hair down in a long plait, her book in her hand. Dammit, it wasn't decent; the woman should show some emotion.

'You've decided on this bed, then,' he said redundantly. 'I'll take the other.' And then in a bout of frustrated nastiness, 'Here for old times' sake, are you? Happy memories of the Captain. Frightened a younger man might be too vigorous, want to lead instead of follow?'

'Go to bed, Gerard,' was all he got from that. 'You knew perfectly well what you were letting yourself in for. Too late for second thoughts.' And her eyes were on her book again.

Perceptive Gerard might be, and usually was, where women were concerned, but the preconceptions he had formed of his new wife, and his own frustrations, were preventing him from making his usual cool-headed appreciation of the situation he was in, and he missed his bride's trembling hands, and the occasional betraying quiver of her lip.

Torry had determined that tonight, of all nights, she would not tempt the tiger. She was wise enough to know that Gerard was trembling on the edge if not of rape then of something like it, and that she was not going to risk.

'I had better say goodnight, then,' he offered her, voice hoarse.

'Yes, goodnight,' she said absently, without lifting her head from her book.

Gerard's control snapped. He strode across the room to the bed, flung the book away, caught her face in his two cupped hands and hissed, 'If I can't have anything else, then by damn I'll have a goodnight kiss from your ladyship.' And his mouth ground down on hers, not kindly, not gently, but with all the frustrated passion of the strong male animal he was: the tiger was on the point of snapping his chain.

Helpless, pinned back against the pillows, Torry endured his onslaught—and then, unwillingly at first, began to co-operate with it. He could have identified the exact moment when reluctant participation changed to acceptance, when from being stiff in his arms she softened in them, so that for a moment he thought exultantly, By God, I've won. I knew she'd never hold out against me. It's not in her. A *horizontale* only exists to peddle her sex, and if I press the right buttons then the machine will roar into life!

But not for long. She was suddenly fighting him

off, her mouth no longer soft, and then her teeth closed on his lower lip, not hard, but enough to break the skin so that blood ran into his mouth, and he started back, as much from the bitter taste as from any pain, reminded that loss of control was all very well if you gained what you wanted, but humiliating if you didn't.

And rape was not what he wanted. He wanted her co-operation, to hear her say, Oh, please, Gerard, please, the tiger's prey begging the tiger to make a meal of her.

He released her, sat back, said breathlessly, 'A kiss was all I wanted, but tell me, is that all you offered the Captain? I wonder he prized you so highly.' But that did not move her, only had her saying coldly,

'Now you have had your fun, Gerard, goodnight again.'

'Fun!' His voice rose. 'Fun! You call that fun? I promise you one day I'll show you what fun is.' And oh, what a feeble way in which to end his wedding-day, as he strode into his dressing-room to find the bottles which he had secreted there against what he had considered the unlikely event of Mrs Victoria Schuyler's refusing to go to bed with him.

Which just went to show that pride, as so often, went before a fall, and taking a bottle to bed was not going to be half so much fun as having Torry Slade beneath him. And some time later, still in his evening clothes, lying on the floor, which was going up and down like the deck of a ship in a high storm, he tried, hazily, to remember when he had last been drunk, and was too far gone to remember that it was thirteen years ago, when he had been a boy of eighteen, trying to prove himself a man.

Neither then nor later could he understand why Torry's rejection of him had hit him so hard. It was not that he was so conceited that he thought every woman ought to be flattered by being invited to share his bed, but the combination of rage with his grandfather, added to the genuine frustration he had felt on seeing her, ready for bed, looking so desirable, had done the damage. So that to the anger he felt for the old rogue because he had left his money tied up in such a fashion was added rage and anger towards her because *she* had been willing to sleep with the Captain — but not with him.

He could not remember, so fuddled was he, whether he had been a crying drunk or not on the last occasion that he had indulged himself, but, shamefully, he was crying for Gerard Schuyler now. For one thing, it was so uncomfortable on the floor of his bedroom — or was it Torry's?

He seemed to remember that at some point, clutching his bottle to him, he had reeled towards the Captain's room to try to find her in his giant bed — to do what? And then had stopped, sinking into a sitting position on the carpet to take another drink from his almost empty bottle.

By now Gerard had forgotten everything, which was the reason for getting drunk, was it not? He only knew that he was unhappy, but did not know why, and that someone — who? — was bending over him, saying, 'Yes, what is it, Gerard?' in a soft, worried voice.

'Feel sick,' he muttered, sinking sideways on to the floor.

'Oh, no,' said the voice, slightly alarmed, and the hand that was on his forehead was removed.

Gerard wanted it back. He sat up. A horrible mistake: nausea overwhelmed him. For some reason standing up seemed a good idea. No, it wasn't, it was a bad one. He sank to his knees; someone seized him, supported his head, directed it down and he was overwhelmingly, disgustingly sick. Spasms racked him again and when he thought that he had finished the dry heaves took over even though there was nothing left for him to throw up.

The hands that were holding his head laid it down on the carpet when he had finished. Unknown to him the hands removed the china washbowl into which he had vomited, brought a damp cloth and began to sponge his sweating brow. His sickness having gone, he had broken out into a hateful cold sweat. Someone put a pillow under his head. Timson? he thought fuzzily, for even when he opened his eyes they would not focus and the small light that there was made him feel so ill that he groaned and closed them again.

'No,' he muttered. 'Wan' my bed. Uncomfortable.' The floor would not stay still, and he was chained to a giant wheel which turned and turned, his feet to its centre, his head on the rim.

'Wanna be sick again,' he mumbled, and so he was, but only a little this time, and the same kind person was helping him, wiping him clean again, and then, some time later—how long?—was half lifting him, half dragging him, finally getting him to his feet, saying in his ear, 'Walk, Gerard, if you can.'

'Can't,' he managed, but he did, and somehow, hanging on to his saviour, he must have achieved his bedroom again where the someone manhandled him on to his bed and began to remove his clothing, stopping at intervals to wipe his sweating face.

After that, Gerard remembered nothing, forgot even what had happened to him before he was gently laid on his bed and the covers drawn over him, so that when he woke in the morning he had no idea of how he had come to be in his bed, reasonably clean, dressed in his nightshirt, with a head that defied description.

Only Torry Schuyler, having finally, with great difficulty and with his unwilling, uncomprehending assistance, managed to get him into his bed, shook a sorrowful head at him, and then before she left him, and she had no idea why she did it, she kissed her unconscious husband on his still sweating brow, the only caress he was to receive from his wife on his wedding-night — and he had no idea that he had been favoured with it.

CHAPTER SEVEN

MRS VICTORIA SCHUYLER was bored. She was pacing the terrace which lay above the ornamental garden at Moidore Castle in Lincolnshire, warm in the sun of an afternoon in late spring. Beside her walked Lady Daisy Gascoyne, talking idly of anything which came into her head, little of it interesting to Torry.

She had been married to Gerard for only three weeks, a marriage distinguished by cold civility in private and warm looks and words in public, when he had come home one evening and said to her abruptly over dinner, 'I intend to go to England in a few days' time, Mrs Schuyler. I am sorry to give you so little warning, but matters there need my attention. I have wrapped up my deals here, and Jevons Shreve is well qualified to keep things ticking over. . .whereas my man in London. . .'

He had watched her struggle with herself. One thing that Torry had not bargained for was how much being Mrs Gerard Schuyler was bound to change her life. Now she was being wrenched out of New York, away from her newspaper, and all her interests. But it was the inevitable result of the bargain which she had proposed, and for a certain time she and Gerard must keep up their charade, except that, as both of them knew, she was being compelled to change her life more than Gerard was required to change his.

'Suppose I said that I wish to remain in New York?' she had said coolly.

'Come now, Mrs Schuyler. . .' Gerard was always formal with her '. . .you are my loving wife. "Whither thou goest, I will go", and all that. . .as the Bible says. I am sure that you would wish to be as obedient a wife as Ruth. If I need to visit London, then perforce you must come with me. Besides,' he had added, 'there is Kate to consider, and Ma thinks that we can have a real honeymoon, seeing, as she says, that a week in the Captain's palace cannot really count!'

'Kate?' Torry had said, picking up the first part of his sentence.

'Yes, Kate. Pa point-blank refuses to take either Ma or Kate to Europe. Says he is done with dancing to other people's tunes. Ma doesn't wish to offend against society's unwritten rules by going there without him. She would like us to launch Kate on London society, something I don't object to. I know all the sharks that swim in *that* sea, and can keep them away from her, whereas Ma don't. And you, looking as you do, and behaving as perfectly as you do, will make a better sponsor for her than Ma.'

Torry liked Kate and the feeling was reciprocated. However, she had buttered a brioche, and said coolly, 'I don't really want to go. There is the paper to think of, and now that I have sacked Judith I shall have to leave it with someone I'm not sure of.'

For, to Torry's horror, two days after the grand Schuyler wedding the scurrilous paper, *The New*

York Tattler, had broken the Homer Blackwood scandal with screaming headlines about the preacher's love-nest, and the fact that his secretary had condoned Preacher Blackwood's taking his wife as his mistress, and that the three of them were living in a cosy *ménage à trois* — in the same house as the preacher's innocent wife.

The Tattler had had no evidence, nothing but gossip to back up its claims, but they had been so exact that Torry had guessed with a sinking heart that her second in command had taken the story to *The Tattler* when Torry had delayed printing it.

Judith Reis had not denied what she had done. 'You wouldn't print it because you married that man, preferring to betray the Woman's Movement rather than him, so I went to the *Tattler* with it, and they had no hesitation in publishing it, evidence or not. No, don't dismiss me, I'm going; they'll pay me far more than you do and they don't have the sort of nonsensical scruples you possess.'

Well, that was that. Torry had had to find a new assistant, and quickly, particularly since being Mrs Gerard Schuyler was far more difficult than being the Captain's companion, since society now received her, and Gerard expected her not only to go about with him at night far more than the Captain had done, but to attend women's society functions during the day, and to keep up their farce she had to obey him.

Gerard was speaking. 'If you're worried about the *Banner*, don't be. Van Rensselaer knows a competent man who will keep it going for you while you are away. I've arranged for him to come to see you tomorrow.'

One good thing about his wife, Gerard had thought, she never displayed tantrums and megrims, always considered what he suggested dispassionately, without reproach or foolish reservations of the sort which most females he knew went in for. Even in their altercations, and strangely there had been none since their wedding-night, she had never been petty, always forthright.

If she struggled a little with herself over the need to subordinate her own wishes to Gerard's, the necessity to keep up their bargain, which, after all, she had suggested, had overridden all other considerations, and she had given him her reluctant agreement.

'So, Mrs Schuyler,' he had said. 'You will be ready? And we shall take Kate with us?'

They were not really questions, Torry knew, but Gerard's way of doing things, which she was beginning to recognise. He had never taken too much to drink again after their wedding-night, and she had known by his manner that he did not know, or had forgotten, once he had recovered from his drunken stupor, that she had looked after him when he had been *in extremis*. And why she had done so, and so lovingly, she still did not know. She did not love Gerard Schuyler because she did not love any man, nor had any wish to do so — and particularly she had no wish to love such an arrogant swine as Gerard Schuyler was.

She had told herself, not entirely truthfully, that she had disliked him from the moment she had first seen him, in the church, staring at her, as though she were something offensive brought in from the street on the edge of someone's shoe, fit only for the trash can.

But, on their wedding-night, when she had found him, helpless, on the floor of their dressing-room, when he had clutched at her so fiercely, not in lust, but wordlessly demanding simple help, because he was beyond helping himself, never mind that it was his own fault that he was in such a state, she had felt for him something more than pity — but less, she told herself, than love. For, after all, he could never have foreseen such a wedding, or wedding-night, as she unwittingly and the Captain wittingly had provided for him.

And his body, when she had stripped him, had been such a contrast in its firm youthful masculinity with that of the Captain that she had drawn in her breath. It had been plain by his condition that he rarely drank to excess as he had done that night. And its impressive musculature, with its promise of strength and violence, had served to highlight his helplessness, such strength and such weakness coming together, so that, as she had pulled off his shirt, her breath had shortened as she touched him.

'Yes,' she had said, 'I can be ready, Gerard, as soon as you wish.' For she had felt that after all she owed him something, and the something was co-operation in the few months which they must live together.

In great pomp, therefore, the Schuyler party had been driven to the liner in New York docks, to be escorted aboard to take up residence in staterooms

filled with flowers, to travel in luxury from the New
World to the Old. Both Kate and Torry had been in
a state of excitement, Torry's concealed beneath her
usual calm mask, Kate bubbling over, delighted to
be away from her mother, to be going to Europe
free from the shadow of expecting to be touted
round the Old World as an American heiress looking for a noble husband.

'And if you do find someone whom you like, and
I know that he's not after you just for your money,
then you can marry him — or not — as you please,'
Gerard had said.

They had arrived in London in early April, before
the season was really under way, and for the first
week they had stayed in Gerard's Park Lane home,
touring the shops, the museums and the art gal-
leries, seeing little of Gerard who was busy clearing
up the financial damage done in his absence.

Coming home late, on his first night there, he had
found his wife waiting for him in the drawing-room.
There was a bottle of wine on a small table, glasses,
and cutlery laid out with condiments and damask
napkins.

He had raised his eyebrows before sitting down.
He had felt tired unto death.

'I thought,' said Torry smoothly, 'knowing you,
that you had probably eaten on the run. The
Captain liked to have a small leisurely meal at night,
after a hard day, with no servants present. I took
the liberty of assuming that you might have the
same tastes. I can ring for sandwiches and coffee, or
for a small hot supper: soup, devilled kidneys,
cheese and biscuits and coffee again; I have ordered

the kitchen to be ready to deliver either. This, I am sure that you will like.' And she began to pour red wine into two crystal glasses.

Gerard did not argue with her. Merely said, 'Something hot. I have been eating sandwiches all day and damned bad they were. Kate in bed?'

His wife, who had rung the bell twice to signal that Mr Schuyler wished a hot supper to be brought along, nodded. 'No need to keep her up. I didn't think that you would be ready for small talk.'

'Nor for much at all,' acknowledged Gerard. He was watching her; as always she was graceful in all her movement. She rose, began to set out the cutlery, not waiting for the servants, poured another glass of wine for him, opened his napkin, and generally, he noted, saw to his comfort.

'I started putting things straight today; it should take me about a week to finalise them,' he went on. 'Barring my man here doing something totally suicidal, matters will soon be on an even keel again. One more mistake like this and he'll be on the street. As it is, I've demoted him, relieved him of any responsibility.'

'The Captain would have cut his throat for the first mistake, or had him on the street straight away,' observed Torry calmly.

'So he would,' said Gerard, not explaining himself. He knew that his man had a wife and a new baby. Some unexplained access of mercy had stayed his hand, when before he would have acted exactly like his grandfather.

'Do this sort of thing for him often, did you?' He

was suddenly aware that he was violently jealous of the dead man.

'Yes,' his wife replied, and then was silent when the servants came in with their supper under silver covers, the savoury aromas filling the air. She gained the impression that they were silently disapproving of such informality, but then, what could one expect of Yankees? Torry could not have worried less about their opinion.

'So,' said Gerard, after they had gone, attacking his soup—he had underestimated how tired and hungry he was after his long day, which had ended with him cabling instructions to the New York end of his empire, 'we may begin to enjoy ourselves a little. We have had an invitation to Moidore Castle, Lord Moidore's home, to travel there next week, to stay with him until the full season begins. You and Kate will enjoy that. The Prince of Wales is expected.'

He paused, then said dispassionately, waving a hand at their informal supper, 'Are you going to do this for me, too, as you did for him?'

'Yes,' said Torry, short again, following his line of thought.

'You needn't, you know,' countered Gerard. 'No one here to see you doing the pretty for me. No one to act for.'

'I'm not acting,' replied Torry. 'A man who has been out grafting all day deserves to be looked after when he comes homes late at night.'

'He deserves other things, too,' offered Gerard, looking hopeful, but getting no change at all, since an enigmatic half-smile could not be described as change.

Torry, indeed, made no answer to that, simply remarking, 'Moidore, that's a strange name.'

'So it is,' said Gerard. 'The first Lord Moidore was a pirate with Drake, originally plain Thomas Bulkeley. He brought home a great fortune, tactfully gave a large chunk of it to Elizabeth, Good Queen Bess, and when she granted him an earldom in return asked that he should be dubbed Moidore, seeing that Moidores looted from Spanish galleons had made his fortune for him. Elizabeth was so taken by his bare-faced cheek that she agreed on the spot. Even let him change the name of the castle he acquired and the valley which it dominated, from Rune to Moidore.'

'He sounds like the Captain,' was Torry's only comment.

'Indeed——' Gerard was dry '—so you will be at home there, won't you?'

Torry did not rise to this bait. Gerard decided that he must fish with better flies if he were to capture such a gorgeous salmon as his wife. Did she never unbend, show mercy? He did not know that she had done just that on their wedding-night; had held him so lovingly, had relieved his self-inflicted suffering with such patient care.

The Schuyler caravan had assembled itself again. By train, and then by carriage, Gerard, Torry, Kate, their servants and innumerable trunks and bags had rumbled across country, to end up here, high above Lincolnshire's lowlands in a house which looked like a medieval castle, but was a cheat.

Years ago James Wyatt had been hired by the then Lord Moidore to translate his graceless box of a home into a romantic castle—rather as the Captain had hired his architects to re-create a château from the Loire in New York's streets. The result was everything that could be desired, not quite as grand as Belvoir Castle, Wyatt's other masterpiece, built later, but rather more comfortable to live in, Lord Moidore said, when he took Torry and Kate on a tour of his home.

Gerard had become a friend of Moidore's before he had inherited, when he had been Viscount Bulkeley, and because Tom Bulkeley, behind a mask of aristocratic indifference, was as shrewd a thruster as the founder of his house, and would have made a good friend of the Captain, too, he had used Gerard to help him recoup his family's fortunes, destroyed when his great-uncle had gambled them away on the turf.

He also, Gerard had told Torry and Kate on their long journey to the Midlands—long for the British, that was, as Kate said, although short by American standards—had introduced his American friend to the Prince of Wales's circle, so that he and Moidore had made, and sometimes lost, fortunes for themselves by day, and enjoyed the high life in the evening—a practice which the Prince found admirable.

Many of the Prince's circle of friends were such as Gerard. The heir to the throne, unlike many aristocrats, genuinely admired the self-made men whom he called friends, and, having a genius for friendship, his liking was reciprocated.

Until the Prince arrived time hung heavy on Torry's hands, as Gerard, now sensitive to all her moods, was well aware. Even though they slept, and mostly lived, apart, their apparent care for one another in public, while deceiving many, still remained a sham, but a sham which Kate was beginning to realise for what it was.

'Why did you marry him?' she had said bluntly to Torry one day when Gerard was out riding and the ladies, all dressed in the most elegant of tea-gowns, were seated in the Indian drawing-room, waiting for their lords to return to ply them with the tea which was due to arrive at any moment.

Torry had looked at her, said in a pleasantly equable voice, 'Why does anyone marry anyone? Gerard and I had more reason to marry than most, as you surely know,' an answer which had choked off further discussion.

Kate was enchanting in a young girl's simple dress of pale blue. More than one aristocratic young man had commented on Miss Schuyler's superb taste, rather different from that of most Yankee heiresses who tended to be overdone, 'Wearing,' as one wit had said, 'all their papa's ill-gotten dollars around their neck and on their back at once.'

Kate owed her charmingly modest appearance to Torry, whose own taste was impeccable, being austere to a degree. She went in for beautifully cut simple gowns, little jewellery, and that little carefully chosen—she had refused the emeralds which Gerard had wished her to flaunt with the simple words, 'Do you wish me to confirm for your friends their opinion of Americans as vulgarians without taste? There will be a time for me to wear your splendid gift, but not here.'

'No other woman,' Gerard had replied, a trifle miffed, 'has ever refused my presents. They have always been grateful for them.'

'I am no other woman, Gerard,' she had said, 'I am your wife, and your reputation lies on my shoulders as well as yours. I have no wish to appear to be competing with the heiresses of thousand-year-old names.'

'Ah, but,' was Gerard's shrewd answer, 'by not appearing to compete, you simply compete the more.' For he was beginning to know his Torry.

By her lack of reply, by her simply turning away to straighten her already immaculate coiffure — they were on their way down to a dinner and dance given on their first night at Moidore — he had known that he had said something which struck home. Every day that they spent together became harder to endure so long as she refused overtly and covertly to be more than his wife in name.

If at first he had thought battering-ram tactics might succeed with her, he now knew better. He would have to be subtle. She reacted to all his attempts to sweep her off her feet as she had done on the first night of their marriage, and before. She withdrew herself, endured his embraces, never again responding as she had done the first time he had begun what he later came to call to himself 'his rough wooing', although, God knew, Torry was not at all like Shakespeare's shrew, and would not be won by being coerced, either physically or mentally.

He had no wish to make love to, and subdue, a

block of ice. He wanted her to be his willing partner, as she must have been for the Captain. Nothing less would do.

Gerard became, in fact, something which he had never thought that he would be — the most considerate of husbands. He was so courteous, so kind, both in public and private, that he might have been a model for a young girl's ideal of what every husband ought to be. And he burned for her, how he burned.

But he would not put out his fire by sleeping with others, for he did not want others, he wanted Torry, and here at Moidore where Daisy Gascoyne was offering herself to him again he had refused temptation by saying to his former mistress. 'You cannot be serious, Daisy. Why, I am still on my honeymoon. Later, perhaps, when the bloom is off the rose.'

Which was a thundering lie, for being with Daisy, after being with Torry, he was beginning to wonder how he could have tolerated her empty insipidities. She was good in bed, of course, but for the first time he was beginning to ask himself whether that was enough.

From one of the windows of the massive round tower which Wyatt had built, he watched his wife promenading with Daisy and the others, Kate walking behind with the unmarried girls, here with their parents, enjoying Moidore before they moved on to the delights of the London season where they were all due to come out by being presented at Court. Meantime they must be quiet, be seen and not heard, and not share in the more *outré* of the pleasures which Moidore had arranged for his

friends such as gambling for very high stakes late at
night when all the young things had been sent to
bed.

He knew that Torry missed the busy urgency of
her New York life, he guessed that even when she
had been the Captain's constant companion she had
continued her journalistic career—she must have
persuaded the old man that as he had his public life
and occupation so had she.

But then, she had been the old man's mistress,
not his wife. As Mrs Gerard Schuyler she had to
live up to a whole new set of expectations, particularly since it was important that their marriage be
seen to be a true one.

But she was not fitted to a life of vacuous conversation with such as Daisy Gascoyne, not used to the
longeurs of country house living, however much she
disguised her boredom beneath her good manners,
manners which had already been favourably commented on by the more snobbish of those accustomed to a different sort of American beauty. For
that, too, she was rapidly becoming celebrated.

'Just wait until Victoria is launched on the
season,' Moidore had said to him the night before.
'She will be as big a sensation as the Jersey Lily was
a generation ago—which reminds me, she, the Lily,
is appearing in a new play, *Esther Sandroz*, this
month, and you really ought to go to see her—that
is, if you prefer passé beauties to watching Henry
Irving in *The Bells*.'

Gerard had no wish to see Mrs Langtry, and to
his horrified surprise he also had no wish for Torry
to rival her. The thought of people standing on

chairs to see her enter a ballroom, or buying picture postcards of her, made him feel almost sick. Dammit, she was *his* wife, and he had no desire to share her with anyone else.

The mere thought made him so feverish that, realising that the party of women were returning indoors, he made for the side-entrance which they would use to do so, to meet her, and say, almost fiercely, 'Where have you been, madam? I thought that you were to walk out with me in the grounds this afternoon?'

Torry, conscious of Daisy Gascoyne's raised eyebrows at such a proprietorial comment, replied smoothly, 'I understood, Gerard, that a long walk this afternoon was out of the question, that we were all required to be here to welcome His Royal Highness, and so I indicated to you. We have come indoors to change for tea.'

Gerard was aware of Kate's goggling at his uxoriousness, of Daisy Gascoyne's more prurient amusement. Hell's teeth, he was not accustomed to giving his feelings away so nakedly! He had, indeed, prided himself on not having such feelings. Nevertheless he felt compelled to remark ungraciously, 'So you did, I had forgotten, and yes, do run along to charm His Highness; you might as well add him to your many admirers.'

Well, really, commented Daisy Gascoyne's amused simper, was it, could it be possible that Gerard Schuyler, of all people, was enamoured of that cool piece, his wife? Wonders would never cease, and she shared this somewhat inelegant thought unknowingly with Kate, who hardly recognised her brother in his new persona.

Gerard watched them all move away upstairs to their lady's maids, to change for the third time that day into yet another new costume, not the last they would assume, for later they would all go through the ritual again to appear at dinner like so many swans, necks arched above their low-cut gowns, feathers or flowers in their hair, their constricting clothes designed to betray their essential uselessness since no one could possibly do anything remotely resembling work in any of a society lady's costumes!

Now what brought that on? Was his inward response. Such a thought had never troubled him before, but he had to acknowledge that never before had he had anything to do with anyone like his wife. Her shrewd comments on the life around them, her indifference to the affairs which governed the lives of the other women at Moidore Castle had brought home to him that women, too, could be dispassionate about the life around them, were not confined solely to personal comments about love-affairs, clothes and the latest novel or play.

Noise outside told him that the Prince of Wales and his retinue had arrived. Etiquette demanded that everyone retire, that Moidore himself should be the only one present at the entrance, with a train of servants of varying degree to greet his future sovereign, who might be expected once he had been conducted to his suite to grace afternoon tea with his presence.

And so it proved. Gerard made his way to the large drawing-room, its windows looking out on to an ornamental garden where statues of gods and goddesses stood among the spring flowers. His wife was already there, dressed in a tea-gown uncommonly like the one which she had worn on the evening of their wedding-day, only its *décolleté* was more modest, no hint there of beautiful breasts to inflame him — or anyone else.

How was it that she made Daisy Gascoyne and the others look so shoddy despite their long pedigrees and the careful training from birth designed to prepare them for occasions such as this? He dared swear that Torry had had a hard life, and given his lack of knowledge of it, despite his detective's researches, he was almost willing to bet that she had spent part of it in a high-class brothel learning to charm such creatures as himself and the English aristocrats among whom she was now moving.

But that was knowledge of how to charm sexually. How in God's name had she managed to learn to hold her own in the present company, look so coolly chaste that the very look was itself a challenge?

Tea would not arrive until the royal party had decided whether or not they would attend, or, whether, after their journey, they would take refreshment alone in their suite. In the meantime the company sat about engaging in idle and empty chat.

Kate came over to Gerard, leaving behind a handsome young man who had been asking her questions about her life in America. She was still wearing her young girl's formal blue dress, not for her the mature ease of clothing of Torry and the rest.

'Has he really come, Gerard? Am I really going to meet the Prince of Wales? What fun! Who would have thought it? How absolutely swell! Oh, dear, I really must remember not to say things like that. Torry never does. How does she manage it, Gerard?'

'Ask her,' he said curtly. 'Not me. And yes, you will be meeting the Prince soon, if not now then later. He will be sure to be at dinner tonight — and his Princess.'

'They say that she is very lovely,' said Kate relevantly. 'But oh, Gerard, she cannot be any lovelier than Torry. I shall never look like that.'

Gerard looked from Kate to his wife and silently agreed. But he also thought that Kate had her own individual character even if it were not the same as her sister-in-law's, and told her so.

'Oh, you are always kind to me, Gerard,' said Kate delightedly, 'but you flatter me — just look at her!'

Gerard did. The sight almost made him feel ill. His wife was laughing up into the eyes of the young man who had been talking to Kate, who was Daisy's brother Justin, aimed at Kate because he was penniless, but a nice boy none the less. Gerard felt like killing him. He was appalled by the waves of jealousy which rolled over him every time he saw another man admiring Torry. What could be happening to him? Could it be, was it likely, that he was falling in love with his own grandfather's mistress?

He ground his teeth as young Justin put out a hand to lift Torry up, to lead her to admire a set of mezzotints of the beauties of the last century based on paintings by Sir Joshua Reynolds which adorned one wall. Perhaps it was fortunate that at that moment Their Royal Highnesses, the Prince and Princess of Wales, arrived, to have everyone leaping to their feet, to be genially waved down again by their tubby future monarch.

Albert Edward, Prince of Wales, was neither handsome nor athletic, nor particularly clever in any intellectual sense. What he did possess was *savoir-faire*, an intense and practical knowledge of the world in which he lived, and the ability to judge and also to charm men and women, despite his lack of any of the obvious virtues which those who charmed were supposed to possess.

He was totally unlike his learned father or his dominant mother. For book learning, he substituted learning from the book of life, and was completely without any form of prejudice to guide him in his choice of friends, a fact regretted by the more traditional of courtiers and politicians.

'You're back!' he was addressing Gerard in his guttural voice, more suited to the German he spoke so well than the English of the land he was one day to rule. 'And married, they tell me. Introduce me to your wife.'

The Prince had been, and still was, a great womaniser, and for a moment another spasm of jealousy almost overcame Gerard at the prospect of introducing Torry to a man who, he instinctively knew, would be taken by her charm.

He was not wrong. The Prince's eyes widened at the sight of Torry in her tea-gown, which could not hide the lovely lines of her body, and when, on being introduced to him, she swept him a curtsy of grace and elegance, he turned to Gerard and said, almost as though he were poking him in the ribs, 'Why, you lucky dog! They told me your lady was a beauty, but not that she was one of the first water. I heard that the Schuylers were shrewd in all that they did, but this time you have surpassed yourself.'

He turned to Torry, who was now erect, every woman's jealous eye on her, and more than one man wondered whether here was the woman who would surpass or succeed Daisy Warwick and Alice Keppel.

Apart from her peerless looks, her conversation was so pleasantly lively; she was informed without being pedantic, witty without being unkind or facetious. Gerard, neglected teacup in his hand, watched her enchanting the Prince, heard his rumbling laughter — Torry was telling him of the vicissitudes of running a newspaper devoted to women's affairs.

'And now that you are married,' he demanded, 'you are resigned to being the little woman, hey? Is she, Mr Gerard Schuyler? Are you going to allow this delightful creature to waste her time dabbling in printer's ink?'

Gerard rose on being thus addressed. 'Her choice, sir,' he said, smiling to cloak his anger at the way in which the Prince was looking at Torry, his frank enjoyment of her attractions — there was no doubt, now, that Mrs Gerard Schuyler was destined to be the hit of the season. The only doubt which remained was how far she would choose to go with

HRH, as Gerard called him in private, preferring that to the mocking 'Tumtum', never said to the Prince's face, but often used behind his back, by some of those who to his face were the most subservient.

One of them, Bryce Ledward, a tall blond man, who had arrived at Moidore just before the Prince, and was often in his company, turned avaricious eyes on Torry and mocking ones on Gerard, sensing his resentment at the Prince's interest in his wife, and his inability to do anything about it.

'Prepared to let your wife be one of Tumtum's pretty ladies, are you, old man?' he muttered in Gerard's ear, once the Prince had passed on and was talking to Daisy Gascoyne.

Gerard knew — and disliked — Ledward of old. Rich by inheritance, he had never done a hand's turn of real work, although he was reputed to be a superb athlete who had played both cricket and rugger for Oxford, and frequently took on professional pugilists in the ring, and was altogether a man to be feared. He had a vicious, cutting tongue and had destroyed more than one reputation with it. His behaviour towards women was notorious, but that did not stop him from being one of society's favourites.

Altogether, Gerard decided, he epitomised everything which he disliked the most about some of the British aristocrats among whom he had made his life. Despising Americans, many of them chose to marry their daughters, and live on, and waste, the wealth of the men at whom they privately jeered. Gerard knew that Ledward mocked himself and his family behind his back, and his yellow eyes were feral as he turned and glared at him.

'My wife is discretion itself, Ledward, and you had better remember that.'

Ledward's own eyes narrowed. 'Not what I had heard, old man,' he drawled, 'but then, you know best, eh?'

Gerard's strong hands balled into fists. It was with difficulty that he stopped himself from driving his right hand into Ledward's face and knocking him down for the insult. Only the presence of the Prince, and the damage such an act would do to Torry, prevented him.

'If I hear that you have been badmouthing my wife, Ledward. . .' and his voice was soft with menace '. . .it will be the worse for you.' And how feeble that sounded, he thought disgustedly, and wished that he were back in the States where one man blackguarding another man's wife after such a fashion would rapidly have paid for it.

Ledward had no wish to take the matter further before the Prince. The Prince had already expressed disapproval of some of his ways, and his patience might not withstand a public brawl before ladies, and especially with one of the rich Yankees whom the heir to the throne had recently been favouring.

He contented himself with bowing sardonically, jamming his monocle in his left eye and staring at Torry. A better way of putting a jumped-up Yankee peasant in his place might be to take one's pleasure with his wife. Christopher Sykes had already informed him that Victoria Schuyler was a cold piece who rarely seemed to unbend even with her husband. It would be a pleasure to melt such an icicle, put horns on that brute she had married.

Bryce Ledward did not know why he hated Gerard Schuyler so much — apart from the fact that Gerard had taken Daisy Gascoyne from him so effortlessly last year, without even seeming to try. Perhaps it was the physical power of the man, allied to the cunning which had made him a financial pirate in Leadenhall Street as well as Wall Street, the millions he owned which made 'fat Teddy', another derogatory name of his for the Prince, run after him. Yes, the lovely Victoria would be his next target.

The lovely Victoria, meanwhile, was amused both by the Prince's interest and by Gerard's reaction to it, which she could sense from across the room. She had become as sensitive to him as he to her during the weeks which they had spent together since marriage. She could also almost feel Daisy Gascoyne's and the other women's resentment at the favour showed to her by the Prince.

She suddenly knew that something about her attracted men of power. Not only the Captain had been drawn to her, others had made it known that she had only to show them favour and they would reward her more handsomely even than he might have done. She knew that she fascinated Gerard — she did not flatter herself that he loved her — and now the Prince was another moth circling around the flame.

Gerard took her arm as they moved upstairs after tea, to lie down after the day's so-called hardships and to prepare for dinner. They had a small suite of rooms in one of the turrets, and Torry knew that Miss Clarke would be waiting for her there.

'Send your woman away, Mrs Schuyler, I wish to speak to you,' commanded Gerard.

She always made a point of obeying him, so long as his wishes were not outrageous. She entered her bedroom, said coolly, 'You may leave me for the moment, Clarke. I will ring for you when I am ready.'

The obsequious Miss Clarke had already registered that Mr Schuyler had a face like thunder, and she hurried out of the room, a hard man to cross, being her private thought.

'Now, Mrs Schuyler,' said Gerard formally. 'I have one or two things to say to you, the first of which is that it would be as well to go warily with the Prince. Much though I like him, I have no desire for my wife to be his *mistresse en titre*, so pray do not encourage him. The second is that Bryce Ledward is a man to avoid. He may be a pretty-looking fellow, but his behaviour to women is atrocious; I wonder the Prince bears with him, but he has an old and famous name, and in this damned country I suppose that counts for a lot.'

'I thought you liked English society,' remarked Torry ingenuously.

'So I do, but that does not mean I approve of everything about it,' returned Gerard crossly. The worst of having a clever wife was that you had to bear the cross of her nit-picking comments. 'So, I would be grateful if you avoided him too. He means you nothing but harm. He dislikes me, and would not mind doing me a hurt through you,' he added almost as an afterthought.

Torry looked at him with an almost wicked expression on her lovely face. 'Would it not be simpler,' she offered coolly, 'to issue me with a list of those with whom you think that I might safely converse? It would, I fear, be very short. There seem to be so many that you are fearful of for my sake: Lord Conyers in London, that young man whom you brought home to dinner, although I thought that *he* looked singularly innocent, but I suppose that I might have been mistaken. So far at Moidore you have warned me against your good friend, his lordship himself, Mrs Riley Russell, who apparently has a penchant for young women, and Dainton Harcourt, who, you have informed me, is a notorious lecher. Now it is the Prince and Bryce Ledward. Perhaps you might prefer me to enter one of the orders of nuns who speak to no one, and then you would be free of worry on my behalf.'

'You are pleased to be witty,' said Gerard stiffly, 'but it is for your own good, mind. I am only thinking of you.'

'Oh, of course,' she returned, almost cheerful. 'You are not afraid that I might corrupt them — as I did the Captain?' This last came out so innocently that for a moment Gerard did not quite understand what she had said.

Then, 'Oh, damme, woman. I was doing you the honour of thinking you reasonably innocent. I had quite forgotten how experienced you are. But you swim in deeper waters here, and the fish have more innocent faces but bigger. . .' And he floundered when he reached this. Good God, what *did* fish have?

'Claws?' suggested his wife sweetly.

'Yes. No,' roared Gerard. 'I give up. Go your own way, but don't say I didn't warn you.' Great God, what was coming over him, that he should be fearful for the dollymop whom he had married? She could probably run rings round the lot of them.

But the truth was, he couldn't bear the thought of anyone so much as touching her, and he really must leave before he forgot himself. Torry had turned away, was beginning to pick up the clothes which Clarke had laid out for the evening.

Halfway through the door Gerard looked back around the lovely room, and at his wife, the loveliest thing in it. 'You will think a little of what I have said,' he muttered humbly.

'Yes,' said Torry gravely. 'I will be careful, Gerard. I have spent a lifetime being exactly that. I will not damage your reputation, I promise you.'

But that was not why he had spoken to her so, and they both knew it.

CHAPTER EIGHT

GERARD sat opposite his wife at dinner; she was remarkable in pale lilac silk and white spotted gauze. A band of black velvet ran along her evening gown's neck to a low V at the back from whence depended a garland of pale violets, with their greenery, all made from the most delicate silk and falling almost to the floor. It was the only ornament on her dress, which was otherwise plain, and she wore around her lovely neck a collar of pearls *à la Alexandra*, a fashion set by the Princess of Wales herself, who with her husband was a chief guest at table.

The Princess's sad, grave face had always intrigued Gerard, made him a little uneasy. The Prince was invariably kind to her, went out of his way to defer to her in public, but she had to live with the knowledge of her husband's roving eye, of his many and beautiful mistresses. Tonight, for the first time, perhaps because of *his* wife, Gerard was even more aware of the pain which she must often feel — a strange sentiment for him to experience.

He was also strongly aware of Bryce Ledward, seated opposite him on Torry's left. Ledward was at his most deferential, bending down confidentially to her, speaking in a low voice, making her laugh her low laugh and then complimenting her on it, saying,

'So unlike many of your countrywoman, Mrs Schuyler, so quiet, so discreet.'

Her face took on an expression Gerard recognised, and he thought, almost gleefully, Wait for it, Ledward! Here it comes, the *coup de grâce*!

She looked up at him, perfectly poised, said, and her tone was mild, 'While I have no doubt that you consider that a compliment, Mr Ledward, I cannot be happy at accepting one from which I must infer a slur on all my countrywomen.'

Ledward gave no sign that he was in any way put out by this, merely murmured, 'Oh, I should have known that you were a true patriot, and will remember so in future. Allow me, then, to change my praise so that it is you yourself who are the recipient of it, no comments on others, and allow me also to compliment you on your perfect *savoir-faire* — that you can deliver a reprimand so delicately that the one reproved feels only pleasure at receiving it!'

Gerard thought that he would burst. Damned poseur! And damn the man for getting so gracefully out of the hole he had dug for himself. If only his wife had been equally tactful with him, her husband, instead of reserving her delicacy for such degenerate and effete scions of decayed noble houses. His dislike of Ledward grew.

As course succeeded course, served *à la Russe* from a side-table, Gerard grew more and more morose. He ate savagely through dishes of asparagus soup, devilled whitebait, quenelles of rabbit — ugh! — a quarter of lamb, iced soufflé, orange water ices, and then the dishes of strawberries, cherries and melons, all placed on the table for the guests to help themselves, with hate in his heart for the man opposite who appeared intent on charming his wife — who seemed quite willing to be charmed.

During the serving of the rabbit, the woman next to him, Mrs Riley Russell, a mannish creature with a horse face, and, as he had told Torry, a penchant for women, leaned towards him and said poisonously, 'I understand that your grandfather, Mr Schuyler, was known as the Captain. Am I to infer from that that he was in the Army? Or was it the Navy that he graced?'

Gerard's temper, usually under strong control, suddenly broke free. He looked dangerously at his tormentor, for he was sure that Mrs Russell knew quite well that the Captain did not owe his title to membership of either the US Navy or the Army.

'On the contrary,' he said savagely, aware that Ledward was smilingly mockingly at him. 'My grandfather, God rest him, gained the sobriquet when he was a ragged and penniless barefoot youth ferrying a rowing boat across the small river near his home in up-state New York. When one of his customers mocked him by calling him Captain, and persuaded others to do the same, he told them that one day he would truly be a captain of a fleet of ships which would dominate East Coast trade. You may imagine how they laughed at him — but, as usual, when one mocks the Schuylers, the joke was on them!'

The Princess, who had heard the unpleasantly made question, and Gerard's answer, which betrayed no shame at his lowly origins, said, 'Bravo, Mr Schuyler; one sees that you are descended from a man of enterprise. I must tell the Prince that story — he admires men who have pulled themselves up from nothing — and feel no shame at having done so.'

Ledward, who had deepened his mocking expression in Gerard's direction, now put on a respectful one as the Princess finished speaking.

'And you, Mrs Schuyler,' he said to Torry, and Gerard suddenly knew that, whoever else was aware of her history, Ledward certainly was, 'were you acquainted with your husband's grandfather?'

'Yes——' she was coolness itself '— and a very remarkable old gentleman he was. It was an honour to know him. He was certainly not ashamed of his origins. After all,' she went on, still in her most charming mode, 'if one goes far back enough into the history of most noble families one would discover similar stories. Or so I am told.'

Gerard could have kissed her, or done something even more to his taste. Ledward chose to laugh heartily. 'Oh, one of my ancestors was a humble grazier,' he replied, 'and another perished under the axe on Tower Hill. I believe that your husband's family have not yet achieved a similar honour, eh, Schuyler?'

'Oh, we're not noble enough for the axe,' said Gerard carelessly; 'the rope would have to suffice.' All in all he thought that the palm ought to be awarded to the Schuylers, husband and wife both, for quick-witted table-turning. We could rule the world together, she and I, he thought.

He looked around the table as he attacked his rabbit. He might not be the most handsome man present, far from it — he could not hold a candle to Bryce Ledward's blond good looks — but there was no other woman there who could match Torry. He burned for her all over again.

And so apparently did Ledward, if his expression as he spoke to her was telling the truth. Suppose she had the bad taste — no, the bad judgement — to be taken in by such a shallow swine? Would she consent to do with him what she had done with the Captain but would not do with the man who passed as her husband? To be fair, when he was trying to be amiable, Ledward possessed the charm of the devil, and tonight it was all for Torry.

So much so that when the ladies withdrew and port and cigars were the order of the day Ledward was twitted by several of his fellows to the effect that American manners appeared to please him these days.

'Oh, they please us all,' he drawled. 'The almighty dollar rules here, as it does in the States.' The look he gave Gerard was inimical.

The Prince chose to intervene. 'Come, Ledward,' he growled in his guttural voice, his cigar at a jaunty angle in his rubicund face. 'Our American friends do us more favours than we do them. Their fairest daughters grace our peerage and their wives adorn our court. And you, Schuyler, have benefited more than one of us to my certain knowledge. Come and talk to me about your latest killing. There are times when I wish that I had been born to play ducks and drakes on the Stock Exchange instead of being confined in a royal palace.'

His rumbling laughter filled the room as Gerard,

thus commanded, took the seat by the Prince's side which he had indicated with a wave of his cigar. 'Brandy for Schuyler here,' he called, and Gerard, who—usually—had a distaste for alcohol strange in a man of pleasure, did not deny him, and pretended to drink the burning stuff with pleasure. He took after his grandfather in his abstemiousness, and, looking at the shrewd face of the man by whom he sat, wondered how much of the Prince's insistence that he drink with him whenever they met was mischievous, a use of his princely power.

Well, what was power, if you could not use it? And later, following his royal patron into the drawing-room where the yawning women had been entertaining themselves, he was compelled to watch Albert Edward turn his charm on Mrs Torry Schuyler.

She was equal to him, though, but it was plain that the Prince liked everything about her, from her classic taste in dress to her low voice, on which he complimented her as Ledward had done.

'A soft voice,' he said, 'is an admirable thing in a woman, Mrs Schuyler,' and he proceeded to talk to her, his own voice low, until Gerard, to his horror, felt like going over and punching him in the face. As earlier he wondered what on earth was wrong with him, and when, after the Prince had moved on, she was similarly favoured by some of his sycophants, eager to please the woman who appeared to be pleasing their master, his inward rage grew.

He could not say that she was encouraging them, except that simply for her to *be* was encouragement. He resolved to have a word with her when they retired. She was certainly making enemies among the women however much she pleased the men — no, correct that — *because* she pleased the men.

At last the wretched, interminable evening drew to an end. One of the women sang to the piano, a man challenged him to a game of billiards in the salon which adjoined the room. Gerard refused. He had no mind to be going up to his suite with Torry any later than he needed — they always left together, unlike some husbands and wives present.

'Take no note of Ledward, Schuyler,' said Moidore bluntly to him shortly before he caught Torry's eye and signalled that he wished to retire. 'I dislike the man, but he pleases the Prince, and is a favourite among the women. No country house party seems complete without him, somehow.'

'Great God, what an epitaph,' said Gerard nastily. 'I can conceive of no worse fate than to be valued for such a talent.'

Moidore laughed at him, blew rings at the ceiling from his cigar. 'Oh, well, Schuyler, we can't all be like you — great thrusters, building a new world for the next century!'

'You, too,' mocked Gerard, suddenly recovering his good temper, for Moidore was a sterling fellow when all was said and done. 'You, too.'

Moidore nodded. 'Up betimes, then,' he said. 'Go for a long ride. Mustn't grow fat.' And as though not intending it his eyes came to rest on the rotund figure of his royal guest.

Diplomatically, Gerard said nothing to that, merely nodded at Torry, eyebrows raised, and she came gracefully and obediently towards him, making her adieux as she crossed the room.

'You have her well trained, your good lady,' drawled Ledward in his ear; he seemed to have materialised from nowhere.

Gerard ignored him—safer so—took Torry by the arm, more firmly than he needed to, and steered her towards the great staircase which led to the upper floors, past portraits of long-dead Bulkeleys on the walls and the priceless loot on shelves and in cabinets which they had collected from four continents.

Husband and wife did not speak until they reached the drawing-room in their small suite.

'Madam,' said Gerard, 'I would have a word with you before you retire.'

'A short one, then,' said Torry, turning away from him. 'I'm tired, and this is your second word for me today.'

Anger and desire ran parallel in Gerard. He wanted to seize her, make her look at him as she had looked at *them*, smiling, wanted to. . .wanted . . .to. . .wanted. . .

'And I'm not. Not tired,' he said roughly, his voice as unkind as he could make it, almost as though he were speaking to a recalcitrant servant.

He noted with savage glee that his wife was visibly surprised, and no wonder. Since their night of bargaining and their wedding, he had been consistently pleasant and careful in his manner to her. Startled, her head lifted and her tone became placatory as though she were humouring a child, he thought angrily.

'Well, I am tired,' she said gently, 'and we have another long day tomorrow.'

'Doing nothing,' he almost jeered at her.

'Oh, that's the hardest thing of all,' she riposted, 'doing nothing,' and now her tone matched his. 'Such effort is required; I have not learned the trick of it yet. Daisy Gascoyne, now. . .' She paused and Gerard could have sworn that she had named that particular woman to provoke him.

'Yes,' he answered her. 'Do go on. Daisy Gascoyne, now. . .?'

'Has the art to a T,' she returned gravely. 'I need my rest if I am to match her. Such unparalleled languor. Such mastery of the art of saying nothing and making it sound infinitely witty. It must take the blood of a hundred generations of earls. I cannot compete with her on that.'

Gerard came out with the unforgivable. 'Try to match her in other ways, Mrs Schuyler. Why not? You must know that she was my mistress. Demonstrate to me, in person, that you are more than her match in my bed. You surely know how to do that.'

'Not very gentlemanly, Gerard,' she reproved him.

'I am not a gentleman, as well you know, madam,' and there was a conscious pride in his voice as he claimed this. 'I have never pretended to be one and I never will, and I want my wife—in bed with me, not flaunting herself at other men all night. If you wish to flaunt, Mrs Schuyler, flaunt at me, your husband.'

'Now, Gerard,' Torry returned, still gentle, those wonderful eyes looking earnestly at him, that damask cheek so near to him, that superb unattainable body so near. . .so near. . .so near. . .

He began to walk towards her; the yellow-brown eyes were now all gold, flaming, a tiger's, his shoulders were hunched, his fists lightly balled, he was on his toes, alive, inflamed, aroused. She continued speaking, hiding her sudden fear of him. 'We had a bargain, Gerard, remember. No, do not come any nearer to me. A bargain, I repeat, and well you know it. You agreed to it of your own free will.'

'At pistol-point, madam. At pistol-point. And now I do not wish to keep it.'

He was so near to her, so near. He could smell the scent of her, violets, mixed with fear. Gerard knew fear; he had inspired it so often in others, and always to his own advantage. He had had no intention of behaving like this when they had walked upstairs, no intention of sexually threatening her as he was doing. He had been riven by jealousy, true, but being alone with her, here, in her beauty, desire had mastered him completely.

He had not touched her. He did not need to. What he wanted was plain in every line of his muscular body. His need for her naked. Oh, he had felt this for her many times since their marriage, but on this occasion he would not deny himself, repress his feelings. Oh, how he longed to lose himself in her, his wife, who was no wife.

'Bargains,' he muttered, his voice hoarse and impatient. 'You equivocate like a lawyer, woman. I want you, Torry, oh, how I want you.'

He was not pleading with her. He was telling her, arrogantly. His shoulders had hunched even more.

He was a great cat on the prowl for his mate — the feral eyes told her so, the thickened voice. Torry backed away from him, until the wall behind her allowed her to back no more. For the first time the marks of fear were plain on her face and in her voice. Her control was slipping.

And yet. . .and yet. . .he could have sworn that she was excited as well as he, that her reaction to the formidable male animal who faced her was not solely fear, but fear laced with desire, which heightened the fear. . .which heightened the desire. . . If he could reach to the core of her now, she was his.

'Oh, Gerard,' she breathed, her eyes on his. 'No, be reasonable, I beg you.'

She might as well not have spoken; he was beyond reason, but denied it.

'Oh, I am full of sweet reason,' he said, 'which tells me that the words of the wedding ceremony were said by you willingly, not coerced from you at gunpoint.' And now he was upon her and with one rapid thrust he laid his hands on her shoulders and pinned her to the wall, no time for her to resist, no place for her to go.

Why should she not practise with him the arts with which she had enslaved his grandfather — and others? Why should he be the one forever excluded from her bed? Was he so repulsive to her? There were times when he could have sworn he was not. The frustration of the long day and the longer evening drove him on.

'No, Gerard, no.'

'Yes, Torry, yes.'

He used his body to hold her against the wall,

struggle though she might, and he was now so aroused that not only did his erect self, throbbing against her, tell her of his passion, but everything else about him. He took her face in his hands, meant to kiss her forcefully, brutally, show her who was master despite all bargains.

Only, feeling the softness of her, at the last moment he was suddenly gentle with her instead, kissed her, not wantonly on the mouth, but delicately on her closed eyes — which told their own tale of her mixed feelings for him. She opened them again as he finished celebrating them, only to close them with a gasp at the sight of his almost feline mask so near to her that his individual features had disappeared.

And now, with kisses so gentle that they were like a moth alighting, he roved about her face, as, paralysed beneath him like an animal, either so taken with desire that it made no effort to free itself, or so fearful that it had lapsed into catatonia, she was held against the wall, and hardly needed his hands or his body to keep her there.

So near, he thought exultantly, so near. Paradoxically, had she fought him, he might have been the more provoked, his will and temper aroused as well as his body. Strangely, as his kisses ran down her face, reached that tender mouth, she accepting them passively, this time like an animal awaiting final death, except that it was the little death of love with which she was threatened, she felt to him like a virgin stricken by finding for the first time what passion, out of control, did to a man.

Shame rose in him, challenged his arousal, his determination to have her, come what may.

For the first time, in this encounter, their mouths touched, and hers was so soft and sweet that guilt and desire warred in him.

'No,' he said, but to whom he said it, and what he meant, he did not know, and even when he pushed her lips open with his tongue and her mouth opened on a strangled sob—fear? or desire?—and he entered that in lieu of entering anything else, and he felt her proud rigidity begin to melt beneath him, guilt began to overcome desire.

For, shame whispered, what he was about to do was rape. Nothing else; disguise it how he might, call it by any name he pleased, he was no better than an East Side ruffian holding down his victim while he took his pleasure. Could he bear what she might think of him afterwards?

More, what would his pleasure be worth, bought at such a price? For she had begun to shudder, pulled her head away, moaned, 'No, Gerard, no. If you do this, I may forgive you, but you will never forgive yourself!'

Instinct whispered to him, Take your mate. For, however much she resists you now, she will be your willing partner before the act is over. You were made for one another.

Conscience said, Not so, that is sophistry, designed to justify violence, and where will your self-respect be afterwards? Lust in action is what you are about, and you love her, do you not? And love is more than taking one's pleasure willy nilly, with no thought of your partner.

It was only afterwards that Gerard was able to put into words these conflicting emotions which tore through him at that last moment before consummation when he held her, ready for the taking.

He had admitted it to himself at last. He loved her, and because he loved her he must respect her, and let her go. He stepped back from her as suddenly as he had attacked her, raised his hands as though surrendering, and said violently, 'God forgive me. You have unmanned me twice, made a beast of me when I attacked you, a cur when I stopped. You have won, madam, and have done so by using your tricks on me. Who taught you so cunningly to play the virgin assailed, about to be ravished so that I could not continue? I commend your teachers, and you, for your performance.'

Torry, apparently exhausted, slid down the wall into a heap on the floor. There was nothing graceful left about her. She put her face in her hands, made no answer to him.

Sardonically, before he left her, all passion spent, Gerard looked down at her, the last little waves of desire running quietly up the beach of his mind, nothing like the pounding surf which had had him nearly taking her for his own.

He remembered how he had admonished himself in the first days of their marriage as to the way in which he might win her. Be subtle. Subtle! He had been as subtle as a charging bull, but unlike the bull he had gained nothing by it. At the last fence of all, something had stopped him.

Later, much later, on his bed, still dressed, he rationalised what could not be subject to reason.

For he had stopped because it had struck him in a blinding flash, a true revelation, that he loved her. And how and why he loved her he, Gerard Schuyler, did not know, only that he did.

Inconveniently, improbably, true love, which had eluded many men, had touched him with its magic, and he was five fathoms deep, drowning in a sea of passion for the one woman whom he would have sworn could have had no attraction for him at all!

CHAPTER NINE

'MRS SCHUYLER! A word with you, if you would be so good.'

Torry turned to see Bryce Ledward walking towards her, a smile on his face. They were in the long picture gallery at Moidore Castle, where Moidore's ancestors, predators all, hung on the walls. Three hundred years of nobility had not dimmed their aggressive acquisitiveness.

Looking at them, Torry was reminded of Gerard — and of the Captain. Something in their stance, the gleam in their eye, a sense of 'What I have I hold', was similar. The Bulkeleys had once been new men on the make, like the Schuylers, and after her experience of the night before she shivered a little.

And their women were all beautiful — or the painters had made them so. They could choose the best, always the best, and had done so over the generations. But Bryce Ledward with his smoothness was a different animal altogether from the assembled Bulkeleys. The danger he carried about with him was of a different order.

She compelled herself to smile at him a little. A cool smile, which offered nothing. She had been practising it for the last two months on Gerard. Ledward took the smile for more than its face value and said easily, 'I had hoped that you had seen me.

That we might speak together. I know you spend a great deal of time in the picture gallery and the library next door. They are interests of mine, too.'

Torry did not doubt it. She knew from his conversation that, athlete and man of the world though he was, the intellectual arts had not passed him by, as they had passed many of his fellows — including the Prince. This, she thought, made him the more dangerous, not less.

She gave a slight bow, said, still cool, 'It seems a pity that when one has the privilege of visiting a great house such as this one does not inspect and enjoy its treasures.' A colourless speech, she thought in all conscience, not likely to make him wish to spend time with her, if her conversation were of such platitudinous dullness.

Ledward, however, broadened his smile, came the closer to her, and said softly, honouring her with a slight bow as he spoke, 'You are a most diplomatic lady, Mrs Schuyler, and I know that I will offend you all over again by what I am about to say, but I must say it — you are not at all like your fellow Americans. You give so little away.'

Torry bowed her head slightly, said stiffly, 'You know my sentiments, Mr Ledward; do not provoke me to repeat them.'

'Oh, come.' He was all charm. 'Bryce, if you please. Your husband and I are not exactly friends, acquaintances merely, but he would not dream of being so formal with me as you are.'

'I am not a man, Mr Ledward,' responded Torry curtly, and prepared to leave him.

He put out a hand, to detain her without touching

her, but making it plain that he wished her to stay. 'Oh, I know *that* very well, Mrs Schuyler. I wish you would allow me to call you Victoria. Somehow, Torry is all wrong; it denies your very real dignity and—your innocence.'

'My innocence? What is that to you, sir? Pray allow me to leave. This is the kind of conversation which I most dislike, since it demeans women by supposing them fools.' She had not raised her voice, but scorn rode on her face.

Ledward laughed softly, not at all put out. 'Oh, Mrs Schuyler, you are a wonder, are you not? Many think that charming little air you have, almost of a chastely bred young girl, *jeune fille bien élevée*, must be a nonsense because of your notorious past history——

At this, Torry could not contain herself. Usually in command of herself, something in his knowing tone piqued her and her cheeks flamed. She had known that, inevitably, some of her past history would be known to the people whom she met in England, but so far no one had said a word. Discretion had been all, and now this.

Ledward had stopped speaking to watch her face—nay, her whole body, he dared swear—blush. It supported a private belief which he had been holding ever since he had first seen her, virginal in white, at Drury Lane Theatre, in a box with Gerard, and had asked who the delightful Vestal was, to be told that she was Gerard Schuyler's soiled dove of a wife, married, rumour said, though none knew the exact truth, to gain his grandfather's money.

'And his grandfather's mistress into the bargain,

they say,' his informant remarked with a grin. 'Want a bout with her, do you, old man?'

'Yes, perhaps,' he had said thoughtfully. *That* a dollymop? Never! He would have bet a fortune on it, and talking to her, watching her, always watching her, something about her drew him, and that something was a belief that she was very much not what rumour said.

And the marriage. Now, what a strange thing that was! Armed with what he thought he knew, he had watched Gerard and Torry like a hawk, both in London and now here at Moidore Castle. He would have liked to be able to bet on the true nature of their marriage.

'Of course your history — or what people think is your history — is known, but most men are afraid of your husband, and — '

'You are not?' queried Torry swiftly.

Ledward gave a lazy smile. 'More frightened of you than of him, my dear. No, do not turn away. I dare hazard a guess that so long as our conversation is impersonal you will be as severe with me as you are with him, and everyone else. It is a novel way to conquer hearts, but I grant you that it seems to work. But suppose I change the rules of the game, and speak to you of what I dearly wish. . .'

'I do not want to know what you dearly wish, Mr Ledward. I only know that this conversation does not please me and that *I* wish to leave. You would not follow me to my room, I hope.' She added this because as she moved away from him Ledward followed her.

'I didn't mean to drive you away,' he said lazily.

'Don't go, Victoria. You have no idea how much you fascinate me, nor how much I could add to your pleasure.' He paused before throwing his bomb. 'You do not wish to remain a virgin forever, I hope.'

Torry felt herself go white, then red. She clenched her right hand inside the folds of her pale-grey morning dress and said coldly and collectedly, 'You seem to forget that I am a married woman twice over, Mr Ledward. Which is perhaps not surprising, since you appear to have forgotten your manners as well. Suppose I told my husband of the freedom with which you have seen fit to speak to me?'

'Ah, but you will not, if my suppositions are true ones,' he replied with a grin. 'Because, shrewd though Gerard Schuyler is, he has not fathomed the truth of you, madam.'

The eyes he turned on her now burned with admiration and with a sly knowledge. Oh, what a beauty she was, and if his guess were correct what a pleasure to be the first to possess her! What plots had they been hatching, these Schuylers? And why should he not join in? The woman was fair game, so bad was her reputation.

'Come,' he said, 'enjoy yourself with me, and he will never know, seeing that he thinks you what you are not.'

'I have no control over what you think,' replied Torry, compelling herself to be indifferent. 'And if you do not allow me to leave without causing me further annoyance by your effrontery, I shall. . .'

'What?' he drawled, suddenly all aristocratic languor, jamming his monocle in his eye to survey her, like a parody of wicked Sir Jasper in a bad melodrama threatening the heroine. 'What shall you do, madam? After all, I have been flattering you. Nothing I have said demeans you, far from it, for I have been denying your bad reputation, not reproaching you with it. And most women, I can confidently assure you, would welcome my attentions, not reject them.'

Torry saw that he was enjoying himself, and suddenly bold, for after all he could not actually assault her here in public where any guest or servant might see them, she swung round and began to walk briskly away from him, to reach the double doors leading into the library where she knew that Dr Finch, the curator at Moidore Castle, would be protection for her by his mere presence.

She could almost feel Ledward's hateful stare behind her. She had not gone many paces before he had called out to her, gently, 'I live to fight another day, Victoria, never fear.'

'A parcel for you, sir,' said Timson, coming into the drawing-room in Gerard's suite, finding Gerard sitting at an exquisite writing-table decorated with marquetry flowers, more suited in its delicacy to an effete eighteenth-century dandy than to Gerard's strong and powerful body.

He thought his master looked weary, and speculated with a grin on the reason. Well, it wasn't because of going several rounds with madam last night, that was for sure. Timson knew perfectly well that sir hadn't laid a finger on madam since their marriage — but he wasn't telling.

He might mock his master gently in the servants'

hall, calling him 'The great American bison', but Gerard had been kind to him, and his mockery did not include giving away Gerard's secrets. Rather, he hugged them to him, knowledge being power, as the saying had it. Meantime, he smoked the cigars which Gerard accepted as presents but did not want, and drank the light wines which Gerard despised and handed on to him, and inherited any of Gerard's clothes with which his master grew bored.

Besides, Gerard never abused him, never treated him as that Ledward treated his man, but spoke to him as though he were a fellow human being, and not a trained ape. He was not sure that Mrs Victoria Slade, as was, deserved him, but she was pleasant to him, and considerate, and never let the bison down in public, which was more than you could say for some of the women. . .

'Nothing to do, Timson, have you?' said Gerard with a grin, as he opened his parcel, his man seeming to have gone into a trance. He watched Timson walk out of the room before inspecting what had been forwarded to him.

Letters and papers, and two newspapers from America. He sighed, thought that he really ought to employ a private secretary — a thing which he had always done without: they knew too much. But since his obsession with Torry, work, which had been his previous obsession, had come to seem less important.

He flung the whole lot on to a side-table, to deal with later, but after a time the sight of them reproached him for his dilatoriness. Whatever was coming over him, that a woman should interfere with his orderly life?

Fatal to think of Torry. He wondered where she was, whether she was happy. He was sure that she was not. First there was his appalling behaviour last night to trouble her, and secondly, she now had no occupation, and, whatever else, she had been occupied in her previous life, and their bargain and subsequent marriage had deprived her of that.

If she were his true wife, what then? Surely, she would have occupation enough. Gerard pushed the thought away irritably, and to stop himself from thinking of her — for, after all, what was she but a high-class whore? And one didn't think of or consider *them*, and no man was fool enough to let himself fall in love with one, no man but Gerard Schuyler, that was — he picked up his mail and began to riffle through it.

A moment later, his face purple, his feral eyes glowing yellow, the hairs on his body bristling, he cursed, a string of oaths so violent that he shocked himself.

The reason for his anger was the screaming headline in the newspaper open before him: BLACKWOOD LAWYERS ACCUSE SCHUYLER BRIDE OF HYPOCRISY. During their absence in England Homer Blackwood had been sued for adultery by his secretary, Merton Spencer, who claimed heavy damages for the seduction of his wife.

In court, Homer's lawyer had called Judith Reis as a witness, and had compelled her to admit that the original evidence had been gathered by Victoria Schuyler before her marriage, and that Judith had used the evidence after she had left Victoria's employment, and had then been hired by *The Tattler*.

Homer's lawyer had questioned Judith about Torry, her relationship with the Captain, and her marriage to Gerard, raising the cry of hypocrisy and of tainted unsupported evidence, coming from a woman of great notoriety and loose morals. . .

Yes, the person who had come off the worst from the Spencer-Blackwood case was Torry herself, not his lecherous cousin Homer, and his heart sank at the prospect of even further dirty linen being washed in public. He thought of Kate, and how the scandal would stick to her, except, cynically, he also thought that Schuyler dollars might wash her reputation clean enough for her to accept some English lord—if she wanted one, that was.

But Torry! And he burned all over again. The paradox of his anger at her for being what she was, as against his inordinate rage at her reputation being so blown on, did not strike him. He only knew that what hurt her now hurt him, and, brave though she was, this must hurt her.

Not that anyone would say anything directly to her, but the knowledge that everyone she spoke to would be aware of the exact truth of her. . .

He stopped cursing, a useless thing to do. He looked at the other newspaper which contained more of the same, and he knew that without a doubt Homer Blackwood was going to get away with his wrongdoing, the red herring of Mrs Torry Schuyler, formerly Mrs Torry Slade, having been raised.

It was necessary that he speak to her as soon as

he could, that she know of this from him, and from no one else.

Later, he was cursing again, but inwardly this time. He had shown her the newspapers and her response had been as cool as ever. It had been as though she were reading of someone else. She had handed the paper to him when she had finished, raised her eyebrows, and said levelly, 'So? It is only what the whole world thinks it knows, after all.'

It was as though, Gerard thought, Torry were enclosed in one of those glass balls which, if you up-ended them, rained snow and frost upon their miniature occupants, so remote did she appear from him and the world. If she had admirers, were they able to pierce the glass, allow the perfect figure inside it to break free? Had she been like this with the Captain? With her first husband, that mystery man of whom he knew nothing? Had they entered the glass ball, to share it with her? Or had she stepped from it to. . .engage with them? He could not bear to think of the reality of the two relationships. Had she dissolved beneath their caresses, clung to them in abandon, either real or pretended? Had she. . .?

Despite all that he had said to her, and their weeks of living together, she remained an enigma; the invisible barrier which she had erected around herself remained unbreached.

Torry looked at him, saw that he was distressed for her, and because of her, and, touched a little by his concern, she said, 'You knew that this might happen before you married me, Gerard. It is unlike you, I think, to care what others say about you and yours.'

Gerard knew that was true, knew that his feeling hurt on her behalf was untypical. To justify himself, a new experience, he spoke, and despite himself his voice shook a little. 'But never before have the Press printed anything so explicit, so vilely designed to destroy — in order to save my worthless cousin. If we were back in New York I should be in danger of going for him — and killing him!'

'A good thing, then, that we are not in New York. Gis once said. . .' She stopped, his sucked-in breath, his expression warning her that he was near breaking point and that to refer to the Captain in any way was calculated to take him beyond it.

'Ah, yes,' he replied stonily, keeping his voice level with difficulty, 'Gis once said? Why stop at such an interesting juncture? Do tell what Gis said; I am aching to know.'

The beautiful violet eyes looked straight into his. He read pity there, and he rejected it violently; he did not want her pity. He wanted. . .he wanted. . . Inconvenient, unwanted desire rose in Gerard. Yes, it was like being a boy again, to be so roused merely by the sight of her, by the spectacle of her apparently effortless self-control. Was she made entirely of ice?

'Gis once said,' she resumed, as though nothing had passed between them since she had mentioned his grandfather's name, 'that it was futile to care what other people thought of you. What you were, what you thought of yourself and the world was all that mattered, and to let such as that ——' and with one beautiful finger she flicked at the newspapers lying on the table before them '—distress you was to sell your soul to the others.'

'Quite a philosopher, my grandfather,' he heard himself saying bitterly, the bitterness because he evidently did not live up to the standard which the old man had set, and by which she apparently judged all men. 'And no doubt you made an apt pupil.'

'I learned a lot from him, yes,' she admitted.

'This damnable calm you always display, I suppose, is owing to him.'

'Would you rather that I ranted and raved, Gerard? Surely not. That would be to satisfy those who wrote this, and would be of no benefit to either of us.'

He wanted to say, I could reach you if once you lost your perfect composure, proved yourself human, were moved by passion, showed weakness even. Instead he turned away from her, for to see her was temptation itself, and it was his control, so perfect, so unassailable until he had first met her, that day in the church, which was now always in danger. 'And Kate?' he ground out. 'She is not to be hurt by this, you think? Will not be dirtied by association with it? Or will you teach her your arts, so that she can no longer feel? What did you feel for him, Torry? For the Captain? Can you feel nothing of that for me?'

Always it came back to the Captain. The dead old man seemed to stand between them in every possible way. Lover and mentor, who, from the grave, had imposed his will on the pair of them, so strongly that he was the ghost at their table, the ghost who kept him from her bed, who walked beside Gerard to whisper into his ear that he had possessed her first.

Gerard shook his head as if to clear it. He had not meant to seem to plead with her, to beg her to give him what she was so plainly withholding, and when she did not reply he said fiercely and unforgivably, 'Or do you only feel for others, and never for me? Could you not even pretend to feel something for me, as you must have pretended to do for all your other lovers?'

She made no answer to this, for, although he did not know it, she was almost beyond speech, or rather she was terrified that she would break, and would tell him all those things of which she had vowed never to speak to anyone, certainly never to any man.

Had Gerard remained silent, then her defences might have been breached. Words she could reject, and when he threw at her one last defiant sentence, one last bitter reproach, 'Or are you so touched by frost that you feel nothing for anyone any more, not even yourself?' she made no answer to him.

He flung away from her to leave her standing alone in the pretty room and so never saw the two great tears which ran down her face.

Kate heard, of course. Not only imported newspapers but letters arrived at Moidore, telling of the open scandal which surrounded Gerard Schuyler and his new bride. She headed for the great drawing-room which looked out across the surrounding countryside, the castle being sited between the flat country of Lincolnshire on one side and the rounded woodlands of Leicestershire on the other.

She found Torry seated on her own — most of the other women rose later than the Schuylers — sat by her, and said, 'Oh, Torry, it is useless pretending. I have seen the newspaper with the accounts of Cousin Homer's trial in it, and I think that he has behaved disgracefully in pillorying you, Gerard and the Captain as he has done.'

Torry looked at her, thought of what Gerard had said, and answered her with more warmth than she usually displayed. 'He is fighting for his life and his reputation, Kate, and will use any means to save himself.'

'But to do this. . .' Kate's honest indignation further warmed her sister-in-law, who said equably,

'My dear, you are very young, but you are, I know, as hard-headed as all the Schuylers. You must be aware that I have no reputation, and so to attack me is to attack nothing. It is Gerard and yourself who have most to lose.'

'Oh, Gerard!' Kate dismissed him. 'Gerard has no reputation left, either. Do you think that I don't know that he is a financial pirate and has been a womaniser? As for myself, I am a Schuyler, and we stand to be shot at. It will make no difference to Justin, you know. He won't think any the less of me. He has already taken into account that I am an American and therefore something of a savage, even if I don't wield a tomahawk, but money washes everything clean, you know that, Torry.'

So she did, and if it were a pity that young Kate

was already aware of the harsh realities of life for Yankee heiresses then by Torry's reckoning that was a good thing, not a bad thing, for Kate would go open-eyed into any relationship she might form with Justin, or any other young aristocrat who took her fancy. In her own way she was as shrewdly pragmatic as Gerard, and at the moment love, lust, or whatever it was he felt for his wife, was not blinding her judgement, as it was, to some extent, blinding his.

What Torry also knew was that Bryce Ledward's pursuit of her was beginning to cause more gossip, and that, inevitably, Gerard was going to be enraged by it. The fact that Ledward had no attraction for her, that on the contrary he made her shudder even more than most men did when they came too near her, was something of which she could persuade neither Ledward nor her husband.

In the small world which was Moidore Castle it was impossible to avoid him. He sought her out, talked to her, in public of impersonal things, books, ideas, paintings, even a little politics, while in private he pursued her remorselessly, and without causing scandal she could not hold him off.

But, of course, not holding him off was also scandalous, for he contrived to behave as though they shared a private life, and however much she tried to avoid him he was always there.

'No,' she said to him one afternoon when he had cornered her in a far corner of the park where she had thought to escape him and all men, for since the scandal had broken in the Press more than one had tried his hand at breaching her icy calm. 'Leave me, I beg of you. I do not want your company, and I know that my husband dislikes the insistent way in which you choose to favour me.'

'Good,' was his only smiling answer. 'That pleases me. The ineffable Gerard Schuyler deserves to suffer a little, and that I should be the cause. . .'

Torry rose, began to walk away from him, but he followed her to the border of a small ornamental lake.

I could jump in, she thought. Let the waters close over my head. Why did I ever suggest that ridiculous bargain to Gerard? Why do I care what he feels? Why does it trouble me that men — and women — might laugh at him if they thought me faithless to him so soon after our marriage? Ledward suspects the truth of us, but no one else does, and what a joke it would be on Gerard, to allow the world to think that Ledward might have succeeded in his campaign against me.

'Mr Ledward,' she said. She had swung round to face him, and in her gown of rose-pink and silver-grey velvet she had never looked more beautiful. 'If it were not for the further scandal it might create, I would ask His Royal Highness himself to protect me from you. Indeed, if you persist further, I shall have no other recourse. Let that be a warning.'

Bryce Ledward suddenly knew that he could never succeed with her. Whatever the truth of her, she was so staunch that he could not prevail against her. His hatred for Gerard grew. What had the swine ever done that he should deserve such loyalty from the peerless and spotless creature he suspected Mrs Victoria Schuyler to be?

Damn him! And damn him again! If he might not bed his wife then he had a double hatred for him, and before he left Moidore he would make sure that, whatever else, Gerard Schuyler would pay for being a cursed Yankee, for being Victoria Schuyler's husband, and for the misbegotten loyalty which that same Mrs Schuyler showed for him!

Gerard had been out riding with Moidore and some of the other men, Ledward among them. They had walked into breakfast to find the dining-room empty — the women of the party rarely rose before half-past ten, and nine was just striking. Moidore led the way, and they began to inspect the food waiting for them on the sideboard, lifting the gleaming silver covers to reveal eggs, bacon, kippers, kidneys, smoked haddock, sausages, mushrooms — the spendid English equivalent, Gerard always thought, of French cuisine, honest food honestly presented. It was one of the things he liked best about his adopted country.

The assembled men carried their filled plates over to the long table, poured out coffee and tea. Gerard always took tea — English coffee left much to be desired. His stay at Moidore was coming to an end; London and the season beckoned them all, Moidore included, and this elegant and civilised country house living would come to a temporary conclusion, to be resumed in the autumn when the season was over.

Ledward, seated opposite Gerard, was in a savage mood, only lightly concealed by his veneer of good manners. He was baiting Justin Otmoor over Kate, in a veiled manner, of course, but the drift of his comments that he was after her merely to shore up the ruined fortunes of his family, since otherwise no one would ever marry an American, was plain.

Gerard suddenly had had enough of it. First Ledward was pursuing his wife, and now, by implication, was badmouthing himself and the Schuylers through Kate. Justin was too well-bred to say very much for fear of causing scandal, but Gerard made his own rules.

'Bad form, as you say, isn't it, Ledward,' he said sourly, his knife and fork put down so that he might speak easily, 'to comment on the ladies, even by implication? If you wish to be unpleasant about Americans in general, or the Schuylers and myself in particular, then do so, but leave Kate out of it.'

The table fell silent. Moidore, bluff face alert, opened his mouth to say something, then closed it again. Let Schuyler and Ledward battle it out at last; better so in the long run, perhaps, he thought.

'Oh, charming,' sneered Ledward. 'An American as an arbiter of good manners! What's the matter, Schuyler, the truth hurts, is that it?'

Gerard controlled himself with difficulty. Why was it, these days, that the superb self-control which had always come to him so easily was in danger of cracking? He willed himself to be calm, placed his hands in his lap, out of sight, lest the tension in them betray him.

'The truth?' His tone was a jeer. 'What the devil do you know about truth, Ledward? Not something you peddle in, is it?'

'Peddle in!' Ledward shot back at him. 'Hark to

the huckster talking.' He too had lost his usual calm
control, and the normal veneer of good manners
which kept social life among the upper classes an
apparently ordered affair was disappearing with it,
so that Moidore opened his mouth, to speak this
time, but too late, for Ledward, colour high, was
boring on, determined to hurt the Yankee swine
before him.

Mimicking Gerard, he flung at him, 'And what
the devil do you know of manners, good or bad, or
truth come to that? What's the truth about you,
Schuyler, and that damned prissy wife of yours?'
and all the frustration he felt at Torry keeping him
at arm's length came boiling out in one unforgivable
torrent. 'What with the Yankee Press *peddling* her
blown reputation, and yours, daily, I wonder that
she dare show her face in decent society. . .'

He got no further. Primeval rage had seized
Gerard by the throat. The conventions of the polite
world in which he had come to live suddenly meant
nothing to him. He was his grandfather's grandson
with a vengeance. The Captain had once publicly
flogged a rival who had cast a slur on him and his
family, and the old Adam was in him and would be
out.

'Damn you,' he said, and the ferocity and strength
of will in his face and voice was a revelation to the
watching men. 'Damn you for the cur that you are
to speak of my wife so.' And, standing up, he picked
up his plate of scrambled eggs, bacon, mushrooms
and sausages and smashed the whole lot into
Ledward's face before anyone could stop him. 'If
that doesn't silence your lying tongue, nothing will.'

For a moment there was a shocked calm, both at what Ledward had said, breaking all the taboos which governed what was supposed to be the done thing, and Gerard's instant and violent response. And then, suddenly, bedlam reigned. Ledward, shaken more than stunned, sat paralysed in his place as Gerard, once he had released the plate, began to launch himself at his tormentor across the table-top, to finish what he had started. The men around Gerard seized him by the arms and pulled him back, those next to Ledward restrained him.

Ledward was incoherent between rage and shame at the insult put upon him; Gerard, admonished by the man who was holding him, young Justin, said grimly, 'English breakfast *à la mode de Schuyler* ought to settle his hash for good. Eggs and bacon will never taste the same again!'

Moidore's voice rose above the uproar. 'For God's sake, gentlemen, remember where you are! The Prince is in the house; suppose he came in to see this! Ledward, you were wrong to speak of Schuyler's wife publicly in such a fasion, and later, when you have both regained your senses, you must apologise. Schuyler, while I understand why you acted as you did, you were wrong to do so, and you too must offer reparation.'

Both men glared at him. Gerard roared rather than said, 'I apologise to you, Moidore and gentlemen, for allowing my anger free rein here. I was wrong. And you,' he snarled, voice ferocious, turning to Ledward, whose look at him was equally so, 'I challenge you, damn you, to any form of duel or combat you see fit to satisfy me with.'

'Gerard, Gerard,' said Moidore urgently, 'the days of duelling are long past here, unlike. . .'

He paused; his anxiety to end the matter had destroyed his ability to be tactful, for Gerard said, still violent, 'Unlike my own savage country, I suppose you mean, Moidore,' and then to Ledward, roughly, almost in the manner of a Bronx hoodlum, quite unlike the courteous man he usually was, 'OK, OK, Ledward, six-shooters, or what? I won't take my challenge back.'

Moidore saw that the only way to end this, for those around both men, offering advice, begging them to shake hands, were being ignored by the furious would-be combatants, was to allow Gerard and Ledward to pursue the matter to its bitter end, with the hope that later they might see sense.

Ledward, taking out his handkerchief and beginning to wipe his face and his suit clean, said, suddenly cool and sure of himself, 'Oh, pistols won't be needed. We don't live in the Wild West here, Schuyler. You may meet me in fair fight at the National Sporting Club in proper form, Queensberry rules, over as many rounds as you please, when we return to town. I'll be delighted to give you a good hiding.'

'Be quiet, man.' Moidore was suddenly in command. 'You've named your weapons. Now, Schuyler, what do you say to that?'

'Satisfied,' ground out Gerard, wrenching himself free from those holding him. He knew of Ledward's reputation as a bruiser, and some of those present began to protest that such a contest would not be fair.

'Oh, be damned to that,' said Gerard. 'I'll meet him when and where he pleases, bare knuckles or gloves, Queensberry rules or not. Be happy to spoil his pretty face for him.'

'That's it, then,' said Moidore, satisfied. 'I'll be arbiter, and peace-maker too, if possible. The Prince will be here at any moment, and he must not know of this, nor the women either.'

But, of course, the Prince, and then the women, soon found out what had occurred at breakfast — everyone except Torry, that was. For some reason, her perfect calm daunted even the women among whom she found herself, and no one dared to tell her what her husband had done.

Kate bearded Gerard in the herb garden where he was strolling alone, and took advantage of their privacy to say, 'Oh, Gerard, is it true? Did you really decorate Bryce Ledward's face with your bacon and egg for being unpleasant about Torry? And is it true that you are to fight him in some gymnasium in London when we go there in ten days' time? Whatever does Torry think about it all?'

The look Gerard turned on her was so fierce that Kate quailed before it.

'Torry thinks nothing about it, because she knows nothing of it ——'

'But she should,' Kate could not help protesting lucklessly, to be faced by a Gerard whom she had never seen before. He had always been gentle with her, and she had sometimes been surprised to learn that people were frightened of him. She knew now why they were, his face and voice were so forbidding.

'You are to say nothing about it to her, Kate, do you hear? Not a word. I'll not have her troubled. And if I learn that you have told her anything, anything at all about what Ledward and I got up to—I suppose that ass Justin Otmoor had nothing better to do than tell you everything—I shall send you home on the next boat with the most unpleasant chaperone I can find! You hear me, Kate?'

Why, I do believe he loves her, thought Kate in wonder. For all her lack of years she was no one's fool, and she had never before seen her brother so moved by anything. His cold imperturbability was a byword in the family, but now his agitation was so extreme that the only explanation could be that he cared for her—no, loved her. Did Torry love him?

'Not a word,' she said fervently. Gerard had taken her arm when he had warned her of what he would do if she disobeyed him, and when she gave him the answer he wanted he let go of it.

Kate rubbed the released arm, and Gerard was suddenly ashamed that, once again, faced by what he thought was a threat to Torry, his self-control had snapped.

'She's sure to find out, you know,' said Kate, fascinated by this new Gerard. 'And yes, Justin did tell me, because I asked him what all the women were whispering about. Does the Prince know?'

'Probably,' said Gerard gloomily. 'You saw how he favoured us both last night and virtually cut Ledward.'

'He's kind,' said Kate. 'I wonder what he thinks about you boxing Mr Ledward?'

'Fighting him,' Gerard corrected her, suddenly

himself again at the prospect of ruining Ledward's
beauty — particularly since everyone else seemed to
think that it was *his* ugliness which was going to be
enlarged. 'I don't box — that's for effete English
aristocrats.'

Gerard had no illusions about his looks, but he
was also unaware that many women preferred his
rugged grandeur to Ledward's smoother attractions.
He was a Norse god, rough and wild, thought Kate,
seeing him for the first time as a man rather than as
a brother, unlike Bryce Ledward who was a Greek
god, soft and decadent for all his athletic prowess.

'And now hush,' he ordered her, for Torry,
accompanied by Daisy Gascoyne, was walking
towards them, and for a moment they all chatted
together, before Kate, who was already showing
signs of being a true granddaughter of the Captain,
surprisingly managed to manoeuvre Daisy into
accompanying her on a detour to the lake, leaving
husband and wife together.

'Gerard,' said Torry, who was wearing a walking
dress of deep navy wool and a black straw hat
decorated with the violets which were almost her
emblem, 'is there something which I ought to
know?'

Gerard, who had offered her his arm, began to
walk her out of the herb garden, down a woodland
path to a vista where there was a small temple.

'Such as?' he replied, giving the air of a man
without a thing on his mind.

'I don't know,' said his wife thoughtfully. 'But
there seems to be an air of suppressed excitement
about the party. I first noticed it at luncheon yester-

day, but no one has informed me of anything untoward. And the Prince was so very particular with us last night, and I was wondering whether that was to demonstrate his favour to us or his displeasure with someone else.'

'Oh, your imagination is misleading you,' he said airily.

'I do hope so.' Torry was thoughtful. 'I should hate to say the wrong thing out of ignorance — that it was the wrong thing, I mean.'

Did she know? Was she testing him? How inconvenient it was to have for a wife a woman as shrewd as she was. He could see why she had been a good journalist. And when and where had she learned to read atmospheres so correctly? For, of course, the Schuyler-Ledward feud was the subject of everyone's discussion in private.

Gerard decided that Torry really did know nothing, and said comfortably, hoping that she would remain ignorant, 'You really shouldn't trouble yourself about such things, my dear. And as for saying the wrong thing, you have been saying the right thing so supremely well, I cannot believe that you will suddenly lose your touch.'

Torry remained thoughtful, despite this comforting and somewhat unexpected praise. Gerard was right to believe her ignorant of what had passed at breakfast the day before, but she knew that something had happened, and thought that it involved him. It could not be too bad, because the Prince had shown them favour so markedly. Well, she supposed that he would tell her some time, and in the interim she would try to read the runes, as her first husband had said, and they might tell her the truth.

Dutifully she admired the little temple, allowed Gerard to sit her down, and they rested there peacefully, like an old married couple, happy to enjoy the mild spring sunshine, and not at all like a man and wife who had never shared a bed and who were determined to part as soon as they had established Gerard's claim to his grandfather's estate.

Only somehow, and for all their cleverness, both of them were only dimly aware of what was happening: the relationship between them was slowly beginning to change. . . For if Gerard was suddenly fathoms deep in love with his originally unwanted wife, Torry's feelings were contradictory too.

Gerard looked sideways at her pure and austere profile. He shivered a little, and whether it was desire or a strange fear which affected him he did not know.

'My dear,' he began, and the illusion of a years-old marriage was preserved. 'My dear, I would wish to apologise to you for the other night. I can only say that the mere sight of you. . .'

He paused as Torry placed her lace-gloved hand lightly on his knee, saying, 'No, Gerard. There is no need. We have an unusual relationship and it is only natural that at times it should be. . .strained.'

'Strained!' He laughed, a sad laugh, then said, a trifle bitterly, 'What a word to use, so polite, so little like what passed between us.' He was silent, and when she did not reply said abruptly, 'I had not meant to frighten you.'

The hand was withdrawn. 'I was foolish,' she

admitted, 'to be so strongly affected. But I had not anticipated——'

'And if I am honest,' he interrupted her a trifle roughly, 'and it may comfort you to know it, nor had I anticipated that I would act as I did. I do not usually lose my self-control so swiftly and completely.'

It was not the kind of confession he was used to making, and that he made it at all told the listening woman that when she had used the word strain it had been an understatement, and, further, that in apologising at all he was making her an enormous concession. The Gerard Schuylers of the world were not wont to apologise.

'I shall try not to behave so again,' he finished stiffly. 'I will attempt to keep to our bargain, although, God knows, it will be a hard thing to do.' Why was he talking like this to the Captain's whore? As though she deserved his respect. Had not she and the Captain engineered this situation? And God knew that they had wrought better than they might have hoped.

For she was not merely Gerard Schuyler's wife as the result of their conspiracy—he was trapped, penned, caught in the snare which they had made, and into which he had fallen. For, improbably, ridiculously, and every god in the pantheon must be laughing at him for it, he was in love with her, and could not talk himself out of it.

And what was more he had given her what he had rarely given to any woman. He had ridden through life taking what he wanted when and where he had wanted it. He had never been an exploiter of women such as he knew Ledward and others to be, but neither had he given overmuch thought to those whom he had made his mistresses. They, and he, had gone into their liaisons open-eyed, and he had never been one for seducing house-maids and shop-girls.

He would have liked to tell her that, for his behaviour the other night might have given her a different impression. He shook his head, almost as if to clear it, for these days all his speeches and actions where she was concerned were taking him into unknown territory.

What territory? The territory of a man in love.

No, he did not want this, not at all; he wanted to be uncomplicated Gerard Schuyler again, but that Gerard Schuyler had gone; the woman sitting by his side had destroyed him, and had created someone else, and that someone had to learn who he was and what rules were needed to run his life in the alien land in which he found himself.

CHAPTER TEN

LEAVING Moidore was nearly as elaborate a business as arriving had been. The Prince had only stayed there for ten days, and then had moved south back to London. Official duties called him, and for once Ledward had not left with him. The Prince had informed him gravely the night before he had left that his services would not be required.

He had been cool to his one-time favourite ever since he had been informed of the ugly insult he had put upon Mrs Schuyler, and had gone out of his way to be pleasant to her, but not in a fashion which might provoke further scandal. The Princess had been friendly to her as well, saying, 'You must visit us at Marlborough House, Mrs Schuyler. I have greatly enjoyed your company here.'

Torry had murmured vaguely something to the effect that the feeling was mutual. The Princess was such a gentle creature, wandering around the castle with her little camera, snapping groups of courtiers and guests against the supposed medieval splendours of the castle, driving into the countryside, Torry sitting opposite to her in the landau, both of them chatting serenely while admiring the beauties of the Lincolnshire landscape.

Later, she would send to Torry copies of the photographs which she had taken of her and Gerard, stiff in their best clothes, Moidore standing between them smiling—and one which showed the Prince with them, a dog at his heels, his hand on Gerard's shoulder but his eyes on Torry.

Torry had never thought to be in such exalted company, nor that such exalted company would be so easy to live with.

She said as much to Gerard in the first-class compartment of the train which took them Londonwards. She and Kate were surrounded by flowers, boxes of chocolates, books, newspapers and magazines.

Kate had rapidly commandeered *The Strand*. She had turned to the latest Sherlock Holmes story and was reading it eagerly, occasionally exclaiming over it, to Gerard's amusement. Gerard was examining *The Illustrated London News*, but put it down when Torry said, 'I was astonished to find how unassuming the Prince and Princess of Wales were. I suppose,' she added thoughtfully, 'that I foolishly imagined that they went everywhere wearing gold crowns, with bowing courtiers backing away from them. But they looked and behaved more like Herr and Frau Saxe-Coburg than the royal pair they are.'

'That was because you behaved yourself perfectly—were not servile, but did not presume either. Had you done so, you would have been left in no doubt that one day His Royal Highness would be the King-Emperor.'

'I hear that he gave Bryce Ledward a right royal wigging before he left,' remarked Kate, abandoning Dr Watson for a moment.

Gerard gave her a warning glare, for the wigging had been over Torry, and she still remained unaware of his quarrel with Ledward and the coming boxing match, or fight, as Gerard was pleased to think of it.

'Yes,' he replied repressively. 'Best not to offend Albert Edward.'

'Or any other man of power,' said irrepressible Kate, who had rightly read Gerard's look at her, and thought that he had nothing to learn from the Prince about the art of handing out rebuffs, even if he weren't a member of the British royal family.

But I suppose, she thought, that we Schuylers are something of a royal family, in America, at least. And it was no wonder Gerard fitted in so well with the life here, for she had immediately seen that her brother was popular with the aristocracy and gentry who surrounded him, and not solely because he was a rich Yankee on whom they wished to batten. Lord Moidore was obviously both a friend and a confidant.

And as for the women, well, there was no doubt that Gerard could have taken his pick, except that, once married to Torry, he had seemed to ignore them, absent-mindedly, and the Gascoyne woman had not liked that at all. Odd to think that Daisy would be her sister-in-law if Justin chose to propose and she chose to accept him.

She returned to Sherlock Holmes, and wished that life would work out as neatly and justly as fantasy so often did.

'I wonder,' said Torry idly, as she picked up her novel, 'what Mr Ledward did to earn the Prince's disfavour?'

'Trumped his best trick at whist which His

Highness had just taken with an ace, when there was no need,' replied Gerard irrepressibly.

'Small-minded, if true.' And once again Torry, answering him before she resumed her reading of Mr Henry James's satire on liberated American women, *The Bostonians*, had the impression that something was being kept from her, a feeling which she did not like. Gerard had a habit of mentally sliding away from her whenever Bryce Ledward's name came up, and Kate was not much better, for she put down *The Strand* magazine and began a line of chatter about the passing scenery which appeared to have no aim other than to steer the conversation into neutral waters.

The rest of the train journey passed without incident, which was more, they all later reflected, than could be said for Torry's and Kate's launching on London society.

The season had already begun, and Gerard, who knew everybody, was invited by that everybody to all the great houses and attended all the manifold events which made up the calendar of society's doings. If Kate was a little of a sensation with her delightfully frank and fresh charm, the American girl at her best, as more than one great lady commented in this, her inaugural season, then Torry was something else.

Back in New York Gerard had fantasised on how his wife would strike London society, and at Moidore Tom Bulkeley had told him that even without the patronage of the Prince and Princess of Wales she would be a sensation.

And a sensation she was. It was Mrs Langtry and

Jennie Jerome, who had married Lord Randolph Churchill, the Duke of Marlborough's brother, all over again.

It mattered not a whit that she was married. People stood on chairs in ballrooms to see her. Pirated photographs of her appeared in shops for sale — she was nicknamed the American Lily, in a sly reference to Mrs Langtry who had been the Jersey Lily. Gossips speculated as to whether she, too, would become the Prince of Wales's latest mistress.

When she and Gerard rode in Hyde Park — she rode splendidly — or they drove there, Kate in attendance, crowds followed them. Everything about her was admired. Her beauty, her dress sense, her manner, her informed conversation, that 'stand off and don't touch me' air, as more than one man commented, were all, taken together, enough to drive any man wild, as they had driven Bryce Ledward wild, and all society knew of what had happened at Moidore and the fight which was due to take place as a consequence of it.

Coarse wits nicknamed Ledward 'Bacon and Eggs' behind his back, fuelling his hatred of Gerard and his desire to humiliate him in the ring.

The only person who did not know of the coming bout between the two men was the innocent cause of it. Torry, indeed, was faintly amused by the furore which she caused. She remained unaffected by it, thought that perhaps her dubious past was part of the attraction, and her even odder marriage to Gerard.

And Gerard? If once he had believed that it

would amuse him to loose Torry on London and see what would happen, he did not find it so when his fantasy had come true. Jealousy rode on his back, whispered in his ear. She was his, his, no one else's! But oh, he knew that she was not. Not his, not anyone's. Had she ever been anyone's? Had she kept her inner self inviolate even when she was pleasing the Captain and his predecesors?

He could not believe it. He would never have imagined that he could be caught in such toils, would want her so desperately and be able to do nothing about it—except protect her. And why should he do *that*? Dollymops, ladybirds, whores did not require protection, could not be the subject of a decent man's love—if he were sane, that was.

But he was not a decent man. He was Gerard Schuyler, who made his own rules. Only somehow he had lost that power, and the more he yearned over her, the worse he felt. At least Ledward left her alone, except that he was yearning too, also watched her enter ballrooms, stand, surrounded by admirers, a faint smile on her face.

Leonardo da Vinci should still be alive, to paint a new Mona Lisa, Arthur Balfour remarked on meeting her, echoing Gerard's own thought on his first seeing her, and his remark flew round London, reached the Prince, reached Gerard, who ground his teeth—and redoubled his preparations to teach Bryce Ledward a lesson which he would never forget, and which would warn others not to speak of her lightly.

* * *

'She does not know? She has no idea?' drawled Daisy Gascoyne to Kate, one night at the opera. Kate was in the Gascoynes' box, ethereal in white, looking not at all like her true sturdy self, Justin Otmoor beside her; all society knew that they were a thing.

'No,' said Kate. 'Gerard does not wish her to know.'

'Oh, Gerard,' said Daisy dismissively. 'I shall tell her.'

'No,' said Kate, and her voice, although she did not know it, was a female version of Gerard's at his hardest. 'If you value my friendship, with you, and with Justin, you will say nothing to her, and you will see that others say nothing, too.'

Daisy frowned at the veiled warning. Stupid to lose Kate for such a thing—the Schuyler millions were needed to put Justin's estate back on its feet, and she knew instinctively that, much though Kate cared for Justin, there was a core of steel in her, and to cross her might mean that the millions would be lost.

'Someone is sure to tell her,' she remarked tentatively.

'I trust you to see that no one does,' was all Kate had to say to that. 'After all, Daisy, your word is law, and if the Prince agrees with Gerard and does not wish her to know, and I can tell you that for a certainty, then it would be foolish to risk his displeasure as well.'

'The Prince!' Daisy's look was thoughtful. 'And is he hopeful, Kate? She has smiled on no one else. Is she holding out for him?'

'Never! You don't know her,' retorted Kate, who thought that she did, and although she was unaware of it she, Bryce Ledward, and Timson, Gerard's man, were the only ones who had read the enigma who was Mrs Victoria Schuyler correctly, and for their different reasons none of them was telling what they thought they knew.

'You are as hard as Gerard,' complained Daisy. And then, 'Oh, very well, have it your way. From her behaviour I would not have thought that she needed protecting from anything — or anyone. But if that's the way you both want it. . . Is he in love with her? Gerard I mean. Surely not!'

'No business of ours.' Kate was cheerful, having got her own way. There were times when she thought that she was even more like the Captain than Gerard was, except that, unlike the two men, she would not be able to engage in the boxing match which was due to take place in a few days' time, and on which all society was placing bets, everyone talking about it covertly, no one mentioning it overtly. Margot Tennant, beauty, wit and rebel, had been reported as saying that in society one might do as one pleased, so long as one did not do it in the street and frighten the horses!

Well, a boxing match to be held at the National Sporting Club, as though two friends were engaged in amicable contest, and not as the deadly rivals they actually were, was not going to be held in the street, so the horses were safe, thought Daisy wryly.

She also thought of defying Kate, and telling Torry all about it, just for the fun of it. And then she thought of the Schuyler millions. . .and the

share of them she might have, through Justin. . .
and thought again.

Gerard did not know why he wanted Torry kept in
the dark about his match with Ledward. He told
himself it was to protect her, but how could that be?
Everyone knew. And even if Torry did find out, he
could not believe that it would disturb her lovely
calm.

So why? It could only be that the passion which
he felt for her was translating into something deeper
even than he knew. It was not mere lust, but
something more, and overwhelmingly had become
a desire to protect her.

He was thinking this as he sat over breakfast,
Torry opposite him, already immaculate, Kate *en
jeune fille*, hair down, wearing a little girl's dress,
looking quite unlike the strong-minded female who
had kept Daisy Gascoyne in her place.

'I shall be out tomorrow evening,' he said suddenly. 'I have an engagement with Moidore and
some of the men, a stag party,' he improvised. 'One
of Moidore's cousins is to be married at the
weekend.'

Now, this was true at least, that Moidore's cousin
was to marry, but the stag party was the following
night, and Gerard's engagement was really with
Bryce Ledward, and Moidore was to be there as
Gerard's second. A professional referee had been
hired, to see that all was according to Queensberry
rules, and there would be quite an audience present,
Gerard knew, for the match had been presented as
otherwise than it was.

The pretence was that two amateur athletes were meeting to test one another in a friendly contest. That was surface decoration. Everyone knew the real truth, but everyone was, of course, pretending that he or she didn't. . .

Torry bowed her head and said gently, 'I think Kate and I will enjoy a night in for a change. If it is possible to grow tired from a constant round of pleasure, then I think that I am tired, just a little.'

'Missing the *Banner*?' ventured Gerard.

'Yes.' Torry was serene. 'I'm not really used to being idle.'

'Not all that idle,' said Kate proudly. 'Since they have discovered how businesslike she is, Torry has been elected to every committee in London. This afternoon we are meeting to discuss a bazaar to help fallen women, and Torry will be chairman.'

Gerard's eyes slid towards Torry, who said, mischievously, 'Doubtless, knowing a little of my history, they chose me since I might be supposed to have some knowledge of the subject of our charity.'

Gerard could not help laughing. He rose, said, 'Well, better that than total idleness, I suppose. Do not expect me home early tomorrow, my love. I anticipate a long and lively night,' and as he passed her chair he deposited a kiss on his wife's head. That act, and his previous comment, had been designed to deceive Kate. He thought of what Torry had said, and of how hard-headed she was beneath her calm serenity.

She must know what was said behind her back, and indeed the quip which she had just made had been made — also behind her back — by Daisy

Gascoyne at the time of her appointment, and had been duly retailed to Gerard by one of Daisy's rivals. It had not made him love either of the women, and he raged internally that Torry should be the subject of such comments. But if she were able to dismiss the whole business so lightly, why should he be troubled? After all, he was going to get rid of her, was he not, as soon as he decently could, once the Schuyler millions were indubitably his?

Nevertheless, hearing her come upstairs to her suite of rooms, he walked over to her door and knocked gently on it. She showed her surprise when she admitted him, for since the scene at Moidore they had rarely been together in private, Gerard not trusting himself to be alone with her.

'Gerard!' she said, and her surprise was manifest. 'What is it?'

He looked about him. Her room was as lovely and ordered as she was. Before they had left for Moidore she had called an interior decorator in, and during their absence it had been refurbished. It bore the impress of her whole personality. It was uncluttered, free of the bibelots, the gewgaws with which most fashionable women surrounded themselves.

Classic simplicity, he thought, and then, What did the Captain make of her? Out of bed, that was. He dismissed the thought and said, diffidently for him, 'May I come in?'

She nodded, but, he noted with a little pain, retreated before him, keeping her distance.

'It does not trouble you too much?' he began, without preamble. 'The gossip, I mean.'

'Since no one ever says anything directly to me,' Torry replied, 'no.' Now this was not strictly true, for Bryce Ledward had been direct, had he not? But she would not confess to *that*.

'You are quite unlike any other woman I have ever known,' said Gerard, the comment wrung from him, for he had previously thought all women much the same, lumping every member of the female sex together, indistinguishable, like eggs on a grocer's counter, all looking alike, and all behaving the same.

Shows how muddled I am becoming, and all because of madam wife, he thought, to maunder about eggs *behaving*. What next?

What next was even worse. What undid him he did not know. Her little smile, perhaps, after he had admitted her difference and by doing so had admitted that women had characters, too, were not something called woman, undifferentiated.

Perhaps it was, he later thought, the softening of her face, a little movement of the body which betrayed that she was not all steel, might be moved. Whatever it was it had an effect on him so strong that it almost unmanned him, drove him to behave as he had never done before.

Since brutal assault had failed because he could not maintain such selfish ruthlessness, then other means might suffice. Not that Gerard thought this consciously at the time. The mind had vanished; the body had taken over and had its own rules.

He fell on his knees before her — at ten o'clock in the morning! — clutched at her skirts, hid his face in

them, then looked up, his hands rising to clasp her
to him.

'Of your mercy,' he began — was this Gerard
Schuyler speaking? 'Of your mercy. You know what
I want. You married me. Let us be married. . .truly
married.'

He had never thought to behave so humbly that
he would beg a woman for what before she had
always willingly granted, and he had, as if by right,
taken. To be so occupied by a woman that she
dominated all his waking hours was new to him,
unknown territory. For, after all, what were women
but toys, playthings to pass an empty hour, to grace
the end of the day, refresh the tired warrior, the
businessman home from his bloodless kills?

Real life was not about women, did not involve
women. They were what you came home to when
the business of living was done. They were to be
remembered only when the front door closed behind
you in the evening. They were your partner in bed,
the mother of your children, the means by which a
man renewed himself to face the workaday world.

She put out a hand to stroke his glossy black hair,
absent-mindedly, no passion in her action. Perhaps
an infinite pity. Gerard did not want her pity, he
wanted her, Torry. He wanted her to give herself
willingly, to be his partner, to be more than someone to share a bed with, to be more than that, much
more, to be. . .

He was in agony, and shuddered beneath her
hand. He felt her begin to turn away from him, and
clutched her the more tightly.

'No, you are not to walk away from me. You

always walk away. You walked away from Ledward, from the Prince even, I saw you. Don't walk away from me. Don't retreat, advance. Why don't you advance? Is that how you win, by retreating? Did you retreat from *him*?' He meant the Captain.

He felt her withdraw even further, and groaned. The Captain, always the Captain. He could forgive her the other men, but not him, never him.

'We had a bargain, Gerard.' And her voice was calm. How could she be so calm when he was on the rack?

'Damn the bargain,' he said violently, his voice muffled in her skirts, for he would not let her go. 'I should never have agreed to it. When I made it, I thought. . .'

'What did you think, Gerard?'

'I thought that either I could prevail on you to break it, or. . .'

'Or?' Her voice was implacable in its cool certainty, but he could feel her betraying body quiver.

Mona Lisa! She was rightly so named. Would he ever know what she thought, felt? She should think—for him! Feel—for him! Not lock herself away.

'I thought. . .that it would not matter. . .that I could look at you. . .think of the Captain. . .and feel nothing. Would feel nothing if you. . .capitulated. . .or if you held off. . .and now. . .'

'Now?'

'Would you have me grovel?' he burst out, looking up at her, to see her looking down at him. Compassion? Was it compassion on her face? Damn her compassion! No, if that were all she had to give he would take that. . .

'Now!' he exclaimed. 'Now I know that every rule by which I live has failed me with you. What do you want? No, don't answer. You have what you want. You have no feelings, are a true whore. The payment at the end of this charade is what you are waiting for, while I, I suffer and burn. No! A true whore would give me what I want, and laugh. Oh, I don't want that either.'

He let go of her skirts, dropped his head into his cupped hands and prayed to be unfeeling Gerard Schuyler again, so that he might leave the house, find any woman, no matter who she was, so that he might lose himself in her, forget the anguish of wanting what he could not have.

Once, he could have behaved so. Not now, never now. In learning what one woman could mean to him, he had learned what all women were, and he could never go lightly among them again, taking what he wanted, regardless of their feelings.

Before, he would have denied that this could happen. He would have believed that if she were to refuse him he would take his revenge on her sex.

Instead, loving truly had changed him, and tomorrow night he was going into the ring to defend her, to punish the man who had tried to blast her reputation publicly when he had failed with her privately. And more, his pride would have it that she was not to know what he was doing for her, for he would not buy her love that way. It must be freely given, or he did not want it.

'Gerard.' She was speaking, still calm; he dropped

his hands away from his burning face, slowly rose, to look down at her now, where before he had looked up in worship.

'Yes?' he said, hopefully.

'Gerard, I would not have you suffer.' How calm she was, but were there fires burning beneath that marble surface? He hoped so, oh, he hoped that she, too, suffered a little as he was suffering. 'But you must understand that. . . I cannot love you. I don't think. . .' and the calm voice trembled '. . .that I can love anyone. I offered the bargain in good faith, because. . .because. . . I thought that you were. . .like me. I was wrong, and I apologise. I didn't mean to hurt you.'

'Flesh and blood,' he said bitterly. 'I have found out that I am flesh and blood. At least you have given me that. Because I have learned to suffer, I have discovered that I am as other men are. . .' He fell silent.

'I could give you what you want. Sell myself to you. . .to make you happy. But I don't think you want that, and I am. . .incapable of giving you more.'

'No —— ' he was passionate ' —I can't believe that. I won't. If I can feel, truly feel for another, as I always thought was impossible, then why shouldn't I make you share my feelings? I always swore I would never beg anything from anyone. Allow me to break my rule by begging you to let me try to. . . make you feel.'

They were close now, and she was not pushing him away, nor turning on her heel to leave him. She had begun to tremble, the lovely mouth was quivering, the beautiful violet eyes were full of tears.

Tears! For him? Or for herself? Did it matter? She was lying. She could feel, he knew it! He moved even closer, and she did not reject him; he held her refulgent eyes with his, orange glowing on violet, let them mix, meld, to make another colour — green. Green was the colour of jealousy, but was it not also the colour of life?

He was not begging her now, nor was he simply taking; he put his hands on her shoulders oh, so gently, not begging, not demanding, his eyes still on hers — until he bent his head and claimed her lips as a prize.

He had felt her shudder as he touched her, but she did not push him away. For one heart-stopping moment, as her mouth softened beneath his, as the shuddering ceased, he thought that he had won, and then the world, the God-dammed world, the world which always claimed him, claimed him again, and the longed-for, almost achieved idyll was shattered.

There was a rapping on the door, a voice, the voice of Timson, apologetic. It had her moving away from him, startled, mouth trembling, eyes wild. 'Sir, there is an urgent telephone call for you; the man would brook no delay.'

And what delay can I brook? thought Gerard savagely, but his answering voice was cool. 'I'll be along in a moment, Timson; tell them to hold the line.'

She had turned away again, had retreated, he knew as soon as he saw her. She was behind her defences, and they would have to be breached all over again, but he knew now, he told himself, what he had to do. Not rough wooing but tenderness; tenderness, would win her, he was sure.

She might say that she could not feel, but he knew that she was wrong. For one moment there she had been liquid beneath him—it was the only word—ready to be loved. Only Timson's intrusion had prevented her from surrender.

Let him deal with Ledward, and he would return to claim her as his prize. Knights of old went into the tourney wearing their mistress's favour, to defend her honour, or to make her the Queen of Love and Beauty. Well, he would take her favour, whether she would or no; and that afternoon, coming home to find that she had not yet returned from a committee meeting at the Wales's London home, Marlborough House, he went into the lovely room where he had so nearly won her, and found her handkerchief, tucked into a small bag with her embroidery, removed it, kissed it, and took it with him to Moidore's dinner party, given to Gerard and his backers on the night before the fight.

Sitting there, joining in the masculine fun, knowing that the handkerchief was in his pocket where he occasionally touched it, a small secret smile on his face, he knew that even the old-time knight could not have felt more for his willing lady than he, Gerard Schuyler, did for his unwilling one.

CHAPTER ELEVEN

'TORRY, whatever is the matter?' It was the evening of the day on which Gerard had bared his soul to Torry. Kate had come into the drawing-room to find her sister-in-law alone, sobbing bitterly, her book and her canvas work abandoned on the sofa beside her.

There was alarm in Kate's voice. She had never seen Torry other than calm, perfectly composed, but the woman before her was unrecognisable.

Shortly before Kate's entry, Torry, who until that moment had remained the sphinx who had allured and defeated Gerard, had given a loud sob, had put down her book and allowed the misery which had been curled inside her like a hard ball to burst free from its bonds and envelop her, as though it were a succubus. Or did she mean incubus? she thought later, the difference between an incubus, which meant that she was enduring a nightmare of oppression, or a succubus, which might mean that she was a kind of wraith which sucked men's souls from them, being obscure in her misery.

She only knew that the tears which she had kept at bay since she had first needed to shed them at the early age of sixteen, and had refused to do so, could no longer be denied. Gerard's hopelessness that morning, the sensation of his hard arms about her, his mouth soft and tender on hers, his living pain at

210

her rejection of him, had pierced the armour which she had worn for nearly twelve years.

And, once pierced, the tears were falling, and who were they falling for, Gerard or herself? She did not know, nor did she care, for abandon was bringing relief. Like a river in flood bursting into a valley to carry away all the debris which lay in its way, her tears were washing away everything which she had lived with for so long. The inability to feel for others, because she could not feel for herself, had been washed away as well.

Living with Gerard, she had made herself a hostage to fortune. And how strange it was that another's pain should crack the shell of indifference which surrounded her, so that her pity had always been given to ideas, causes, and not to the warm and suffering individuals who lay behind the ideas and causes.

And that it should be Gerard, hard, proud, confident Gerard who should unlock her was another mystery. Perhaps it was because he had shown her the vulnerable man beneath his apparently unshatterable self-confidence that his suffering should move her. Since if he could feel so deeply, who had so much, who had denied his humanity with every word and act he committed, then there was no one in the world who was invulnerable — and that included herself.

Dimly, she heard Kate speaking to her, heard the note of alarm in her voice.

'Oh, Torry! What is it? Is there anything I can do? Please, let me help you. Is it Gerard? Has he been unkind?'

At Gerard's name Torry sat up, fetched out her inadequate pocket handkerchief, and began to wipe her streaming eyes. All her bright and cool beauty had gone. Her face was swollen, her damp hair had come down. She tried to speak, but could not do so for sobbing. Twelve years of stoicism, of refusal to show emotion had been destroyed in an instant, and she was incapable of resisting the emotions which swept over her.

'No, not Gerard,' she managed. 'He has not been cruel to me. It is I who have been cruel to him. Oh! Oh! Oh!' And her sobs redoubled, and she began to rock herself to and fro, clutching herself with her arms, as though to feel them about her might give her relief, except that they didn't, and the strange rocking redoubled until Kate took her into her arms and began to croon over her, trying to hide her alarm at the state to which Torry was reduced.

'You? Cruel to Gerard? I don't believe you.'

'Oh, I was, I was,' hiccuped Torry. 'He was so hurt, so miserable, and I did nothing to help him. I rejected him. Oh! Oh! Oh!' And her wails grew louder still, until Kate fetched out her own handkerchief and began to mop up the hot tears which fell like rain.

'And there is nothing I can do, nothing.' She looked earnestly and painfully at Kate. 'I can't tell you, no, I can't tell anyone, but oh, I can't believe what has happened to me, no, no, no. Oh, I love him, and I cannot do anything about it.'

'Love him!' exclaimed Kate. 'You love Gerard! But how can that be a bad thing, make you cry like this? And if you do love him, why were you cruel to him?'

Torry, who had looked for a moment as though she might recover herself, dropped her head in her hands, and the river began to roar down the mountainside again.

'I can't help myself! And then, a moment or two ago, quite out of the blue, I suddenly felt for him, and I knew, I knew. For the first time, I knew that I cared for someone, quite desperately, and I was so unkind to him. Like an inquisitor. . . I know I hurt him cruelly, and once I would not have minded that I had done, but now. . .oh, oh, oh, I know he will hate me, he must, he must. . .' And her wailing grew the louder and she began to rock again.

Kate gave up. She was certain now, quite certain, that Gerard and Torry had never been truly man and wife, something which she had begun to suspect early on in this so-called honeymoon. But since no one else seemed to think so, she had concluded that in her inexperience she might be mistaken. She now knew that she was not.

For a moment she debated whether or not to tell her sister-in-law about tomorrow's fight, but decided against it. It was plain that Torry was distressed over her behaviour towards Gerard, and to learn that he was about to fight Bryce Ledward over her would merely add to her burden.

And if Torry had just confessed that she loved Gerard, she was now also sure—and Torry had just confirmed it, more by what she had not said than what she had—that Gerard loved Torry!

What a pair of ninny noddies they were, thought

Kate prosaically and sensibly, that they did not simply settle the whole thing by going to bed together, and how fortunate that what she felt for Justin and he for her was not so profound and complex as what lay between Torry and Gerard.

Oh, yes, she loved Justin and he loved her, but the strong passion which her brother and his wife felt for one another was something which she instinctively knew she would never experience. Yes, *she* was the one like the Captain, able to stand outside life, not cold-bloodedly, as Torry had tried to do, but warmly, involvedly — but letting others make fools of themselves.

'There, there,' she said, still rocking Torry, whose sobs had begun to subside, once she had confessed her true feelings for her husband. 'Why don't you tell him that you love him?'

'Oh, if it were only so simple,' said Torry, lifting her woebegone face up to meet Kate's kind eyes. 'What a sensible girl you are. And surely, being sensible, knowing my history, why do you think he should believe any such thing? He quite despises his love for me. . .because I am me, if you see what I mean.'

Kate, thinking of Torry's reputation, knew exactly what she meant, but said, 'If Gerard really loves you, what you were shouldn't make any difference to him.'

'So says logic,' sniffed Torry, 'but love isn't logical. It's the Captain, you see. . .' She fell silent, then muttered, 'I shouldn't be telling all this to an unmarried girl of seventeen.'

'Oh, but I'm not your usual unmarried girl of

seventeen,' returned Kate incontrovertibly, 'and I shan't be unmarried long. Justin is winding himself up to make me his countess, and I'm sure I shall say yes. I quite fancy wearing a coronet on the day Albert Edward is crowned—oh, and taking the *pas* before Daisy Gascoyne at every dinner we attend.'

'Don't you love him at all?' asked Torry, forgetting her own miseries on hearing this sane appraisal of what being an English peeress meant to Kate.

'Oh, yes, but not madly, passionately. We are friends, you see, and will deal well together, and we shall be faithful to one another, because to be unfaithful is not sensible, and Justin loves his home, and the country, and we shall breed dogs and farm his acres, and come to London for the season and go home to the children with some relief at the end of it.'

Torry was so fascinated by this that she stopped crying, and said, almost shyly for her, for she knew that Kate had been talking to distract her, 'You will not tell Gerard, will you? About my foolishness and. . .'

'That you love him?' offered Kate practically. 'No, but I think you ought to let him know, in fairness.' Only to see her sister-in-law shrink away.

Wise for her years Kate might be, but she had no idea of the complexities which surrounded Gerard and Torry and how difficult it was for them to break through the nets which bound them. . .

Unaware of all this, Gerard spent the next day preparing himself to meet Bryce Ledward in the ring. He had said and done nothing when he left to

give Torry any idea what he was doing other than
go to the stag party of which he had told her. Kate
had said to him before he left that Torry still had no
idea that he was about to fight Ledward over her,
and that she had warned the other women in their
circle to say nothing of it to her.

It had been strangely hard for him to deceive
Torry, especially with Kate's reproachful eyes
staring at him over the shining plates, the perfect
cutlery, the excellent food which his household,
impeccably run by his new wife, had served up to
him.

Like ashes in his mouth, he thought grimly, then
said again, 'Do not wait up for me, either of you. I
am likely to be far from capable of maintaining
sensible conversation when I reach home.'

Kate stopped him in the hall as he was struggling
into an overcoat held out to him by Timson; she had
made some excuse to leave the table before Torry,
and her voice was now added to the message of her
eyes. Later, thinking of Torry's strange confession
to her, she was to wish that she had defied him, but
at the time the authority which streamed from him
like power from the sun kept her from doing anything other than try to reason with him.

'You have still not told her?' Kate was aware of
Timson silently supporting her, wondered what the
valet knew, what he thought of his master's goings-
on, forgot that as Gerard said curtly,

'No business of yours, Kate; I don't want to
discuss this further.'

He walked to the door; Timson picked up two
pigskin leather bags and followed him, giving Kate

a sympathetic glance. She watched Gerard climb into his motor, watched Timson place the bags on the seat beside him, watched the chauffeur who had saluted him as he climbed aboard drive off, and wondered for which masculine hideaway Gerard was bound.

Turning, she saw Timson's sad eyes on her. He said, face impassive, as though he were informing her of the time of day, 'I shouldn't worry about him, Miss Kate. He usually knows what he is doing.'

Kate ignored this thundering breach of protocol and said passionately, 'Not always, Timson, not always. We are none of us always correct in our actions and judgements.'

'Mr Gerard more than most,' he said quietly, still looking straight ahead, still impassive. 'And he does not want Mrs Gerard to be troubled over this.'

'Is that a warning, Timson, or advice?'

'Oh, I wouldn't presume, Miss Kate,' he said smoothly. 'I think that, like Mr Gerard, you always know what's what.'

For one brief insane moment Kate wondered whether she ought to go to Timson for advice, since he seemed to be more aware of what was happening than anyone else.

Gerard had spent part of each day since he had returned to London working out in a grimy gymnasium in the back streets of Bermondsey where a professional pugilist nicknamed Flash Harry had helped to sharpen him up for the coming contest. The place reminded him of home in its cheerful

raunchiness and lack of any deference to class,
either Gerard's or the proprietor's own.

'Useful feller, ain't yer?' his instructor had said
on his first visit, after discovering that he did not
need to be nearly so tender with Gerard as with the
occasional gent who found his way riverwards.

'Rusty,' Gerard had said briefly and ruefully.
Years ago as a young man he had visited the Bronx
for tuition, and had transformed his performance in
the amateur ring as a result. He had thought himself
fit, but it was only by his third visit that he had
begun to feel ready to take Ledward on.

'Got the killer instinct as well,' his new friend had
said amiably, a grin on his battered face. 'Not many
gents got that.'

'No good fighting without it,' had been Gerard's
riposte, 'and it will have to make up for lack of
practice.'

'Who're yer fightin'?' he had been asked and on
his naming Ledward the pug had looked thoughtful.
'He's useful too, but. . .' and he had eyed the
awesomely compact muscle of Gerard's body
respectfully '. . .not a killer, I would say, but
dangerous. Watch out for tricks.'

Moidore, who had come along on this last morning—he was to act as one of Gerard's seconds—
also looked respectful when Gerard stripped off for
this final training bout. He watched in a little
wonder as Gerard engaged in only a light work-
out—'Mustn't take the edge off yer,' his partner
said. 'I wish I was going to be there tonight.
Couldn't smuggle me in, could yer?'

This interchange took place at the end, when

Gerard, blowing lightly, was having his gloves removed by a dwarf who had once fought the flyweight championship of the world, and who had packed a lethal punch which bore no relationship to his size.

'Tell you all about it when it's over,' said Gerard; the dwarf was now towelling him down, before rubbing oil on his pinkened torso. 'It'll be a pleasure.'

'Confident swine, yer friend,' said Flash Harry to Moidore. He had gained his name in his palmy days when he had dressed like a swell and had escorted posh ladies to the Café Royal where he had met Moidore, who had recommended him to Gerard as a trainer.

'Need to be,' said Gerard, overhearing him, and tossing this offering over his shoulder. Moidore was half amused, half impressed at how laconic his friend had become since they had entered the gym. It was as though someone else had taken Gerard over, someone hard and deadly, and for the first time he wondered whether it was Ledward who was going to get the shock in the evening's bout.

He knew that the betting was heavily against Gerard, and that lunchtime, after he had left Gerard at his London office, he rang his bookmaker and placed a heavy sum on Gerard's winning.

'Stand to lose a lot, my lord,' the bookie had said. 'Sure you want to risk as much as this?'

'Stand to win even more,' replied Moidore, who thought that Gerard's laconic mode must be catching. 'On second thoughts, double it.' He had not told Gerard what he was going to do; he did not want to put his man off, and thought that Gerard would try the harder if he knew that all the money in London was against him, Ledward's prowess as a boxer being so widely known.

Moidore's surprise at Gerard's physique was mirrored in the response of those present in the hall when he entered the ring that night and divested himself of his flashy dressing-gown to reveal that he was wearing equally flashy red satin shorts.

Ledward, smooth in discreet blue, his shorts black, had stripped off to reveal the body of the perfect athlete in the classical tradition. Straight and tall, with wide shoulders, a narrow waist and long, beautifully long legs, he looked ready to be immortalised on the Parthenon, a study by the ancient Greek sculptor Apelles.

Gerard was something else again. Most of the watchers, seeing his size and bulk, had expected him to be soft when stripped, but he was solid, remarkable in quite a different way from Ledward, no narrow waist, a man of compact muscle, no fat at all, and although no one could say that his body lacked impressive proportions it was of quite a different order from Ledward's, particularly in the power of his thighs and calves. If Ledward was a deer, Gerard was a bull.

For one moment, entering the ring, having his gloves laced by Justin Otmoor, his other second, staring at Ledward, a cold stare, wolfish, Gerard wondered what he was doing here, in a foreign country, among men who were from a different class and a different culture.

And then he remembered Torry, and the insult the effete swine opposite to him had put on her, and the vow he had made that he would spoil his pretty face for him, recalled him to his duty. Idly, dispassionately, he let his gaze wander around the hall.

There was a large audience, and the pretence that this was a friendly match governed the whole way it was conducted, although every man in the hall knew the truth, and that this was a fight to a finish between two men who intensely disliked one another over a woman whose reputation was, to say the least, dubious.

No one said this aloud. Betting was vigorous, had been so for some days, and the hall was alive with excitement, and blue with cigar smoke.

The MC, a burly man, wearing an elegant evening suit, called the two men together into the centre of the ring. Facing one another, the contrast between them was marked. Ledward looked the epitome of light, Gerard of darkness. Anticipation had Gerard stooping a little, hunching his splendid shoulders, making the contrast even stronger.

The dislike he felt for Ledward was mirrored in Ledward's eyes as dislike for him. The MC, who had been briefed by Moidore, said, 'Still time to call this off, gents. Apologies are always in order, I understand.'

Both men spoke together, Gerard's rude, 'Not bloody likely,' drowning out Ledward's politer refusal.

'Then, gentlemen, I will inform you of the rules under which this contest will be conducted.' Which he did, at boring length, Gerard, thought — he was anxious to get this over—and when he touched gloves with Ledward in the centre of the ring his grin was the most savage yet.

And yet, when they began, the watching spectators, who had arrived in some anticipation, were acutely disappointed, for Gerard proceeded to behave in a manner which promised no contest at all.

Straight and erect, Ledward danced around the ring, like the figure of a boxer in a book of instruction come to life, his right hand tucked beneath his chin, his left hand extended. He advanced on Gerard, his purpose both plain and fell. And Gerard retreated. Worse, he retreated after such a plodding, flat-footed fashion, that he was almost a bad joke to the watching men. His shoulders were hunched, his chin was on his chest and both hands were tucked close in to his body, so that the view Ledward was getting, although Gerard was almost exactly the same height, was of the top of Gerard's bent head.

A round of this, Ledward advancing, Gerard stolidly retreating, had everyone yawning. 'What the devil are you doing, man?' growled Moidore in exasperation, thinking of the money he had invested in a victory for Gerard. 'He'll take your head off when he catches you.'

'Won't catch me,' mumbled Gerard, who had visibly felt Ledward's growing impatience as he chased his flat-footed enemy around the ring.

'Well, you know best,' sighed Moidore, meaning, of course, that Gerard didn't, and his impatience grew as round two followed round one in being a total write-off.

The hall began to hum, particularly when Ledward, impatient, aimed a flurry of blows at Gerard's head, most of which he evaded by ducking and weaving with a speed and skill that belied his clumsy progress.

'Damn you! Stand up and fight,' roared Ledward at the beginning of round three, when despite beating constant tattoos on the ever-retreating Gerard's ribs, he had not once managed to land a telling punch, and Gerard had not thrown one.

'Damned if I'll oblige you,' snarled Gerard, who by now had the measure of his man and was confident that he could take him as and when he pleased. Neither Ledward nor the watching men, who had begun to halloo at Gerard for not fighting, knew anything of the new style of pugilism which was beginning to transform Yankee boxing, and of which Gerard, with his remarkable physique, had become a master, as his Bermondsey trainer, who had visited the States, had instantly recognised.

Round four, he thought grimly, was when he would make his strike. Ledward would by then be thoroughly frustrated and would make mistakes, and he ended round three in the heavy-footed plod which had been his hallmark since the fight began. Moidore muttered fretfully in his ear in the interval between rounds three and four, 'I hope to God, Gerard, you know what you're doing.'

'Watch me,' said Gerard, and as he rose to his feet he flung over his shoulder at Moidore, 'The last, Moidore, positively the last you'll have to endure, I promise you.'

Ledward had also decided that this was to be the last round. Face grim, still erect, ready to unleash his straight left on Gerard, he advanced on him — to meet a tornado, or, as some awed watchers later said, a windmill.

Gerard was suddenly everywhere. His flat-footed plod had gone, but, still crouched, he unleashed a rain of blows, not to Ledward's head but to his body. Heavy punishing blows which Ledward could not avoid, and which left their marks on his torso; nor could he touch Gerard, whose bobbing and weaving was now purposeful, not to say lethal.

Uproar reigned, as the bout was transformed, and as Gerard followed up his punishing blows to the body with as many to the face. Ledward went reeling backwards, the effortless superiority which he had exhibited in nearly every bout he had ever fought gone.

Never before had he encountered a man who fought as a professional might fight and, worse, after a manner which was unknown to him. The savagery of Gerard's attack was equalled only by its accuracy. He had promised himself he would ruin Ledward's pretty face, and he proceeded to do so, remorselessly.

Years ago, in his late teens, when he had first sought help to improve his performance, the pro who had taught him had said that he could make a champion of him — 'If you weren't a rich man's soft son, that is,' he had added drily.

The taunt, for taunt it was, had angered Gerard

so much that he had nearly taken up the man's challenge, but always, later, at the back of his mind was the thought that one day what he had learned might prove useful.

Now, under a rain of blows, Ledward went down, to rise again and again, and Gerard thought later that, whatever other attribute Ledward might lack, at least he possessed courage. But the thought did not stop him from taking Ledward apart, and half the crowd were baying for blood, and the other half for the suddenly unequal contest to be stopped. Moidore was not the only one to guess that Gerard was refraining from landing a knock-out blow, but was systematically punishing Ledward for the insult to Torry.

Finally, almost at the round's end, the referee parted the two men. Ledward, dazed, was rising from the canvas, face swollen and bleeding, to meet Gerard, who was wading towards him yet again, to be stopped by the referee's right arm; his left was holding Gerard back.

'Enough,' the referee said, as a white towel came sailing in from Ledward's seconds, appalled at what was happening to their man.

Gerard, having wound himself up, found it hard to stop. The rage which had consumed him ever since the fatal breakfast at Moidore Castle was not quite burned away. With difficulty, he stepped back, allowed the referee to direct him towards his seat in the corner of the ring after holding up his hand to signal his victory, and then watched as Ledward was half carried to his stool by his backers.

'Good God, man——' Moidore was respectful

'—who taught you to fight like that?' And then, with a grin, 'You've saved my bacon, and I've made a hundred thousand on you. I stood to lose a fortune if Ledward had won.'

'The Bronx,' said Gerard. 'I learned in a boxing booth in the Bronx from a champion.' He was suddenly exhausted. 'And pity the poor devils who've lost fortunes over this night's work,' he added. He was light-headed, and thought savagely, He'll not badmouth her again, and nor will any man.

Privately Moidore was thinking the same thing. Gerard had shown him a man who would stop at nothing to repay an insult. 'Be ready,' he warned his friend, who might not be completely *au fait* with English customs. 'Protocol says that you must shake hands at the end, however badly you feel about each other. No, keep your gloves on, that's the way of it. He's ready to leave the ring, but God knows what he'll feel like tomorrow.'

'Dreadful, I hope.' Gerard was not mollified, but under Moidore's prodding he stood up and advanced to the centre of the ring, where Ledward, now recovered, face battered, disfigured and sullen, the marks of Gerard's fists on his body, touched gloves with him at the MC's bidding.

Well, that's that, Gerard thought, and a good thing it's over, and for a moment he didn't know whether he was glad or sorry at what he had done, only knew that it had had to be done.

And then, as he was preparing to leave, he heard Ledward call his name, and turned towards him, body relaxed, for he was now tired beyond belief through exertion and achieved success.

'Yes?' Gerard said. 'What is it?' Thinking that in an access of public school chivalry Ledward was about to offer some kind of peace.

But quite the contrary, for as he stood there, hands and body lax, Ledward said, 'Damn you to hell, you damned Yankee peasant, and your wife, too,' and struck him, as hard as he could, on his unguarded chin, so that Gerard dropped like a stone to lie helpless on the canvas, outraged noise filling the hall, and a shocked Moidore having to be restrained from attacking Ledward, before falling to his knees to discover what damage had been done to his friend.

Justin Otmoor, who had also watched this final turn with horror, roared at Ledward, who stood there, gazing at his fallen enemy with triumphant dislike written on his face, 'By God, Ledward, there's not a house in England that will receive you after such an unprovoked attack,' only to meet Ledward's indifferent stare.

Later, when he realised the enormity of what he had done, for he had publicly broken the code by which the society of which he was a part lived, Ledward was to regret his action, but at the time he was filled only with a savage glee, to see the damned Yankee brought low.

Moidore, satisfied that Gerard was not seriously hurt and was immediately trying to rise, turned to Ledward's shocked seconds who were trying to lead their man out of the ring, stood up, face fierce, and added his voice to Justin's. 'Take him away,' he

said, 'out of the sight of honest men. You are
finished, Ledward, you understand me? Every door
will be closed to you.

He turned back to Gerard, who was now propped
up against Justin's knee, and was ruefully rubbing
his bruised jaw. 'Come on, old man,' he said gently.
'Let's find a doctor for you in case you have concussion, and then I'll see you home.'

'Home,' muttered Gerard groggily. 'Don't want
to go home. She. . . Torry. . .mustn't know. . .
mustn't see me like this. . .' He lapsed into silence.

'Not know!' exclaimed Moidore, astonished. He
assumed that Gerard's mind was wandering.
'Dammit, man, she must know. She's your wife!'

'No.' Gerard tried to stand up, but, the effort too
much for him, he fell back, and said with difficulty,
'No, I say. Take me anywhere but home; I don't
want her distressed by this,' and suddenly putting
out a hand he grasped Moidore by the lapel of his
evening dress coat. 'Promise me, Tom, promise me.'

Moidore regarded him dubiously. 'Oh, very well,
if you say so. I'll take you to my place off Brook
Street. You'll be private there. But what do I tell
her? She's bound to wonder why you don't go home
tonight.'

All Gerard wanted was to make sure that Torry
was not hurt by any of this. 'Tell her. . .tell her. . .
that I'm called out of town, on business, anything.
Only, promise.' And when Moidore gave him a
grudging yes he uttered a great sigh and, relieved,
allowed Justin to help him up and lead him away,
applause for his performance following him to his
dressing-room.

CHAPTER TWELVE

How, when and where she was going to let Gerard know of her changed feelings for him Torry did not know, nor did she even know whether she could give Gerard what he so plainly desired—herself. She did not even want to know whether he was in love or in lust with her. Whatever his feelings, hers for him had become paramount. Living with him, coming to know him intimately, her admiration for him had grown daily.

And when had admiration ripened into love? Was it recently, in London, or at Moidore, or had it been the day when she had first met him, or the day when he had sat in her office, her gun trained on him, mocking her, his impudence making his harsh face attractive, or the evening when he had quoted Herrick to her. . .or. . .or. . .?

She did not know, and when he did not come home on the night of Moidore's cousin's stag party her disappointment was great, and then when he did not return on the next day, she having merely received a message from Lord Moidore that Gerard was called out of town, and did not know when he would return, she faced another dreadful possibility.

Had she lost him, driven him away? Had she, by her conduct to him on the morning when he had begged her to make their marriage a true one, turned him away from her for the last time? Was he comforting himself with Daisy Gascoyne or with one of the many other women whom she knew he attracted? And if he were, was it not her fault? He was not to know how difficult it was for her to contemplate being his wife, any man's wife. . .

Outwardly calm, inwardly boiling, fear that she had lost him making her feel sick, it needed all her fabled self-control to keep herself from crying out, screaming, hurling herself at Kate again.

On the afternoon of the third day she and Kate were due to visit Marlborough House. Torry was on one of the Princess's committees for the relief of poor children, yet another society bazaar was in the offing, and Mrs Schuyler's valuable services were needed.

Kate had also been invited to spend the afternoon with a group of young people, children of the stars of London society who made up the committee, and afterwards the two parties would take tea together.

'Do you feel well enough to go, Torry?' asked Kate anxiously. Torry's calm could not conceal from her the distress her sister-in-law was in.

Wherever was Gerard? Kate's thoughts were feverish. What was he doing? Was he badly hurt? Surely not; Lord Moidore had told her that he was staying with a friend and that the doctor they had summoned was observing him, he had a light concussion, but it was thought better that he did not exert himself by going home. Kate could only imagine Gerard's annoyance at being compelled to rest, and also knew that he could not yet be quite himself if he were causing Torry undue anxiety by staying away so long.

Daisy Gascoyne and Justin had told her of the fight, and all society except Mrs Gerard Schuyler knew that Bryce Ledward, after being humiliated by Gerard, had disgraced himself irretrievably by his attack on him, unprovoked and made without warning.

Kate had half a mind to tell Torry the truth, but she had promised Gerard that she would keep quiet, and so she must, but it was against her better judgement, and the look she gave Torry when they parted in the vestibule was a worried one.

The room the committee met in was what Torry would have called the fussy end of interior decorating, pretty, but full of frills, scent bottles, little ornaments, frivolous books, small tables and innumerable photographs of the Prince and Princess of Wales's family in silver frames scattered about the room.

On the wall, facing Torry, was a portrait in oils of Albert Edward when he had been a young man. He was vaguely handsome, with prominent blue eyes, but already showing the tendency to run to fat which made him so unlike the tall and handsome man his father, the late Prince Consort, had been.

All day the feeling that something was being kept from her had been stronger in Torry than ever. She had the feeling of being watched, that when she looked around eyes slid away from her, and people spoke in whispers. Once, she thought that she heard Gerard's name, and wondered vaguely if she was becoming mentally ill: she must be imagining things.

The meeting was a busy one. She found herself asked to do a great deal of management, for the women present had discovered already how competent she was, and that her years in New York had fitted her to organise and to command.

The Princess of Wales finally closed the small notebook before her, looked around the table and said, 'Thank you, ladies. I am most grateful to you all for your attendance and your co-operation.' She began to rise, but her lady-in-waiting leaned forward and whispered in her ear, so that she sat down again, smiled at Torry, and added, 'Oh, I had quite forgot, a word with you, Mrs Gerard Schuyler, before we adjourn for tea, which I gather is waiting for us in the blue drawing-room.'

The sense of being watched was stronger than ever. Torry rose herself and bowed as the Princess walked over to her. 'I will not detain you long, Mrs Schuyler. I suppose that, like me, you are only too eager for a little refreshment, but I felt that I had to assure you that in your time of trouble my and the Prince's thoughts are with you. We hope that your husband will soon be restored, and you will be pleased to learn that the Prince has expressed his displeasure plainly at what Mr Ledward has done, by barring him from his company in future. No, he will never be received by either of us again.

'Please give Mr Schuyler my best wishes and His Highness's hope that he will soon be quite restored. It was very brave of you to attend today, but I know that you would always do what you see as your duty.'

Torry stared numbly at her. What on earth could the Princess be talking about? Gerard hurt? There was a buzzing in her ears, but since the Princess

seemed to think that she, Torry, knew what was
what, then she must keep her wits about her. She
found herself bowing again and saying, in quite a
normal voice, 'Accept our thanks for your gracious
condescension, madam, and the Prince's too. I
know that I speak for my husband as well as myself.'

This ambiguous and time-serving answer, for had
the Princess chosen to question her Torry could not
have offered any sensible reply, seemed to be satisfactory. Alexandra, Princess of Wales, still beautiful, still elegant in middle age, moved away, and for
once Torry was grateful for her celebrated vague-
ness. A more acute person might have realised how
much at a loss Mrs Schuyler was.

The Princess gone, Torry found herself feeling
faint, a sensation which accompanied her into the
drawing-room, where she made straight for Kate,
who was talking to Daisy Gascoyne.

'Kate!' she said, and the note in her voice had
Kate swinging around, alarmed, Daisy Gascoyne,
too. 'And Daisy,' said Torry, whose colour was
coming and going. 'Is there somewhere private we
may go? It is urgent that I speak to you both.'

Daisy, a *habituée* of Marlborough House, said
rapidly, 'There is an ante-room over there. Are you
ill, Victoria? You look ill.'

'Not ill,' said Torry, equally rapidly, 'only angry.'
For anger was beginning to succeed nausea, and she
followed Kate and Daisy into a small room as fussily
furnished as the rest of the house.

'Kate, Daisy,' said Torry, even before Daisy had
closed the double doors, 'I must ask you to tell me
immediately what Gerard has been doing such that

the Princess has commiserated with me, and why and how it is connected with Bryce Ledward. I have been deceived, things have been kept from me, and it is no good staring at me, Kate. I mean to know.'

'Oh, Torry,' said Kate sorrowfully, 'I knew Gerard was wrong to keep things from you,' and she began to tell her sister-in-law of all that had passed since Gerard had thrown his bacon and eggs into Ledward's face.

'His breakfast, in Bryce's face.' And despite her worry and distress Torry began to laugh; she could almost see Gerard doing such an outrageous thing. 'But why?' And then, when both women stared at her, she said, 'Oh, yes, of course,' and coloured. 'So, then they fought, and after he had been beat, he hurt Gerard, wilfully. Where is Gerard? I want to go to him. Why has no one told me of this? No, you need not answer that, either. It was Gerard, wasn't it? Trying to save me pain.'

She said nothing more, only sat down abruptly; her legs seemed to be failing her. Kate said rapidly, 'I'm not sure where he is. Lord Moidore took him away and sent for a doctor. He didn't want you to know what was happening, and swore us all to secrecy, Daisy as well. Everyone has been so good; Justin has been a positive tower of strength, hasn't he, Daisy?'

Daisy nodded, and ex-mistress and wife stared at one another numbly. 'Moidore says that he is not really hurt,' Daisy offered. 'I have been so worried that. . .that I knew why Gerard did not want you to know until the whole wretched business was over. I never did like Bryce Ledward, and it was a truly rotten thing to do. Such a cad. None of us will ever receive him again.'

Which was Ledward's epitaph, Torry thought, and then Kate said earnestly, 'I don't think Gerard will be away much longer; Lord Moidore told me today that he seems much better, and is getting very cross about the doctor's making him rest. . .'

'I can imagine.'

Torry had recovered herself. She rose, smiled at the two women. 'We are breaching all protocol, I think. We had better return to the others before the Princess thinks we are hatching a new Gunpowder Plot.' And she led the way to the door, immaculate as usual, in bronze silk, her carriage as graceful and assured as ever, all signs of her recent distress gone.

Daisy took Kate by the arm and whispered to her as Torry passed from their sight, 'I was determined to hate her, you know, because of *him*, but she is quite remarkable, a match for him in every way. I wonder what she is thinking, what she will say to him when he at last returns?'

Kate began to laugh. 'Oh, I would rather not know, I think. Gerard needed someone like her. Anyone weak he would have danced on and reduced to cinders, but Torry. . .' And she shook her head, and went to drink tea, quite demure, the model of every *jeune fille* there ever was, as Torry was the model of every perfect wife!

'I don't give a. . .' roared Gerard indignantly and obscenely. 'I'm going home today. You've been a brick, Moidore, an absolute brick, to give me refuge and keep the fools away, but I know I'm better now, and I must go home. Torry will think I've run off with Daisy Gascoyne, or done something equally unforgivable, and the worst effects of that swine's blow seem to have worn off.' And he rubbed his jaw experimentally.

'None of which,' he added, 'means that I'm less than grateful to you for your kindness, Moidore, although I know I don't sound like it!'

'You sound like Gerard Schuyler feeling better,' retorted Moidore affectionately. 'And I agree: stay away much longer and your wife will begin to worry about you for quite the wrong reasons. And, Gerard,' he added, as Gerard, a triumphant grin on his face, began to make for his bedroom to abandon the nightwear, dressing-gown and slippers to which he had been confined since he had been brought to Moidore's tiny *pied à terre* off Brook Street, kept for the occasional ladybird Moidore ran, and used for other, business purposes as well, 'you really ought to tell Victoria what you have been doing. She's a strong woman, you know. Won't faint, or have the vapours,' but Gerard's face set in obstinate lines, and Moidore began to laugh. 'Oh, do go and get dressed; no talking to you with that expression on you.'

Gerard reached home. The first person he saw, other than the butler who ushered him in, was Timson, coming down the stairs, one of Gerard's frock-coats in his hand.

Gerard, pulling off his greatcoat, having put down his bags — he had refused Moidore's offer of a footman to accompany him home — said, 'Do you happen to know if Mrs Schuyler is at home?' He had a sudden desperate desire to see her, to reassure her as to his absence.

'Madame and Miss Kate are out, sir, at Marlborough House, and will not be early back,' said Timson smoothly. He had laid down the coat he was carrying on a table in the black and white flagged hall, took Gerard's greatcoat from him, and when Gerard made to pick up his bags again said reproachfully, 'Sir, allow me. You do not yet appear fit. You would care for tea, or something stronger, served in your rooms, I suggest.'

Gerard was about to tell Timson what to do with his suggestions, graphically, when he suddenly felt as weary as he undoubtedly looked.

'Oh, very well,' he said ungraciously. 'If you must act as my nursemaid, you must.' And, allowing Timson to relieve him of everything, he walked slowly upstairs, followed by Timson's soothing comments to the effect that sir must have had a bad few days since his. . .recent experience.

Gerard only just refrained from calling down some rude comments on over-officious valets, but had to confess, when Timson arrived in his private drawing-room, a footman and a maid in tow, carrying trays of tea, sandwiches and a splendid selection of cakes, that to half lie on the sofa enjoying it was a soothing experience.

Timson stayed to make up the fire, and watched his master's grey face turn rosy.

'You have all you wish, sir,' he said gravely, making for the door, where he hovered gracefully for a moment, like an elephantine butterfly.

'Tell me, Timson,' said Gerard, Wedgwood cup and saucer put down, his plate laden with cucumber sandwiches, thinly cut. 'Why do I get the impression that you are bursting to confide in me? Shouldn't it be the other way around? That I confide in you?'

Timson sighed. 'I am sorry to be so obvious, sir. I suppose I ought immediately to have congratulated you on your sterling showing against that apology for a gentleman. I am only sorry that we are not still at Moidore so that the servants' hall there could have had a dinner to celebrate his downfall. Most gratifying.'

Gerard surveyed him warily. He had hired Timson when he had been penniless and abandoned in New York, his previous master having lost everything in one of the city's gaming clubs. Gerard had been twenty-one at the time, already worldly-wise, about to start on his piratical career. 'And is that all? All that damned hovering for that?'

'Not quite, sir. I should also say how delighted the staff are that you defended madam so successfully. You will allow me to say that we all — I know I speak for my fellows — respect your choice of a wife, a most estimable lady. . .'

'And?' prompted Gerard, who was beginning to enjoy himself, and was quizzing Timson between wolfish bites at his sandwiches. 'Do go on, Timson; knowing you, I am sure that there is more.'

'And, sir, in the circumstances, I think that perhaps I ought to tell you of something of which you may not be aware, if you will pardon the liberty, sir.'

'I've pardoned so many liberties of yours,' was

Gerard's only answer, 'that I am sure I can grant you one more. Continue, before I beat it out of you.'

'It concerns your wedding-night, sir.' Timson was all deferential respect. 'If you will allow. I was aware that you took a case of the best Nuits-St-Georges to bed with you that night — a strange choice, I thought. I could not but observe that you sought comfort from the Nuits, rather than madam. I took the liberty then, as I took the liberty now, to go to your room at about two in the morning, to see if I could be of assistance.'

He thought Gerard's eye on him was dangerous; he continued hastily, 'I suppose, sir, from several things which you have said to me, that your memory of that night is a little faulty. When I arrived, you were, to say the least of it, dreadfully foxed, quite helpless — most unlike you — but. . . I was not needed. Madam appeared to be well capable of looking after you. She was not aware of my presence, and I never seek, sir, to obtrude in your private life. When I was sure that she was capable of. . .wrestling you into bed, I retired.

'I believe, sir, from what you have subsequently said, that you thought that I was your Good Samaritan that night, but, alas, much though I should have liked to render you that service, I was forestalled. It was your lady wife who cared for you. I thought that you would like to know.'

Gerard had stopped eating. He put down his sandwich which had become stuck in mid-air in his suddenly nerveless hand. He remembered little of that long night; he had assumed, if he had assumed anything, that the person who had held his head, cleaned him up, undressed him and put him to bed was Timson, and had half hinted so to his valet, grudgingly thanked him.

Trying to remember, he recalled the soft voice, the warm cheek against his. . . Torry! It had been Torry!

'You are telling me the truth. It was Mrs Schuyler who. . .'

'I would not lie to you, sir.' Timson was all wounded integrity. 'It was she who ministered to you. And seeing how nobly you defended her, it occurred to me that you ought to know how much she is worth defending. A kind lady, madam. A lady in every sense. One cannot say that of many. You will forgive my impertinence, sir.'

He moved to the door, turned at it to say, 'You would like some hot water, sir, for another cup of tea. I fear that your present one may have grown cold while we spoke.'

Gerard, whose thoughts were far away, came to himself with a start. 'Yes. . .no, Timson. I should like something stronger. A good red wine perhaps. I'm sorry I should have got drunk on Nuits-St-Georges when methylated spirits would have done as well. I wonder that you did not reproach me for that.'

'A lesser master, sir, and I would not have hesitated. But you, like madam, are always considerate. Will that be all?'

'Oh, I'd say that was quite enough, wouldn't you, Timson?' Gerard's grin was broad, but his mind was far away. So, his graceful and elegant wife had performed the most menial services for him on their wedding-night, and he had not so much as known, and therefore had never thanked her.

He was constantly discovering new things about the woman his grandfather had wished on him, and he wondered what there was still to learn!

Presumably there was still much to learn about Timson as well, for as he ghosted out of the door he turned to give his master one last piece of wisdom, unasked for, and the more surprising for that.

'If I may say so, Mr Gerard, sir, I think that I ought to recommend to you an old maxim which a previous master of mine always found of use. Appearances may be deceptive — but I suppose that you, of all people, do not need to be told that!'

Torry and Kate were late back from Marlborough House, and the butler who came towards them, and took Kate and Torry's parasols and shawls from them, said urbanely, 'Mr Schuyler is home again, madam. I thought you would like to know.'

Before Torry could answer, Kate said hurriedly, 'Oh, good. Don't wait for me, Torry. I'm sure that, in the circumstances, you would like to greet Gerard as soon as possible.'

Torry inclined her head, said nothing, but moved calmly up the stairs towards her rooms. She had no intention of seeing Gerard immediately; she needed to think carefully about what she would say to him when next she met him, her thoughts having been in turmoil since she had discovered how fiercely and gallantly he had defended her good name.

She passed Timson on the stairs, who bowed

gravely and said in his most colourless manner, 'Shall I inform Mr Gerard that you are home, madam?'

She gave him rather more than she had given Kate; she stopped, smiled at him vaguely, and said coolly, 'Oh, I think not, Timson. I am rather tired and would like to refresh myself. Time enough for me to see him later.'

Timson's answering bow was irreproachably neutral. 'As you wish, madam.' And, unknown to her, he watched her all the way up the stairs, a benevolent smile for once cracking his impassive face.

Gerard's body, particularly his torso, was still sore, and he had a slight residual headache, he discovered, as he levered himself into his formal evening dress without Timson's help. He had sent the valet away—something which he occasionally did—after Timson had indicated to him the complete set of clothing laid out for him on the bed, yet another reproachful look on his face, but Gerard needed to be alone, to think up a useful plan of campaign which would bring Torry into his bed.

Lying on the sofa at Moidore's hideaway, he had come to terms with himself and his feelings for her. No more dashing assaults, but instead loving kindness, and an endeavour to persuade her that what he wanted most to do was protect her from the cruel world.

Never mind what she had been to the Captain and the others; it was what she might feel for him which was all important. He was struggling with his black tie, and damning his clumsiness, when the door opened, and he heard her voice.

'May I come in, Gerard?'

He could see her approaching him in the mirror, after he had given her a hoarse, 'Of course,' and, to distract himself, added, 'And you may do something about this tie for me; I seem to be all thumbs this evening.'

She was not wearing one of her classic evening dresses, but a tea-gown in cream and the palest cinnamon, a supple and flowing thing, informal, and her hair, instead of being dressed high, was loosely arranged, finishing in a great knot at the nape of her neck.

Her expression was so enigmatic that he could see why A. J. Balfour had called her Mona Lisa. She stopped before him; he bent a little so that she might take the black tie and begin to knot it carefully, saying as she did so, 'If it is not to your liking, Gerard, tell me, and I will do it again.'

She was so near to him that the essential scent of her was strong in his nostrils, paralysing him, so that when he did not reply she said, the tie in her hands, 'Your business went well, Gerard, I trust?'

'My business. . .' he began hesitantly, forgetting the lie which he had made Moidore tell her to explain his absence.

'Yes, the business which called you from town. I take it that it was urgent, seeing that you left so quickly, and without warning.'

She stepped back, admired her handiwork, and added coolly, 'I see that it must have been onerous. You look very tired. You must not overdo things, Gerard. Even the strongest of us may pay a price for that,' and she looked him in the eye, her smile more engimatic than ever.

Gerard found himself trembling at her nearness, the beautiful picture which she presented of cool and controlled elegance, even in her informal wear — which had him saying, 'You do not intend to dine with me, madam? You are not dressed for formal dining.'

Her smile was dazzling. 'After your exertions, Gerard, I would have thought that you might have preferred not to dress formally but to eat alone with me, in either your room or mine, without ceremony or servants. You look as though you need to be troubled as little as possible.'

Did she know? Had she been told? There was something about her, not only the slight mockery of her smile but the very way in which she was holding herself, which troubled him.

She had moved away from him as she spoke and he followed her, taking her gently by the arms, saying, 'And what exactly do you mean by that, Mrs Schuyler. I have had Timson in here talking in riddles, and out of them. Are you riddling me, madam? And why?'

It was Torry's turn to tremble. She had once thought that provoking Gerard was like prodding a tiger with a stick, and she had been quite consciously speaking with a double meaning, and, being Gerard, he had not answered her in like manner, but had cut straight through to what he thought was the heart of the matter.

'Why should I speak to you in riddles, Gerard? I have no need to do so, have I? Your life being such an open book, I mean. Unless you have been writing something in that book, Gerard, of which I know nothing.'

Oh, she did know, he was sure of it. Had Kate told her? But, of course, there were a hundred who might have told her, and after the fight had probably taken pleasure in doing so.

He tightened his grip on her, bent his head, and kissed her, not on the face, but in the hollow at the base of her neck, where a pulse trembled, and trembled the faster because of the gentleness of the kiss.

She made no effort to pull away; neither did she co-operate with him. He lifted his head, and Torry saw the golden flecks flaring in his dark amber eyes as he said, 'And do you always tell me what you have written in your book, Victoria? What you wrote in it on our wedding-night, for example.'

This did surprise her, he was pleased to see. So far, the initiative had rested with her, but now it had passed to him.

And despite himself, because he wanted to go slowly, her nearness, her softness, the informality of her dress, and the knowledge when he had pulled her to him that she was wearing no carapace of corsets beneath it, to come between the softness of her body and his, had roused him, so that he had begun to sweat gently and his breathing was becoming affected.

'Our wedding-night? I was not aware that anything had happened of which you do not know.'

'Now, Mrs Schuyler, a man who drinks himself into near insensibility is hardly aware of whose kind hands held his head for him while he vomited, who cleaned and stripped him, and dragged him into his bed. Did you perform those offices for me, madam? And why should you have done so?'

Torry made no effort to move from his constraining arms, though he could feel how her body trembled beneath him.

'Common humanity, sir, common humanity.'

'Ah,' said Gerard, gently savage, 'so you are human after all, Mrs Schuyler. There have been times when I have doubted it,' and he bent his head to kiss her again, and this time he did not stop at once but, starting again with the delightful hollow in her neck, he let his lips travel upwards until he found her mouth — and still she did not pull away from him.

Only when at last it was he who pulled away he found her smiling up at him, oh, so innocently, and saying, 'It does not hurt you to kiss me, then, Gerard? Your. . .overwork. . .has not left you too sensitive? You must tell me if you find too much contact. . .distressing.'

'Oh, you witch,' he said thickly, for his self-control was beginning to slip. 'You know, don't you, what I have been about this last week? Who told you? Was it Kate? I asked her not to.'

He held her a little away as he spoke, and the smile she gave him when he had finished speaking was pure delight. He had seldom seen her so easy with him. 'Don't blame Kate. She was as quiet as the grave. . .quieter. It was the Princess of Wales who let the cat out the bag, by accident — you know how vague she is — and then I compelled Kate and

Daisy Gascoyne to tell me what you had done. Why did you do it, Gerard, why?'

Gerard had never thought to be shy. But the beautiful eyes looking at him so gravely had that effect on him. He hung his head like a green boy and growled, 'I could have killed the cur for the way he spoke of you at Moidore. I ached to have to wait to half kill him in the ring.'

'And then he attacked you, and hurt you,' she finished. And, to his astonishment, she put out her hand to touch his strong chin, the chin which Ledward had struck, still bruised and a little swollen. She stroked it gently. 'You did it for my sake, Gerard, for me?'

It was neither a statement nor a question, but something between the two, and when, head still hanging, because to be more definite might mean that he would go too fast for her, although she was now going fast with him, he muttered, 'For you, Torry, for you,' she took his chin in both hands and kissed him gently on the mouth——

For Gerard to give a deep groan and change the kiss to one which was fierce and powerful. Moved by something elemental which had begun to stir in him when she took the initiative, he clutched her to him, and when the long and passionate kiss was over he said, 'Oh, Torry, I love you so. I would do anything for you, anything. I want to love you, and to protect you. Damn the Captain, damn everything; nothing matters but that. . .' And he found himself saying something else, something which he had never thought to say to any woman. 'I love you, my darling; be my wife, I beg you, my true wife.'

And he dropped his head to claim her mouth so fiercely that she moaned beneath him, and when he released her she sighed,

'Oh, Gerard, yes, if that is what you want, but do be gentle with me, I beg of you.'

And if he was a little astonished at such a plea from one with such a history — and in the cynical mode which he had abandoned he might have questioned it, or thought that it was a ploy by which she excited her lovers — he took it at face value, said hoarsely, 'Oh, I will try, my love,' and began to unpin her lovely hair so that it fell about her shoulders, held her face for a moment, and then dropped his hands to part her tea-gown, to pull it down to discover, as he had hoped, that she was ready for him, no barriers between the pair of them.

For a timeless moment they stood there, his mouth on hers, his hands exploring her body, until impatiently he said, 'If this is what you want, then not here, not here,' and, lifting her easily, he strode with her to his bedroom, holding her in one strong arm as he first kicked the door to behind him, and then locked it, before laying her on the bed, her gown falling from her, to show him that beneath it she was as lovely as he had hoped, a vision in alabaster, faintly tinged with pink, her nipples like the buds of tiny carnations lost in a vision of cream, like sea whipped up into foam around the island of Paphos, the goddess Venus's island of love ——

For him to join her there, ripping off the tie which she had so lately fastened for him, his shirt, to reveal the strong body which had surprised the audience at the fight, revealing his heavily muscled back and chest, the black mat of curling hair which began at his throat and narrowed down to his trousers, which he also removed, showing her at last the full power and the strength of him.

She gave a little cry as, kneeling on the bed, he took her in his arms, his face so alive and fierce, the yellow eyes burning with such fire, that as he began to stroke and caress her again, his own arousal hard against her, she hid her face in his broad chest and said, voice muffled, 'Oh, Gerard, I'm frightened,' and she was trembling, and whether it was passion or fear which she felt the most neither of them knew.

Well, if it pleased her, the married woman, the lover of his grandfather, to act the frightened virgin, then he would not deny her, and, hearing her plea, he held her still for a moment, whispering into her hair, 'Oh, I shall never hurt you Torry, never,' and knew, at last, that for him love meant not only passion but also an overwhelming desire to protect, to fight off anything which might hurt his mate, or the cubs which he hoped she would give him.

Slowly, slowly, he made love to her, with a patience which he did not know he possessed, and slowly, slowly, her body melted beneath his, and the shiverings were, at last, not those of fear but of desire, so that finally her body wanted and welcomed his.

Gerard found himself using his voice as well as his hands and body to soothe her, and then to rouse her, as though it were a frightened mare he was gentling, like the one which he had tamed when he was a boy.

Just as he had had to woo the animal, to distract its fear, he found himself doing the same with her. Overwhelmingly, the need to do so fired him, so that his own wish to take her straight away was fuelled by the very pains he was taking to reassure her that he would not.

He stroked her long flanks, the perfect breasts, said in her ear, 'Touch me, Torry, touch me, love me as I love you,' so that slowly, slowly, her hands were on him, and as he comforted and reassured her she did the same for him, as though both were virgin, faced with love for the first time, and not absolutely certain what to do, except that the blind demands of nature were telling Torry, as they told Gerard, who needed no telling, that what was wanted was union, loss of the self in another.

All that was left in the world was Torry and Gerard; the room, their pasts, the misunderstandings and doubts which surrounded them were of no moment, only the body reigned, and finally Torry cried, her voice blurred with passion, 'Oh, Gerard, please, Gerard. . .please,' and did not know for what she asked.

And at that demand, the demand of every loving woman to the man who was loving her, Gerard finally cast off the shackles which had bound him, seeing that she was ready and what he wanted she finally wanted.

He could have given an exultant shout as he entered her, except. . .except. . .madly, and improbably, he could not do so without forcing her, hurting her, for the miming of virginity was not mime at all—she had never known another man, and, even in his delirium of desire and pleasure at what he was discovering, for a moment Timson's words flashed through his head — 'Appearances may be deceptive'! — even as such pleasure as he had never known before overwhelmed him, and swept words and thoughts away. Gerard had found his true destiny at last.

The pain which Torry felt when her marriage was at last consummated was as nothing to the ecstasy which followed it. Her involuntary cry, almost of rejection, was succeeded by her cries of pleasure, and she clutched Gerard as fiercely to her as he clasped her to him. The fear which had consumed her ever since she had decided to go to Gerard and give him what he wanted was burned away in the realisation that what he wanted she wanted too, and that together they had, as the marriage ceremony said, become one flesh.

Oh, that such ecstasy need not be so short was the feeling of both of them, as Gerard finally fell across Torry, to lie, his head in her hands, panting and gasping, and, after a time, to turn her above him, so that he might look up at her, not down, feeling the length of her body on his, seeing that desire had blurred her features, as it had his.

Seeing, too, her face change, as she bent to kiss him to thank him, and that alone was enough to rouse him again, so that slowly, slowly, on this second occasion he was able to take his time, and at the end of it they fell asleep, exhausted in each other's arms.

*   *   *

Downstairs, Kate looked restlessly at the clock, and sighed. She had put dinner back twice, the kitchen would be in ferment, and still there was no sign of Gerard and Torry. She debated going up to Torry's rooms, but instinct forbade it. She walked out of the drawing-room into the vestibule, where she found Timson doing what he did best — hovering.

'Oh, Timson,' she said inanely. 'There you are!'

He bowed. 'Exactly so, Miss Kate. Might I suggest that you order dinner for yourself? I think that sir and madam will not be down tonight. I have the distinct impression that supper in Mr Gerard's rooms will be all that they require. I will so inform the kitchen.'

'Thank you, Timson,' said Kate, feeling, for once, quite inadequate. And, as once before, she burned to ask him a very pertinent question, but decided against it. There was really no need. Torry had found out what Gerard had done for her, and consequences would flow. . .had surely flowed. And she was hungry. . .

'Now,' said Gerard, 'I need to talk to you.'

They had woken up to find that the clock said, quite improbably, that it was eleven at night. Gerard had rung for Timson, and within a suspiciously short space of time supper and two bottles of champagne had appeared.

Torry was still lying dreamily in bed. She could hear Gerard talking to Timson and the footman in the next room. He was saying something about the champagne — which he had not orderd — and Timson's answer was as enigmatic as usual. 'I thought, sir, that you would appreciate it, and took the liberty of asking the butler to provide it.'

Moments later, the bedroom door opened and Gerard came in carrying a tray of food which he placed on the table behind the sofa which stood before the fire, and then disappeared, to reappear again carrying a tray with two bottles of champagne on it, and two flutes.

'One of these days,' Gerard announced, pouring out the champagne and handing a flute to his blushing wife, 'Timson will go too far. But not tonight. Most remiss of me not to order champagne — as he virtually told me. On second thoughts, he needed no words: as usual, his face spoke for him!'

Torry, leaning back on her pillows, looking like a houri strayed from the sultan's harem, made no answer, and when Gerard, in his dressing-gown, came and sat on the bed beside her, she still did not speak, merely gave him a drowsy smile over the top of her glass.

'Well and truly loved, eh, Mrs Schuyler?' remarked Gerard with a self-satisfied smile, saluting her with his glass. 'And now I am waiting for an explanation as to how *Mrs* Torry Slade, the late Captain's notorious mistress, turned out to be a virgin. You might have told me.'

'And would you have believed me?' sighed Torry, who found being a thoroughly satisfied wife a most pleasant and relaxing sensation.

'There is that,' said Gerard shortly. 'But I really think that you owe me an explanation, seeing that the Captain is dead, and cannot talk, and your husband—did you ever have a husband, by the by?—is absent, so is also unable to inform me.'

Torry's face suddenly crumpled. She put down the flute, rolled away from him and sank her face into the pillow, from whence a muffled voice said, 'No. . .no. . . I can't. Don't ask me.'

Gerard poured more champagne into her empty flute, took a great swig from his own, and said, without touching her, 'Torry, my dearest. It is quite plain to me that not only were you a virgin, but you were, and by your behaviour have for a long time been, desperately afraid of making love. Knowing that explains so much of you. Rightly or wrongly, I believe that until you face what caused your behaviour our chances of a successful marriage are less than they ought to be.'

An anguished wail came from the pillow. All the impressive self-command which his wife had displayed since he had first met her seemed to have flown away with her virginity.

'No. . .don't ask me. I don't want to think about it.'

Gerard looked at his empty flute, decided not to drink any more, looked at the food temptingly arrayed on the tray before him, and said mildly, 'Do you think, Mrs Schuyler, that you might please Timson and the kitchen—who undoubtedly know what we have been up to, and for the first time, too—by eating what they have sent us?'

Torry surfaced. One dark eye looked pleadingly at him. He picked up a sandwich which oozed pâté and cress, and said, 'I hope you are not as hungry as I am, my dear. Love first destroys appetite, and then, when satisfied, enhances it.'

This, he was pleased to see, provoked a rather weak giggle. His wife sat up, pulled the sheet around her, and put out her hand for a sandwich.

'I have never found,' remarked Gerard judiciously, 'that beds were very good for eating in. They rapidly fill up with more crumbs than the original sandwiches consisted of. Remarkable, that, considering that most of the sandwich has been eaten. At the risk of being blasphemous, there are times when I understand the parable of the loaves and fishes.'

'Beds are perhaps better for other things,' ventured Torry, and then blushed a delightful rosy red. Her rather stiff manner seemed, Gerard noticed happily, to have disappeared, another good effect of being thoroughly loved. He hoped her new, relaxed mode would not disappear with the night.

'Pleased to hear that you enjoyed yourself.' Gerard's grin was broad. 'May I advise a little more champagne? Timson would be most distressed if we sent any back, and I fear that if I drink the lot I shall be unable to do my duty by you again tonight. And that would be a pity.'

The rest of the meal, he was happy to note, was passed in a haze of similar light-hearted nonsense. Finally, they both consumed a really delicate syllabub, served with tiny biscuits—'More crumbs,' observed Gerard. 'I can see that I shall have a rash by morning, the bed will be so burdened.'—and when they had finished he was suddenly back in it, pouring her more champagne, so that she said to him, savouring the last drop,

'A truly decadent way in which to go on, Gerard.'

'Charming, isn't it, madam? Had I known that you were so determined to ravish me, my dear, I would have ordered the room decorated with roses and carnations. You deserve a bower to be loved in.'

He took the flute from her, and placed it with his own on the tray on the table by their bed, and then turned to her, to take her in his arms. 'And now, Mrs Schuyler, time for confession.' And even as he spoke he felt her tremble beneath him.

'No, Gerard, no. . . I can't.'

He kissed her tenderly, nothing of ferocious Gerard Schuyler left. 'May I remind you that by your behaviour it is not very long since allowing me to make love to you was something which you felt that you could not endure? And now look at you, positively encouraging my advances.'

Torry hung her head. 'This is different, Gerard.' Her voice was low.

'Torry, we have been as close as a man and woman can be, but if you keep from me something as vital as the reasons for your surprising virginity I cannot hold out much hope for the future of our marriage.'

This did move her, he could see. She said, voice lower than ever, 'Promise not to look at me while I tell you. You have always been so. . .confident. Here and in the States, you are surrounded, either by women to whom you have made love, or by women who would cheerfully let you make love to them, while I. . . I am such a poor thing.'

'I am not over-proud of my headlong career in the lists of love,' said Gerard gently. 'I will neither look at you nor laugh at you, I promise. And I am longing to know about your true relationship with the Captain. I fear that unless you enlighten me my imagination will be busily at work. Far better that I know the truth. It seems that I have been hating him, quite wrongly, ever since I met you.'

She turned away from him to stare at the wall to the right of the bed, and for a long time said nothing. Gerard made no move to hurry her. He had, he felt, all the time in the world. Finally she began to speak, slowly at first, and then, forgetting where she was, and who had such a loving arm about her, she felt the river begin to run again, the river which had revived the other afternoon when she had talked to Kate, and which had so recently, in Gerard's arms, burst its banks.

CHAPTER THIRTEEN

'IT ALL began,' Torry said, 'when my father died when I was ten years old. . .we were living at Howland's Corner, a small town in Illinois. . .' and, speaking freely to Gerard, she was back in the past again, the past which she had spent long years pretending had never happened.

At eleven years old, already a tall, leggy girl, beginning to mature early, Victoria Schuyler, then Victoria Elliott, was surprised one day when her mother came home with one of their neighbours, Jeb Wadsworth, a widower, to tell her, with every sign of happiness, that they were to be married.

Jeb was a teller in the local bank, a tall, rather gloomy man, Victoria thought. She had never quite liked him, but her mother did. Her mother was older than Jeb by quite a few years, but that did not seem to matter to the happy pair, as the Reverend Thomson christened them when he came to tea and congratulated Victoria on having a new Papa.

Victoria, or Torry, as her father had always called her, although her mother preferred the longer form, felt that she was selfish when the quiet life she had lived with her mother changed so dramatically after she had married Jeb. It was Jeb who occupied her mother's thoughts, not Torry, and she tried not to mind too much, for jealousy was not a nice emotion, both the Bible and the minister informed her, and it was an emotion she had not thought to experience.

One day — she remembered it quite plainly; it was shortly after her fourteenth birthday — her mother called her to her in the afternoon and said shyly, 'What would you say, Victoria, if I told you that you were to have a little brother or sister?'

She threw her arms around her mother in delight, for the jealousy and, if she were honest, the dislike which she felt for Jeb Wadsworth were absent when she thought of the new baby.

'Oh,' she said, 'I have always wanted to be part of a big family,' and she kissed her mother, genuinely pleased at the news.

Her mother seemed relieved, and said as she kissed her, 'Oh, Victoria, you make me very happy. I have always thought that you do not greatly care for Mr Wadsworth, but, although I do not expect you to forget your real father, Mr Wadsworth must be your father now.'

Torry nodded her agreement, rather than speak. Just lately her dislike of Mr Wadsworth had increased, rather than decreased. He had always watched her closely, an odd look in his eyes, she thought, but recently the look seemed to have grown keener, and she wondered why.

What Torry did not know was that early maturity was turning her into a woman, and a woman with a promise of striking beauty. The dark loveliness of eyes and hair, the long and delicate neck, the shapely grace of her body, which were later to attract Gerard, and others, were already there in embryo, slowly destroying the awkward angularity which had marked her early and rapid growth.

By the time her mother was seven months pregnant, and so ill that she was confined to her bed until the birth — to save the baby, the doctor said — Torry had matured even more, and presented a temptation to a man now starved of sexual gratification who had always found his youthful stepdaughter more attractive than the wife whom he had married for her late husband's property.

The dislike Torry felt for him was compounded when she suddenly found him caressing her, touching her, on the slightest excuse. Not that, at first, the touches seemed to be more than innocent — only that they grew in number.

He first kissed her when she had done well at school and came home to tell her mother the good news. He was in the bedroom, talking to his wife, and the kiss on the cheek with which he conveyed his congratulations was a source of pleasure to the mother rather than the daughter.

Only, it was not the last, and the kisses and touchings grew less and less innocent, until Torry became afraid to be alone with him, dodged him, because the fear and revulsion she was beginning to feel at his unwanted attentions frightened her so. And there was no one she could speak to, no one. No aunt, or elder sister, and the thought of telling the preacher, or her mother. . .

Her mother. She could not tell her mother, who lay upstairs happy in the knowledge that soon her child would be born. What would it do to her mother? And worse, it must be she, Torry, who was wrong, not Jeb Wadsworth, since everyone from the preacher down in the little town where she had her home constantly told her what a good man he was, and how fortunate she was that she had a kind and loving stepfather.

Only, they did not know how unwantedly loving he was becoming in private. She would always remember the day her little brother was born. She was working in the back parlour, her exercise book before her, the texts on which she was working around her on the table, when he came in.

'Dear little Victoria,' he said. 'Have you any idea how charming you look, what a temptation you represent?' And he walked over to where she sat, and began to touch and stroke her, first her cheek, and then, more intimately, running his hands down the front of her dress.

She sprang up and said fiercely, 'Keep away. You are not to do that. It is wrong; I do not want it. If you touch me like that, I shall. . . I shall tell Mama.'

He advanced on her, smiling. 'And will she believe you, do you think—or anyone else you might care to tell? I am a sidesman at church, a prominent man in the community. Shame on you, Victoria, for lying so dreadfully about me; that I do this, and this.' And he was upon her, and it was the worst yet; there was no part of her body he left untouched.

Somehow, she fought him off, kicked his shins, so that, face wrathful, he advanced on her again. What might have happened she never knew, for fate saved her, for the time being at least.

The bell by her mother's bed, kept there for

emergencies, began to sound. Her mother had gone into premature labour.

Jeb let her go, using an obscenity far removed from the normal vocabulary of the respectable man he appeared to be, and ran upstairs, leaving his victim dazed and frightened. 'Unclean,' she said to Gerard, who held her closely as she spoke. 'I felt so unclean.'

After that, however, whether because of the new baby or his wife's recovery Torry never knew, he left her alone for a little, and she began to think that the persecution was over, that she might be left to grow up in peace.

But his actions had already damaged her. She was frightened by her own body, her own sexuality, and began to retreat into the cool apparent indifference to men and life of which she had become a mistress when Gerard first met her.

And then, suddenly, why, she did not know, except that by the time she reached sixteen her beauty was already remarkable enough to cause comment and jealousy in her little community, he began again, and it was worse, much worse, for he had convinced himself that such a ripe beauty must be waiting for someone to steal it, and she became so frightened that she was almost on the verge of telling her mother, who loved her second husband more than she had loved her first, and Torry was frightened of what the knowledge of her husband's . . .sinfulness would do to her.

The whole thing came to a head one afternoon when he came home early from his work to find Torry alone, her mother safely at a mothers' meeting at the church, her baby brother, Seth, asleep in his cot.

This time he used his strength to subdue her; he bore her to the floor, and despite her tears, her protests he was on the verge of consummation when the door opened and her mother came home unexpectedly early.

With an oath he pulled away from her, and she sat up, her hair down, her face blurred with tears, her dress torn and dishevelled about her. 'Oh, Mama, Mama,' she said, 'you have saved me,' while he said to her mother,

'She tempted me; look at her. Your arrival, my dear, has saved me from a mortal sin.' And he fell on his knees before her mother, clasping her skirts. 'Forgive me, but she has flaunted herself at me all summer, whispered what her wants were. . . tempted me beyond a normal man's endurance.' And he began to sob.

'No,' she had said to her mother's accusing face. 'No, it is not true. He has persecuted me for years. . .'

Now, in her own maturity and increased knowledge of life, she knew why her mother had behaved as she did, but at the time it had almost completed her destruction.

For her mother moved from Jeb's submissive embrace, advanced on her daughter, and struck her in the face. 'Slut,' she said. 'He has hinted at this, and I have chosen not to believe him.'

And when Torry tried to protest, her words stumbling from an almost paralysed mouth, her mother continued, 'You cannot stay here. You will go to your room, and I shall visit Cousin Howland, ask him for advice; no one else must know how you have shamed us all.'

What could she say or do? That her own mother should reject her! She now understood that for her mother to have done otherwise would have ruined her mother's world, the happy world of her second marriage to a man who had said he loved her; to expose herself and her family and the new baby to the shame which would follow the disclosure that that husband had been on the point of raping her daughter—*that* she could not face. Against everything she would believe the betraying husband rather than the betrayed child.

Torry was locked in her room for twenty-four hours. The next afternoon she was told to dress herself in her best, pack her case and go with her mother to their cousin Howland's home. He was not really a cousin—he had been a friend of her father's and was something of a father to the small town in which they lived. His grandfather had first settled it, and Lewis Howland had grown up to take his father and his grandfather's place. Trained as a lawyer, he had gone for a time to New York, but, involved in an accident, he had come back, semi-paralysed, to take over the town's small newspaper and edit it, and occasionally to practise law, when a lawyer was needed, which was not often—for something to do, he had said once; he did not really need the money.

Jeb drove Torry and her mother in the buggy to the Howland mansion on the edge of town. It was a solid red-brick pile which Torry had visited on several occasions. She liked Cousin Howland; he was always kind to her, and lent her books from his large library and talked to her about them afterwards.

'Now, mind what you say to Cousin Howland,' her mother said fiercely. 'None of your lies about Jeb, do you hear me? He is going to tell us what to do with you; you cannot stay with us. He will find you work, I hope — not here, I trust; I don't want to see you again.'

Torry was in such a daze that she had no answer to make. She could hardly bear the thought of seeing Cousin Howland's accusing eyes on her. She was left in an ante-room while her mother and Jeb went in and saw him — they had been to him the day before with their story, told under an oath of secrecy, and she wondered what more there was to say to him.

Her mother and stepfather came out; her mother said to her, 'You are to go in, and that will be that. Leave your case here. You do understand that you are not going home?'

She nodded a mute yes, and walked into Cousin Howland's study. It was the last time that she ever really spoke to her mother. She turned at the door to see them go, her mother holding Jeb's arm tightly, as though to let him go might be to lose him.

Cousin Howland was sitting in his wheelchair, not in front of his desk as she had expected, but looking out of a big window on to the beautiful gardens which surrounded Howland House.

She stood at the door, hesitant, face white, body rigid, prepared for more verbal onsloughts. He turned his head as she entered and his look at her was so kind that the ice broke, she ran to him, slipped to her knees, put her head in his lap and began to cry all the tears she had held back since her mother had come in and found Jeb with her.

Absently, he stroked her hair. After a time, when her sobs had ceased, he said, his voice kind but neutral, 'Would you like to tell me about it, Torry? When you feel able that is.'

He believed her! Her voice broke when she told Gerard this. At first she had been unable to speak, had, as she had done so many years later with Gerard, sobbed that she could not tell him anything. She had felt so ashamed, so dirtied, as though what her mother had shouted at her had been true, when the truth was that she could not abide the man who had tried to rape her, and what he had done had deprived her for many years of the ability to feel anything for any man.

But gradually Lewis Howland's patience and the hand which had stroked her head had done their work, and she had sobbed out the truth. He had said nothing, so that she had lifted her unrecognisable tear-stained face to stare at him, and said fiercely, 'Oh, you think I am lying to you,' and she had tried to stand up, to run away, where, she could not think.

He had put a restraining hand on her. 'Of course I believe you, my dear. Your mother's husband is . . .known, although everyone would deny what he is. In a small town like this one there are no secrets — but the truth is seldom spoken, and he would be believed, not you, if this terrible story became public. I did not answer you immediately because I was wondering what was the best thing for me to do for you.'

'My mother said——' and Torry had barely been able to gasp out the word mother '—that I should be sent away, to become a mother's help, or a shop-girl; that I could not stay at home after what had happened. Where will you send me, Cousin Lewis, where? Oh, I have lost everything, everything.'

For some reason one of the things which had hurt her most was that she was going to lose the baby. Torry had loved her little half-brother Seth; he was so warm and sweet, a good baby, and she had been allowed to hold him, to dress him occasionally. For years afterwards she could hardly look at a baby because the loss of him had hurt her so.

She was not to know that her mother had suggested that she be put out as a nursemaid, and the only shame she had ever shown was when Cousin Lewis had said to her, gently, 'Don't you think that would be a terrible waste? Torry is such a clever girl; she surely deserves better than that.'

'She deserves nothing,' Torry's mother had said angrily, before her eyes had dropped beneath his cool stare, and then, 'Oh, very well, I leave her to you. But she is not to come home, mind, I am not having that.'

'No,' Cousin Lewis had said enigmatically. 'She is not to return home. I quite agree with you. Not the proper place for her at all.' He hesitated. 'You will accept whatever decision I make, then.' And nodded his head when Mrs Wadsworth agreed, for Jeb had said nothing during this interview, preferring to leave his wife to deal with a man whom he knew had no illusions about who was to blame in this whole sorry affair.

'I don't mind where I go,' said Torry passionately, 'as long as the people are kind, and will not hurt me.'

'Look at me, Torry,' Cousin Lewis said kindly. 'I am not going to send you anywhere as any kind of servant. You are only sixteen, you are already a lovely girl, you will soon be a beauty, and wherever you went you would be. . .prey. Do you understand me? Without anyone to protect you, you would be thrown away before you reached eighteen. Your father's daughter deserves more than that. *You* deserve more than that.'

He looked at her steadily. 'There is one way in which I can protect you, save you from gossip and scandal, silence your mother and her husband, for they would not dare to cross me, and that is. . .' and he hesitated, looked at her keenly '. . .if you married me.'

He raised his hand as she put her own hands over her mouth and said, 'Marry you! But. . .' and before she could finish he added,

'I want a woman to be my hostess, to be a companion, to learn to run my house, and then to take charge of it, but what I do not want, and can never have, is a true wife; you understand me, Torry? But, as my wife, you will be beyond attack, for I, God help me, am virtually the owner of this town, and what I say and do is law. I am the last of the Howlands, and I may live five years or fifty, and when I die you will take my fortune and my place.'

Marry him! She liked Cousin Lewis, liked to talk to him; he was always kind, someone with whom she could discuss those things of which she could not speak to her mother or to Jeb.

'But what will people think?' she faltered.

'Much less than if you are suddenly driven from the home your father owned to be a servant, or if the truth of Jeb's attack on you became known, when, make no mistake about it, you would take the blame. I know these small towns, Torry. Marry me. It is not a good solution, but it is the best I can offer you.'

Of course, she accepted him. She was sixteen years old, just of an age to marry, and he was forty-five, but he would never be her husband in anything but name, and neither her mother nor Jeb would be able to touch her once she was his wife. She would be the first lady of Howland's Corner, for what that was worth, and she would be saved.

She was more than saved, for Cousin Lewis, who had seen the blossoming intellect beneath the blossoming body, chose to train it. He encouraged her to read widely, taught her to write for the paper which he ran in his spare time, and she learned enough to be able to edit it when, at last, he became too ill to do so himself.

Torry remembered her wedding. The excitement it had caused, her mother's resentment, Jeb's odd expression, and the way in which Cousin Lewis had foiled him when it became his turn to kiss the bride, at the end of the ceremony. Sitting in his wheelchair, seeing Jeb approach, seeing Torry's agonised face at the prospect of being touched by him, Lewis had flung what Howland's Corner called a 'conniption fit', and had had to be revived with loving care from Torry and a great deal of brandy. In the middle of the commotion he had given her a great wink, unseen by anyone else, and when they ate their supper that night, the wedding guests having long gone — for the fit had also, as he had intended, cut short the meaningless celebrations — they had laughed together over his naughtinesses.

'I suppose,' said Torry reflectively, when she had reached this part of her story, 'I was as happy with Cousin Lewis as I had ever been in my life. It was like living with a kind teacher. When he realised that he was dying, he said to me one day that if my life in Howland's Corner became difficult after he had gone and could no longer protect me I could always sell up and move away, for I was now able to protect myself in the wider world. He had often talked to me about the wider world, of the women who campaigned for better legal and social treatment for their sex, and how such experiences as mine had convinced him that until society and the law gave women better treatment they would always be exploited.'

She fell silent for a moment, lying warm in the crook of Gerard's arm. 'I used to dream that I would found a paper to defend women, so that girls would not be treated as I was, with even my own mother turning against me.' She fell silent, and then resumed her tale of the past.

Cousin Lewis died when he and Torry had been married for eight years, and what he had said came true. Despite her wealth, her ownership of the paper, once he was dead she was fair game for every man both in and out of town, and particularly for Jeb Wadsworth.

She had found him waiting for her in her office one day—her secretary had been persuaded to let him in. He had not got as far as he did with her when she had been a helpless child of sixteen— Cousin Lewis had talked to her a great deal about how to protect herself.

It had taken a carboy of printer's ink hurled over him as he had closed in on her to blind him temporarily and drive him from the building. After he had gone, she had sat there shivering. Her protector was dead, and only if she went where she was not known, found new friends who knew nothing of the slanders which Jeb had begun to circulate behind her back, could she start again, begin a new life.

Without saying anything to anyone she had left town, sold up, sold everything, and the terrible thing was that it had hurt her more to leave Howland House than to leave her mother and the few relatives she had possessed there. She had chosen New York as a haven because the city was large and anonymous, and there were women there who shared her ideals, whom she could meet and with whom she could join in an effort to change the law and make it kinder to women.

After becoming a reporter, the idea of being an editor again, of running a newspaper devoted to women's interests, had become more and more attractive. But the years had made her careful. She did not want to sink all her capital in founding one, for at this period of her life she had no interest in men, had no intention of marrying, for the dreadful hurt which Jeb had done her on that long-ago afternoon was still with her.

'Oh, I felt so unclean,' she told Gerard earnestly. 'I had begun to think that it must be my fault that he treated me as he did, and, however much Cousin Lewis told me that it wasn't, I couldn't believe him. And all men frightened me, unless I held them at a distance. And women, too — my mother's behaviour had made me suspect everyone. Much easier to remain uninvolved. And then I met the Captain.'

This was the part of her story which Gerard particularly wanted to hear. He had listened in boiling anger when Torry had told him of Jeb and the attempted rape, had had an insane desire to travel immediately to Howland's Corner and beat him to death. But the Captain — how in God's name had she become involved with him? And how had such a notorious womaniser as his grandfather had been not come to lay a finger on her?

'I needed money, capital,' she began. 'I tried to borrow it, and I immediately came up against prejudice because of my sex. I knew from working with Cousin Lewis that if I had been a man, with the kind of collateral which I possessed, a loan would have been granted easily enough, but as a woman. . .'

One day she had gone to a bank on Fifth Avenue, Harden's by name. The banker had received her the day before and had offered her a little hope, had told her to come back on the following afternoon, and he would give her his verdict.

He had bowed her into an ante-room murmuring falsities in her ear. Another man had been waiting, a tall old man, stooped, with fierce amber eyes, who had turned the fierce eyes on her when the banker had finally kissed her hand, and she had—it was almost a reflex action—scrubbed the hand which had been kissed on the skirts of her dress.

Her action had not gone unnoticed and the fierce old creature—he was like an elderly eagle, she thought—had looked after her before he entered the inner sanctum, the banker bowing and scraping before him. He was obviously a man of power, and no wonder, with that face.

The next afternoon she had gone to the bank, to be shown into the parlour. There was sherry wine on the table on a silver salver, with small sweet biscuits arranged on a painted porcelain plate—and yesterday's old man had been seated in an armchair, the eagle eyes on her as she entered.

The banker had shown her to a seat with far more deference than he had displayed the day before. He was almost obsequious. She had looked her curiosity at the old man, and the banker had said, 'Allow me, Mrs Slade——' she had taken the name of one of Cousin Lewis's real cousins '—to introduce you to Mr Ghysbrecht Schuyler. I believe you may have heard of him.'

No wonder that she had thought that he was a man of power. Everyone had heard of Ghysbrecht Schuyler, more commonly known as the Captain, and Torry had wondered why he should be here, why he was present when the banker was interviewing such an inconsequential person as Mrs Torry

Slade, for, rich and powerful though she and Cousin Lewis might have been in Howland's Corner, they were as nothing to the Captain in New York City — nay, in the whole of the Americas which he bestrode as a financial Colossus.

'Sir,' she said, bowing.

'Mrs Slade,' he answered, also rising and bowing. He saw the question on her face, and smiled his smile, the one Gerard gave people when he knew something which they didn't.

'Mr Schuyler has a proposition to put to you, madam, relating to the loan which you have asked of the bank. I do not know what the proposition is, except that I am sure it will be to your advantage. He has asked that he make it to you privately, so, with your permission, I will withdraw. You may ring the bell on the table when you wish me to return.'

Torry inclined her head and said to the old man, wondering what on earth he could have to offer her, 'I will listen to whatever you have to say, sir, but that does not necessarily mean that I shall agree to it.'

'Oh, indeed,' he replied, and although the rest of him might be old — he was over eighty, she later discovered — his voice had remained young, firm and resonant, with a constant undertone of mockery. 'I see that you are a wise young lady. You will read all the small print of what I have to say to you, I am sure.'

'Depend upon it,' she answered him in the same light tone, bowing again.

The banker withdrew, to leave them alone.

'I am assured,' began Ghysbrecht Schuyler, 'that

you are a young woman of great sense, possess a hard head, are doing a man's job on the newspaper for which you work, and will not shriek, faint or indulge in hysterics when you hear what I have to say to you—not that that pompous fool out there knows anything, but he did tell me what kind of a person you are, after I saw you yesterday.'

Goodness, thought Torry, whatever can he want? And then, I think I know what he wants, for the Captain's dealings with women are notorious. Well, if that is what he is angling for, he is in for a big disappointment. I am in no mind to be anyone's darling, let alone the darling of a man old enough to be my grandfather!

Something of what she was thinking showed in her face, and the old reprobate began to laugh. 'Oh, you are quite wrong,' he managed, when he had recovered his breathing. 'Quite wrong. Allow me to enlighten you. I understand that you wish to be granted a loan to finance your. . .feminist. . .newspaper, and that you are having difficulties in obtaining one. Let me assure you that I shall be happy to act as your surety for the full amount which you require, in return for a small service which you may do me.'

Yes, it *was* her honour he was after, the classic proposition, and she was suddenly disappointed in him. Old men with eagle's eyes should not be so obvious.

Except, of course, that he wasn't, and he knew what she was thinking, for he said, almost impishly, 'And if you are thinking what I think you are thinking, then you are mistaken, madam, for what I want of you is quite otherwise.'

He paused, poured himself sherry, and offered her a glass, his keen old eyes on her, tantalising her, she realised afterwards. 'I have recently been very ill,' he offered, putting his glass down, 'and I am lucky to be alive, the quacks tell me. Only, they are wrong, for one of the prices which I have paid for my recovery is that I am. . .impotent. You understand me, madam?'

Torry's face had flamed scarlet, and he smiled his sardonic smile. 'Well, if that is your sole response, then you please me. No offended modesty, although I see, and I am a little surprised, that you are truly modest. I will test you a little further. I am sure that you know of my reputation with women, and now, in my last years, I do not intend to give my enemies the satisfaction of knowing that I am a helpless old fool. If, madam, you will pretend to be my mistress, will accompany me, be my partner, in every sense but the true one, so that we deceive the world together, then I will make sure you get the money which you want, and more beside. But your discretion must be absolute, for if you betray me I shall take the greatest pleasure in breaking you, stripping you of what you already possess. I understand that you are reasonably wealthy in your own right, and very properly do not wish to sink all your capital in a risky venture. Now, what do you say?'

Torry drank down all her sherry in one great gulp. Desperately, she wished to laugh, faced for the second time in her life with an invitation to pretend to be what she was not, for no one in Howland's

Corner had known the truth of her marriage with Cousin Lewis.

And now this monstrous old man was making her the same proposition! There must be something wrong with her, there must, for lightning to strike twice! The sense of being faulty, damaged goods in some strange way, that she could only invite rape or a bloodless union, was strong in her.

She could feel the old man's eyes hard on her, and something in him called to her. Looking at the strong face, the yellow-brown eyes, feeling the rampant will of him, suffering with him the loss of his sexual vitality, and his desire to keep that loss a secret, to die as he had lived, apparently in the arms of a beautiful woman, she found herself wishing that she had known him when he was a young man. Improbably, for all his reputation, she felt that she could have come to love him.

Now, telling Gerard of this encounter, she knew that strength called to strength, that what had happened to her might have been bad in many ways, since it had stunted her emotional growth, but it had made her a woman of power.

And facing her, cold, proud, untouchable and untouched as she was, for the shrewd old man could see all that, and wondered at the title Mrs, the Captain wished that he were young again, to wake Sleeping Beauty with a kiss. And what a beauty! She had not shrunk, shivered, or made some foolish remark when he had come out with his proposition, but had turned those great violet eyes on him, and considered him as shrewdly as he was considering her.

Why not? Torry thought. Why not. Whom was she hurting? No one, and she knew that if the bargain were set out properly he would not cheat her, or rather would only cheat her if she tried to cheat him, and she would not do that.

'Yes,' she said. 'Yes,' and picked up one of the sweet biscuits after offering them to him; and, having taken the biscuit and eaten it, he put out his old hand and said,

'Done; let us shake hands on it,' and then, when they had done so, added, 'And while we leave Mr Moneybags here to arrange the financial side, you and I will draw up our little agreement in secret, for no one must know what we are doing.'

Torry was reckless. 'My late husband was a lawyer,' she said, 'and taught me to read a document properly. I know your reputation, sir; anything you put before me will be scrutinised with the greatest care.'

He gave a crow of laughter. 'Bravely said, madam. And pity that I am not forty years younger. The proposition I would have made to you then would have been quite a different one.'

'And I would not have agreed to it,' said Torry briskly.

So it was done.

'And,' said Torry to the listening Gerard, who had exclaimed at his grandfather's devilry when Torry had reached the point where the Captain had put his proposition to her, 'when I first met you, my shock was profound, for there was the Captain, young again, as I dearly would have liked to know him, only you looked at me in dislike, as Gis never did.'

'Gis,' said Gerard shortly—he still disliked to hear that his wife had been the Captain's intimate, even if only in friendship. 'He had never let anyone call him that. Did he mind?'

'No.' She hesitated. 'It came about quite naturally. You must understand that at first we were very formal with one another; he never so much as laid a finger on me, and we were more like father and daughter, particularly in private.'

She was silent for so long that Gerard began to be a little afraid of what she might be thinking, until she said, her voice reminiscent, 'We became very easy together quite suddenly. It was harder when we were alone; in public we could put on an act, but one evening, after we had come home from some big occasion, and he had escorted me, and everyone had stared at us and whispered, he began to laugh, and said, "Oh, we fooled them properly, girl. How does it feel to know something that no one else knows? A good feeling, hmm?"

'After that things were never the same: we became good companions, I saw a side of him no one else did, a gentler side. He liked me to play the piano for him, to sit quiet in the garden, to watch me sewing or knitting, as though we were both old and mildly content, all passion spent. That last year just before he began to fail, he asked me to go with him to spend the summer at Seahorses. I said no, without thinking, and then I saw his face. It was like that of a little boy who had had his favourite toy taken from him.

'He said, quite quietly, "If I asked you to marry me, Victoria——" he always called me Victoria "—would you come then?"

'I didn't know what to say to him; I could only think, Poor Torry Elliott, two marriage proposals and neither of them real ones. I knew that there must be something wrong with me, just knew.' And she turned away from Gerard, and began to sob into the pillow again.

'No,' said Gerard, recovering her, pulling her to him. 'No, you are not to think that, not at all. Let me show you how wrong you are to think that.' And he devoted the next ten delirous minutes to convincing Mrs Torry Schuyler how much she was loved by her husband, and how much she enjoyed loving him.

When they were quiet again, and she was lying against his heart, his hand stroking her hair, he said gently, 'Is that it, my love, or is there more? I understand why he offered you marriage, but why did you refuse him?'

'Oh, I said, "You don't need to marry me, Gis, I'll come to Seahorses with you, but not for too long—the paper needs me." He understood that, and then the cunning old devil got up to all sorts of tricks to persuade me to stay longer. I think that he knew his time was running out. It was then he began to talk about his family to me, and about you. He told me that he was going to leave me money, and I asked him not to—I knew the trouble it would cause, and he had already given me so much. But he wouldn't take no for an answer.

'I was with him when he died, and just before the

end he said something strange: "Don't cry, Victoria, Gerard will look after you." I didn't understand what he was saying; I thought that he was wandering in his mind, but he must have been thinking of the will. He had bequeathed me to you. I realised at the time of the will-reading what he'd done, and I was furious, at first. And then, when I was thinking of a way out of the impasse he had created, it came to me that if I had engaged in what were effectively two mock-marriages, why not a third? Coping with it would be easy.

'Only, Gerard, I forgot something. Both my two previous men had been old and. . .ineffective, and you—you were quite a different proposition.'

'So I should hope,' murmured Gerard into her hair. 'So I should hope.'

'I felt the ice begin to crack whenever I was with you. It wasn't just that you were so like the Captain, although that was part of it—it was your vitality, even your ruthlessness which called to me. And I was so frightened; I thought that Jeb Wadsworth and my mother, between them, had destroyed my ability to fall in love, or even to feel anything for anyone, and that was why it was so easy for me to accept the Captain's proposition. I truly didn't care what people thought of me,' she explained earnestly. 'And although I had often wished that I had met the Captain when he was a young man, when I met you, and I did, I wanted to run like a hare.'

Gerard's unseen grin as he redoubled his caresses at this confession was broader than ever. Oh, he had beaten the old devil at his own game, and knew that, thinking so, he had never been more like the dead old man whom he had both loved and hated.

'You hardly gave me that impression, my love,' he said. 'Icy you were, frightened you never appeared to be until I began to assault you with my love, and I put that reaction down to a well-trained courtesan pleasing and tantalising her client. I'm afraid I credited you with the most experienced and disgraceful past. Knowing what the Captain used to be, I could not imagine that he would be satisfied by less than the most expert in the field of love.'

'And you will not tell anyone the truth about him,' said Torry anxiously, rising on one elbow. 'He was such a proud man, and even though he's dead, and cannot know, I would not want him laughed at.'

'No,' said Gerard, but his eyes were naughty. 'I shall say nothing, but oh, I shall think a lot. It makes him human, you see.'

Torry sighed and hugged him the closer. 'That's all,' she said. 'There's nothing more to tell you, and you were right — doesn't it bore you, Gerard, always to be right? But you were. I feel better for having told you of the past, although I shall never forget it, for tonight you made me understand that the wounds I received were not mortal and that I was capable of love, could both give it and receive it.'

'A loving husband who is always right will also be helpful, I trust,' said Gerard. 'And now let me make a confession, and one which I think may not be necessary. I never had the slightest intention of allowing our marriage to remain unconsummated. From the moment I saw you in church, I wanted

you most desperately, and, even though the thought
of you with the Captain made me feel quite ill with
jealousy, in the end it didn't matter. At first I told
myself that when I had finally got you into bed I
would use you and cast you off, but the more we
were together, the more I wanted you to be my wife
forever, not just to cheat the Captain. The colder
you were, the more I wanted you, and I told myself
that there was fire beneath the ice, and I would
break through to find it. Why, Torry, why in the
end did you give way and come to me tonight? Was
it pity, or thanks for the fight? I hope it was more
than that, but if it were not then I shall face it, and
try to make you feel for me what I feel for you.'

'Oh, no, not pity,' she said softly, rising to kneel
above him, her dark hair streaming about them as
he had so often imagined, her hands now loving and
seducing him, even as she spoke. 'And not just
because you fought for me and my good name,
which you didn't even believe in, but because you
didn't tell me, kept it from me, did not seek to gain
any advantage with me for what you were doing —
that, Gerard, was true love. Something broke the
ice inside me when I discovered that you felt so
much for me that you didn't want me to be hurt by
knowing that you felt compelled to punish the man
who had defamed me, even though I was unaware
of the defamation and tried to gain nothing for
yourself. I knew then that our bargain had to be
broken, that I wanted you for my love, as I knew
that you wanted me.'

Gerard could not answer her; between what she
was telling him and what her hands and body were

doing to him he was beyond speech, was mere sensation. Together they had at last reached port. For if she understood that to gain nothing from what he had done for her in fighting Ledward was his major aim, then he also understood that she was accepting him not simply to thank him, or to take pity on his suffering for her, but out of true love for him, a love which his own actions had unlocked, had made her capable of expressing.

He turned her beneath him, for one last blazing encounter, before they sank into exhausted sleep, before he could tell her that he would take her on a belated honeymoon to his West Country manor house where they could begin to learn one another and prepare for the years to come.

The entire staff of their London home was in the hall to see them off on their journey to Cornwall. Gerard was smart in his grey town suit, Torry was bridal in cream, carrying white carnations as he helped her into the motor which was to take them to Paddington. Once they were seated together, side by side, Gerard put his arm around her shoulders, fiercely protective.

Kate, left behind under Daisy Gascoyne's chaperonage, soon to be engaged to Justin, watching them, saw the fierce protection and sighed happily. True love, found at last by her brother, was mingled in him with a desire to care and to cherish, and he was as happy as she had never expected to see him, and Torry, too. They were united in their strength as well as in their love.

She turned towards Timson, standing beside her,

his face benevolent, ready to walk down the steps with Torry's lady's maid to follow them in a second motor with the luggage.

He had heard her sigh, smiled, and when she said to him, 'You are ready to leave, Timson? Everything is satisfactory?' he replied, in his blandest manner, watching as Gerard's chauffeur negotiated his way down Park Lane,

'Oh, yes, Miss Kate. I think that we can say that everything in the Schuyler household is satisfactory, very satisfactory indeed.'

Look out next month for Kate's own story. . .

LEGACY *of* LOVE

Coming next month

IMPETUOUS INNOCENT
Stephanie Laurens
Regency

After her beloved father's death, Georgiana Hartley fled Italy to England, to find herself at the mercy of her cousin Charles! In escaping him, she was aided by Dominic Ridgeley, Viscount Alton, who found her a haven in London with his sister Bella, Lady Winsmere.

To Georgiana, Dominic was the embodiment of her dreams, but she possessed few attributes necessary to attract the Viscount—until she learned she was an heiress, and that Dominic had always wanted to buy back the Place, now hers, which had been part of his estate...

TOUCH THE FIRE
Paula Marshall
Book Two - Venice 1896/London 1904

In shock at her husband's unexpected death, the Countess Otmoor, Kate Schuyler as was, deceived her family, and left for the Continent incognito as Mrs Kate Moore, to fetch up in Venice where she met Sir Richard Havilland and his small daughter Sophie. Passion had never touched Kate, but the fire of her feelings for Richard led her into love and she became his mistress. But her hopes for marriage were dashed when Richard discovered who she really was, for the bad feeling between their families was too great—and, eight years later, it seemed little had changed...

LEGACY of LOVE

Coming next month

KETTI
Donna Anders

**Hawaii 1892/3
(Book 2 of Duet)**

Her beloved Hawaii! Ketti Foster knew going home would be the best remedy for a broken heart. Her peace of mind was short-loved, however, when she met the mysterious John Stillman.

Planter John Stillman was captivated by the proud Hawaiian beauty. For the first time in his life he had found a woman whose spirit matched his own. But change was upon them, and the love John and Ketti shared would soon be put to the test.

MOONWITCH
Nicole Jordan

Antigua 1819

When sea captain Kyle Ramsey met Selena Markham on a moonlit beach, her ethereal beauty left him stunned. But when he discovered that she wanted him to make love to her, he was flabbergasted.

Selena's fiancé was betraying her with another woman, and she was sick with rage. Making love to a devastating stranger seemed the perfect revenge...

Their lovemaking carried them to the heights of passion, but society's response was predictable. Forced into marriage, the unexpected lovers charted a stormy course rocked by bitterness and anger. Were they destined to spend their lives in misery? Or could the moon bewitch them once again—for good?

FOUR HISTORICAL ROMANCES & TWO FREE GIFTS!